THE SUNSHINE DAME OF DOOM

Marcos Fizzotti

This book is a work of fiction.

Names, characters, businesses, places, events and incidents are either the products of the author's imagination or used in a fictitious manner. Any resemblance to actual persons, living, dead, or living dead, or actual events is purely coincidental.

Cover by Cesar Santos
ISBN: 978-85-918322-5-5

(It's a zombie book, so be careful!)

TABLE OF CONTENTS

OVERTURE

"So, you're not from around here, are you?"

"Right, I'm not."

"And it's a real bad time to be around these parts."

"Trust me, mate. I got reasons to believe it's the same everywhere."

"Yep, with this epidemic and all, it seems the world as we know is coming to an end."

"And we never knew it that well."

"Speak for yourself, young lady. As you can see, I've lived enough."

"What do you mean? There's no such thing."

"Just take a good look outside! Do you think life is worth living now, that this crap world is worth fighting for?"

"Well, it was kind of crappy before, but people fought for it just the same."

"Yes, by coming in here and drinking themselves to death."

"But that's a good thing for you. Your business bloomed before and you still got a lot of customers now, at least those who are not eating each other. That's a good reason for living."

The bartender laughed.

"Wisdom from the young ones! What's going to be, miss?"

"What do you got?"

"Beer, Brandy, Whisky, Vodka, Shirley Temple, Shirley Steeple, Shirley Church..."

"It sounds appealing. Let me see... Bring me lemonade, and not the kind that makes my gums bleed."

"I'm afraid I'm out of lemons right now, but I got some good old moonshine. It's the next best thing."

"Fine mate, pour it in."

Some strange distant noises roared outside the bar. The bartender kept staring at his customer across the counter.

"Somebody may think you like me, lad." The woman said uncomfortably.

"I saw you before somewhere else."

"Yes, ten minutes ago, when I entered your bar."

"No. I've already seen you before, I'm sure of that."

"It's possible. I got a common face."

The bartender did not take his eyes off her. She shifted position on the stool.

"You're that girl!" He finally jumped.

"Right gender, only the pronoun is wrong. I'm just *a* girl. Make it with an article."

"Oh no! You are that girl from the news! Papers, internet, YouTube, this pretty face of yours was everywhere not so long ago!"

"You're mistaking me for Justin Bieber! Can I have that moonshine now?"

"And to you, it's on the house!" He grabbed the bottle, opened it, filled a glass and slid it toward her."

"This is really not necessary, sir."

"Come on, why are you so embarrassed about? On the contrary, you should be proud. Such an amazing stunt you pulled! An elementary school in the busy hour is attacked, invaded and surrounded on all sides by those horrendous sick dead people that have been eating everybody lately. Teachers and lots of little children are cornered and scared. Local police is stunned and bewildered, they try to invade the school and shoot the monsters down, but nothing seems to work, they just keep on coming. Eventually, the cops run out of ammo and are the first to die. The ones outside call for help, but all other units are busy with similar problems. Those dammed deranged human beasts are everywhere. So, that's it for the school. Nothing anybody can do anymore. Outside the isolation cord around the building, hundreds of parents cry in despair for their sons and daughters, poor innocent souls about to face the most horrible death."

He drank a little from the glass meant to his customer and continued.

"But then, this woman comes. Somehow, she breaks into the cordoned off zone and into the school. And ten minutes later, oh yeah, ten minutes was all she took, teachers run out of the cursed school, followed by hundreds of children, all safe and sound, back to the warm and loving arms of their moms and dads, who cry in relief, thanking heavens for that incredible miracle."

"Look mister, if this is a movie you've just told me, it's a very corny and unoriginal one."

"Oh yes, it would be if it was a movie. But it's not, it's real, it really happened. And that woman, the children's savior, is you!"

"Hoy!" She scoffed. "No offense, my good man, but you've been taking some samples of this poison you sell every day. You're making a terrible mistake."

"No, I'm not. I never forget a face, especially not this face. When you left the school, carrying a little girl who couldn't walk, the last one you saved, an army of reporters took your picture and sent it everywhere. What was left of the police force went into the school to assess situation, but all they could find was the dead monsters you left behind, all with cracked or sliced in half, or even missing heads, because that's the only way to stop them, right, by busting their heads off?"

"I wouldn't know."

"I think you would. The press even gave you a nickname, *Apocalily*, because one reporter found out that your name is Lily."

"Sorry to disappoint you, mate. I don't know what you're talking about."

"Okay. Then tell me your name. And make it with a passport."

"I assure you I'm over twenty-one."

"Not the point and you know what I mean. There's surely no harm in telling me your name and proving your identity."

"Why don't you tell me your name?"

"It's Brian. Now come on, missy! Or should I say Lily?"

She finally had a chance to drink the moonshine.

"You're a loudmouth for a bartender."

"People pay me for that too, honey."

The distant noises from the outside all of a sudden exploded in a loud uproar on the inside.

Horridly deformed rotting skeletons broke into the bar, lacerating three costumers by a booth close to the door, while others ate the guts of a couple sharing a table next to a shattered glass window.

Screams of pain and fear blended with frightful snarls of crazy hungry beasts.

"JESUS!!!" The bartender screamed, leaning against the counter to reach for a shotgun.

The customers who survived the first strike ran scared to the center of the bar, in a desperate attempt to dodge the horde of zombies.

"Good thing you're prepared for this contingency." The woman commented. Then she drank all the content of her glass in a single gulp.

The man was a reasonably good shot and blew two zombies' heads off.

"Keep it coming, lad!" The woman said.
"That's it, only two shells! I'm out!"
"Do you have a pool table somewhere in this place?"
"Listen missy, this is definitely not a good time for a game!"
"Not a game. We can use the cues and balls as a weapon against these bastards!"
"Sorry, no pool table!"
"Then get down!"

Actually, the man was down behind the counter way before she finished that sentence.

All other living souls inside the bar jumped the counter as well, screaming and trying to hide from the impious zombies. Panic-stricken people also ran to the restrooms, but the living dead had already made their way into such area through some backdoors. The place was totally overrun.

The horde of beasts also closed on the woman. She reached for a hockey stick in a sheath strapped to her back and started to assemble it. But some parts got jammed at some point, delaying her actions. The zombies were slow, but steady, almost reaching her head, with dirty twisted teeth ready for the slaughter.

"Why do they make these things modular?" She complained to herself.

She finished mounting the stick. The first row of zombies was upon her, ready to take a bite.

The bartender and most customers were ducking and lying behind the counter, men and women with tearful eyes and dread in their souls, hands covering faces and ears, weeping and praying for their lives.

Loud noises of glasses shattering and wood breaking took the whole place by storm. Nobody knew what was going on. Some of them were too scared even to move. But five minutes later, everything quieted down all of a sudden.

Bartender and customers still waited awhile before having the nerves to stick their heads over the counter. When they finally did it, what they saw was utterly unbelievable. The zombies were scattered all over the floor, some with heads split in half, others even without any head.

But the important thing was they were all motionless, now rendered completely harmless, forming a rotten pool of organs stretching everywhere.

And in the middle of the gore stood the woman, her hands firmly gripping the hockey stick covered in slimy tar, still in a state of readiness, in case some zombie decided to move.

Very quickly she became the center of attention. Her eyes met the bartender's. Like the others, he was gazing at her with open mouth and chin nearly touching his chest.

"It still doesn't prove I'm that girl from the news!" She complained.

ACT 1

"Three black beers!" Vince screamed to the bartender.

"Black beer?" Hector queried.

"Do you have a better idea, bro?" Vince replied.

"What about getting out of here and take a walk around the neighborhood, clear the ideas, get a grip on reality for a change?"

"What neighborhood? What ideas? What reality?"

"This is a three parts question. I'll answer each and every one of them as soon as we are out of here."

"Come on, you know what I'm talking about."

"And I agree with your brother" said Phil across the table, addressing Hector. "There's nothing out there."

"There'll be us when we get out of here." Hector insisted. "Come on, when did this stop us before?" He said turning to Vince.

"This is different, Hec. There was a world before."

"There's still a world out there, a crappy one, but still a world" Hector retorted "One that's not very different from good old Hell's Kitchen."

"What's that supposed to mean?"

"That it's back to the streets for the both of us, bro, as in the good old days, remember?" Hector opened a big white smile, causing his nose to get even larger around the rotund face.

"We can't." Vince frowned. "You're talking about a different life."

"No I'm not! Have you forgotten everything mamma taught us? Let's start over, build everything again from scratch, be the lords of networking!"

People around turned to them with stony expressions and a peculiar look on their faces.

"Keep your voice down!" Phil whispered, feeling all his vertebras contracting at once. "You can't talk like this! People have been disappearing lately, folks who talked exactly like you just did, or so they say."

"Yes, this is yet another thing I'm having real trouble accepting." Hector spoke.

"Then you'd better get used to. Rumor says troublemakers are kicked out of town, you know, for the lamebrains to feast on them."

"Hey, you have some respect when you talk about those souls! They are sick human beings for crying out loud!"

"Not again, Hec!" Vince stepped in furiously. "Now, you're the one not getting a grip on reality! Those bastards are dead, you hear?! Dead and rotting and dilacerating and eating, Jesus, they're not human, man! You saw what they do with your own eyes! They're freaking monsters!"

Hector's forehead wrinkled in anger and the dark cloud of seriousness that fell upon his face caused fear on the other two. He was about to lift a finger at them when the beers came. The bartender left three tall glasses in front of them and walked away, but not before giving them the evil eye.

"You're going to get us all killed." Phil complained.

They took a deep breath.

"Come on bro." Vince said. "Just one for the road and them we walk, what do you say?"

"I drink to that." Phil spoke. "Cheers!"

Hector did not answer. He simply took his tall glass of black beer and swallowed it all nearly in a single gulp.

ACT 2

Lily was driving her modified truck, so modified that the brand and model of such vehicle were long gone. It looked more like a metallic armored, slightly fortified walking peanut.

A sight caught the corner of her eye. In a not so distant prairie, a lonely human being seemed to be surrounded by dead beasts. She took a real harsh turn to the left, leaving a good amount of rubber painting the road.

By getting closer to the strange scene, she got a good picture of what was going on. A young man was trying to keep zombies away with a tennis racquet. Obviously, it wasn't working. He desperately waved the racquet back and forth very near the zombies' heads, but they did not seem to care and advanced to him with furious hunger. "Back off! Back off", he screamed. He didn't have much time.

"I'd better look into this matter." Lily thought.

She left the vehicle and drew two small knives from improvised holsters attached to her belt. When she came to the dead creatures, she looked more like an octopus. In a matter of seconds, all attacking zombies were dirtying the floor with perforated heads.

"Are you all right?" She asked the young lad.
"Yeah" He said breathless and sweating a lot. "Thanks."
"No problem. Two things though. One, this won't do it." She pointed at his racquet. "Those are modern racquets made of titanium, too light to inflict damage. You should try to get your hands on those heavy wooden racquets from days of old. They can really smash a head."
"I can see you know your way around tennis."

"Nope, but I know my way around material thickness. These days, it's important to find good stuff to kill dead folks with."

"Yes, no arguments there."

"Second, dead people don't usually respond to verbal commands like *back off* and all. Sometimes, not even the living ones do. Believe me, I know."

Some snarling and growling sounds were getting louder in the near distance.

"Their friends will be upon us soon." Lily nodded at the corpses on the ground. "We'd better go. Do you want a ride?"

"If it's not imposing..."

"Not at all, where you're heading?"

"Well um... right now, to no particular place."

"What a coincidence! I'm also going to no particular place. I take you there."

"Great!" He smiled.

The man grabbed his bag and walked to the right of Lily's truck.

"Wrong side" she corrected him.

"Oh, okay" and he walked to the left side.

Then, like Willie Nelson, they were on the road again.

Behind the wheel, Lily glanced at the man's bag, which was open due to a broken zipper. She saw some racquets and lots of tennis ball cans inside.

"So, I gather you are a tennis player of some sort." She observed.

"That's very correct. I'm a tennis player of some sort. And I was doing pretty well before this whole mess started. I was number 417 in the world rank, but then I got to the second round of this ATP 250 tournament, that's how we call them, and I jumped to rank 378! Then, I qualified to participate in this ATP 500 championship, more points in this one, with chances to become number 298 of the world if I made it to second round!"

"It sounds like a good climbing. What's the top ranking in this thing, two-hundred or so?"

"No! The top position in tennis ranking is number one!"

"Oh boy... Suddenly the dune turned into a mountain."

"Now, what's that supposed to mean?"

"No offense, but it seems that you made it to the mezzanine of the Empire State, only the flag you were looking for was hanging on the roof, pardon my lengthy analogy."

"Ah, come on! It is still a damn good climbing! It's not easy, you know! Tennis is very competitive! I was kind of half way there!"

"And what happened? Not that I don't know."

"I was already on court, warming up to play the first round of this ATP 500, when all hell broke loose. Suddenly, people started to get sick and turn into those flesh-eating dead fuckers. Even my opponent tried to eat me. I went to my box for help, you know, the place where my coaching team should be, but then I saw my coach and my personal trainer eating my press secretary and my agent, nothing I could do to stop them. I was about to be killed as well. Lucky one of the ball boys had a chef cleaver hidden in his shorts. I don't know why he was carrying such weapon around, but it was a good thing he did. We cut our way through the dead with the cleaver. That boy pretty much saved my life, a brave little kid. Once outside, we managed to find a bus to take the boy away safely, but it was too crowded for me."

He lowered his eyes and continued.

"Suddenly, everything was too crowded for me."

"What about your family?" Lily asked.

"They are in New York. I don't know if they survived this whole mess, probably not. I got no ways to know now. After that day on the court, I tried to get some help, but everybody was too scared to think of anything else other than their skins. I was let down bad. I got nobody in the end."

"Hoy! You got me now!"

"And I appreciate it very much!"

He looked at the dismounted hockey stick in her sheath, sitting beside his tennis bag.

"So, I gather you are a hockey player of some sort." He spoke.

"Actually, I played cricket, but I found out that no other sport gear is more effective in killing walking corpses than a good hockey stick. It chops their heads clean off."

"So, that's your main weapon then."

"Until I find something better, yes."

"Have you ever considered fire weapons?"

"Nay. They make too much noise and even attract more corpses. And ammunition only goes so far."

He was finding rather difficult to make conversation with that girl. He then scanned the interior of the truck with his eyes.

"Nice contraption you got here." He said.

"It gets the job done when you need it, with just a few gallons of diesel."

"Um, don't get me wrong or anything, but do you have some kind of speech disorder or something?"

"None that I know of. Why do you ask?"

"It's just that you talk real funny sometimes."

"I'm Australian." She smiled.

"Oh, all right. Sorry about that."

"Don't worry. I've been getting that a lot since I got here."

"I can imagine."

"So what's your name, mate?"

"Good guess, Mate's my name."

She glanced at him.

"You're kidding, right?"

"Nope, my name is Mate Clarkson, as in *Kelly Clarkson*."

"Well, you'd surely make a lot of friends in Australia with a name like that."

"I guess."

"Anyway, I'll call you *Clark*. Sorry, but from my point of view, *mate* is already taken."

"*Clark*, as in *Clark Gable*, there's a nice ring to it."

"Who's Kelly Clarkson?"

"Oh, she's one of the coolest rock stars ever! Her song *my life would suck without you* is really great! I can only hope she's not a zombie now."

"So, that's how we are calling them, *zombies*."

"Do you have a better idea?"

"No. I guess any possible denomination would be equally demeaning. Zombies they are."

"Anyway, do you think this plague, or whatever they call it, is going on worldwide?"

"I know that at least two countries are affected, United States and Australia. But I guess we can extrapolate it to the whole planet from this."

"Guess you're right. And do you think all social classes are affected, I mean, celebrities and all?"

"If a virus is doing all this, they don't care for bank accounts very much. Actually, if there's one thing, perhaps the only thing that can bring slobs and celebrities closer together is a terrible disease."

"Yes, the slobs teaming up with the snobs. What about politicians? Do you think they turned into zombies too?"

"Well, they were zombies before."

"Got a point there."

"Who's Clark Gable?"

ACT 3

Hector and Vince were walking down dark alleys, passing by run-down buildings, most of them abandoned. But such situation was not new in that neighborhood, which never knew prosperity, not even when the world was breathing the comfortable breezes of normality.

Technology, new inventions, opportunities and ultimately money seem to never reach certain places, fated to stay the same forever, never mind what happens. In a near apocalypse situation, poor areas don't change much, only prosper areas are devastated to become poor areas, like the ones they usually choose to ignore. And we are all the same again. Finally, we are one, as we always were.

"Do you think we can trust him?" Vince asked.

"Who?"

"That Phil guy."

"Never mind. We just share a workplace and some tools with him, nothing more."

"That's right. We don't know him that well. You shouldn't talk the way you talked in front of him."

"Now, what's that supposed to mean? I talk the way I talk. I did this my whole life."

"Gee, you can be really hardheaded sometimes!"

"That's how I made my fortune. That's how we made our fortune. You're hardheaded too, bro."

"That's not what I mean."

"Then what the heck do you mean?" Hector said impatiently.

"Things are totally different now, can't you see?! Now the whole world is the same crap! This thing of *we are in America, everybody can make a buck if they put their minds to it* is over! We have to accept the new situation and adapt to it."

"Oh, you're wrong. You're so wrong. The world is different, but it's still the same world, with the same people in it. Things change. It's part of the game."

"Not like this!"

"It doesn't matter!"

"Yes, it matters! Did you take a good look outside the city? We came from there for crying out loud! We almost died to get here!"

"Big deal! It's not very different from the old routine in Hell's Kitchen. But we made it, didn't we? Yes, I know that a goddamn virus spread worldwide, turning people into rotting freaks who eat everything in their path and our leaders don't seem to care, but then we had World War One, Two, Hiroshima and Nagasaki, the freaking plague on the Middle Age, but the world kept on going!"

"Those events you mentioned are nothing compared to this one, but you just can't accept it."

"Well, I'm not the accepting kind of guy. There's always room for industrious folks willing to rebuild and that's us. And very soon, we'll be right on top one more time, bro!"

Hector opened his big white smile again, but Vince was uncomfortably looking at all sides, as if waiting for thugs to come any minute.

"Keep your voice down, man!" Vince advised.

Hector's trademarked large smile was quickly replaced by his also trademarked scary frown.

"I talk as loud as I want!" He retorted. "You don't tell me how to talk! This is still a free country! I won't hide how I feel!"

"You're going to get us both killed! You saw what happens to those considered troublemakers!"

"They disappeared, that's all. Maybe they just went to the beach."

"You don't really believe that, do you?"

Hector soothed his expression and faced his brother.

"Jesus." He said. "When did you turn chicken, man?"
"It's not that."
"It is. Where's my little brother I could always count on? Remember the old neighborhood? All other kids walking the streets, panhandling money they later used to buy drugs, embarrassing their parents, sometimes even following orders from their parents?"
"Yes, I remember."
"Then, you also remember that mamma dragged our asses to school every morning so we could get some education, while she and sister worked hard to make an honest buck. Daddy let us down bad, but mamma never gave up. And we all helped her, you, me and sister. We never had plenty, but we always had enough. And you were always there for me, man."
"And I'll be there for you till the day I die. But this is not the old neighborhood. Mamma and sister got sick, died, resurrected and tried to eat us, and we had to stick knives in their heads. I bet this kind of shit never happened in World War One, Two, Hiroshima, Middle Ages, whatever. Face it, bro. We're fucked, as in really fucked."
"Trust me. I'll get us both out of this one, like I got us out of Hell's Kitchen."

They arrived at the construction site.

"Another day, another dollar" Vince said.

They went into the small cabinet to pick up jackets and hats.

"Hi Phil."
"Hi guys."

Hector and Vince walked to their respective sidewalk spots and jackhammers, to take up where they left off. But before they could put on their thick gloves, protective ear muffs and glasses, two men in impeccable black suits came to them.

"Excuse me," The tall one spoke "I'm agent Muldoon and this is agent Dressler, we are from the Center of Refugees. Are you Hector and Vincent Dryland?"

"Last time we checked." Vince replied.

"What can I do for you, gentlemen?" Hector queried.

"Don't bother powering up the jackhammers, boys." Dressler, the short guy, answered. "You've just been relocated."

"What?" Vince asked.

"What do you mean relocated?" Hector asked.

"It means you're going from this place to another place." Muldoon responded with irritating arrogance.

"Yes, I realize that, but are you sure this is right? I mean, we've been given this job by your people when we first came in here with the other refugees."

"That's correct, and now we're giving you new jobs." Dressler said also a little too pompous.

"And when are we supposed to start these new jobs?" Vince asked.

"Right now."

"Right now?! You mean today?!"

"Yes, right now usually means today."

"Now, you listen to me!" Hector raised his already loud voice. "Can we at least check with Mister Hanson? He's the foreman."

"That's right." Vince also spoke. "We got a lot of work to do here. We can't simply leave our posts without telling anybody!"

"I know who Mister Hanson is and I'm telling you everything is in order." Dressler informed. "You're coming with us."

"I'm sorry, but this seems highly irregular to me." Hector said firmly. "For starters, how can we know you're really from the Center of Refugees?"

"I don't think I made myself clear, boys." Muldoon retorted. "This is not a request."

Muldoon and Dressler drew stun guns from their jackets pockets and hit the brothers in the waist, not giving them time to make a single move. Electricity seized their nervous systems and they fell cold on the hard ground, paralyzed.

As if coming from nowhere, two other men in black suits came and helped Muldoon and Dressler carrying the petrified brothers to a van parked across the street. Burning rubber, the vehicle disappeared down the avenue in a matter of seconds.

After watching the whole scene, Phil dropped his welder and wiped the sweat from his forehead with the back of his hand.

"There goes two more."

ACT 4

Lily and Clark kept on going. The sunset horizon before them would be a very romantic and comforting view if it wasn't for the fact their world was slowly becoming a catwalk for living cadavers.

"We'll have to stop for some diesel soon." She informed.
"No problem. I can pick up some snacks while you fill it up."
"Just be careful not to become a snack."

He smiled.

"I didn't catch your name." Clark pointed out.
"You're right, sorry about that. My name is Lily Master."
"Lily?!"
"Yes, as in *Lily Allen*."
"Or in *Apocalily*! Hot dang, I knew I had seen you before! You're the kindergarten hero, the one who saved all the children! That was really something!"
"Oh, I can see you're into newspapers too."
"What's left of them anyway. And you were not only on the papers, but mainly on the web. When you left the kindergarten carrying that paraplegic girl on your shoulder, a teenager also filmed you with his cell phone and he uploaded it to YouTube. The video got more than seven million hits in five minutes."
"Then, it's a good thing all communication means are going down because of the plague. They could at least pay me one dollar for each page-view of this YouTube video."
"Well, I don't think money will do us much good in the not so distant future."

He faced her and said:

"Is it me or you're not proud of what you did?"

"I'm not."

"Why? That was great, the bravest feat I've ever seen! Ten minutes and hundreds of children were spared from a horrible death! I'm kind of honored to ride with you."

"Then don't be so honored."

"For God sake, why not?"

"Because it's not fair with the real heroes."

"I don't understand."

"For starters, cops died trying to save those children, but their faces didn't show on the news. Nobody gave them nicknames! Nobody gave them any name."

"Yes, but the fact you saved people in the end made their effort count. They didn't die in vain."

"You're awfully misinformed, *boykie*."

"I don't think so. It was all there, in the papers and the web."

"First, it wasn't a kindergarten, it was an elementary school! Second, I spent a good fifteen minutes trapped in that hell, not ten!"

"Well, fifteen minutes is how long fame lasts, according to some."

"And my fame should've stopped right there, according to me."

"If I had done such thing, I'd be walking on cloud nine right now!"

"Fine, do you want to know why I did it, how things happened? I tell you. I was riding my rig, depressed and bitter. I had just lost my dad to this plague and life had lost all meaning. Then I saw this school coming. I noticed all the fuss of course, the police cordon, the press, folks screaming, I knew there were people in danger. Do you want to know what I thought of all that?"

"Yes!"

"Too bad, I thought. That's right, I was planning to just pass by and overlook the whole mess because I got enough problems. How brave is that? But my truck broke down. Yes, that's why I stopped, my freaking car stalled on me! The engine overheated or something. One more headache for me! I went into the school because I got nothing else to live for, secretly hoping I died in there, putting an end to my miserable existence. Some hero, huh?"

"Well, the outcome was the same. And to me, you're still a hero."

"I'm a fraud with a bad radiator."

"So sorry Lily, but I don't believe you went into that school just because you got nothing better to do with your life. I have this feeling you did all that because you are a great person."

"I don't care what you believe."

An uncomfortable silence followed. Clark broke it:

"Who fixed your truck in the end?"

"The father of the paraplegic girl happened to be a mechanic and he got some spare cables."

"Good. It's the least he could do."

Lily shook her head.

"Then I tried to hit the road, but the bloody press was all over my rig, the flashes of their cameras blinding me. But I didn't talk to them, wasn't in the mood. Later, one damned reporter found out my name and I guess his editor came up with this silly Apocalily thing, a combination of the word *apocalypse* with my name *Lily*, such a stupid playing with words."

"Maybe, but I bet this event changed your life."

"In a way, it did."

"Have you been on the road since then?"

"Even before that."

"Why are you wearing those fingerless gloves?"

"Because I don't like to get my hands dirty. See, I'm no hero after all."

"Then why they are fingerless?"

"Because I especially like to keep my palms clean."

"You don't talk much about you and your past, do you?"

"Why should I?"

"Well, the more you hold information about yourself, the more you look like a badass road warrior."

"Fine! What do you want to know?"

"Tell me about your father. You and your old man were pretty close, right?"

"We had to be. We only had each other. My mother died when I was four, giving birth to my baby sister, but she also didn't make it."

"I'm sorry to hear that."

"It was just the two of us. My father became my world and I became his world. He taught me martial arts, some defense techniques, a lot of those kung-fu, taekwondo, kickboxing thing... At first I thought that was silly, but now it's paying off."

"And what did your father do for a living, I mean, besides being the Australian version of Bruce Lee?"

She smiled.

"He worked in a large telecom industry. Actually, it was the Australian branch of a big American company. He was a competent bloke, that's why he was given this opportunity to work here. Actually, I was even more excited than him. As you can imagine, I went where he went."

"What about the plague?"

"It was starting in Australia. We had news of a fatal disease spreading countrywide like mad, rumors about folks rising from the dead and eating the living. Of course we didn't take such talks seriously, but we were glad to leave the country on those conditions."

"And then you got to another country in even worse conditions."

"Something like that, yes. We heard some folks coughing and sneezing on the plane, but nobody died during the trip. But things were different once at the airport. Chaos was already all over the place, dead people running around trying to dine the living. We heard the locals liked barbecue, but that was a little too much!"

Clark smiled.

"I know what you mean." He said. "Anyway, something tells me you made it out of there alive."

"Daddy could be pretty resourceful when he had to. He was also a kind, loving man, but regretfully some people mistaken this for lack of nerves. Some of his work colleagues who also came to America made fun of him because of that. But my father always knew how to deal with extreme situations, like the one we're facing now. He even modified this truck to make it what it is now."

"Yes, I've been meaning to ask you exactly this, I don't suppose you brought this car all the way from Australia, right?"

"No, we did not. It's a good old American model we acquired in here."

"Then how come the steering wheel is on the right side?"

"My father changed it."

"Your father changed it?!"

"He could never get used to this driving on the left thing. Honestly, neither could I."

"But how he did it?!"

"He never told me all the particulars on how he did it, but you got to admit, we're sitting on the results."

"That's for sure. Anything else your dad could do?"

"He also taught me how to read lips."

"Why? Are you deaf or something?"

"Nope."

"Then what's the use for it?"

"I don't know, quite frankly."

He took a deep breath.

"How did your father die, if you don't mind my asking?"

"Daddy and his colleagues were getting some grub in a snack bar, trying to figure out what was going on, how come dead people were simply rising to eat the living. I was with them. Eventually, the place was overrun by zombies, and they cornered some kids. My father wanted to save them and he asked his workmates to help him. But the same ones who mocked him for his sobriety were too spineless to do it. They just hid behind a table, crying like babies and screaming for help. My father had to save those kids on his own. I begged him not to go, it was too dangerous, but nothing could stop him. He was just that kind of man."

"And the zombies killed him."

"Not quite. Because he was the Australian version of Bruce Lee, he managed to keep the beasts at bay for a while, giving the children time to run back to their parents. But there was this one little girl who was too scared to move. My father got distracted comforting her and a zombie bit him."

"Oh no!"

"He eventually took the child to safety, but we both knew it was all over for him. We had already learnt that whoever got bit by the dead also turned into one of them, and we had to destroy their heads. And my father didn't want me to see him as those things and I was the only one who could stop that. He asked me to bust his head somehow."

"It must've been terrible."

"One of the customers in the snack bar was a hockey player and he fled leaving his bag behind, with a new kind of modular stick inside. Now you can guess what happened next."

"So, your father was the first one you killed like this."

"My world finished that day."

"You had to do it. There was no other way."

"I wasn't so sure, I died with him."

"But you were born again after what you did in the elementary school."

Lily didn't answer.

"Yes you were." Clark insisted.

"I guess daddy would've liked to see me doing something like that."

"Of course he would!"

"So, how did I do in the department of talking about me and my past?"

"Extremely well!"

"Oh thank you."

"But you still look like a badass road warrior."

ACT 5

"Do you think we lost them?" Paul screamed in despair, hands compressing the steering wheel to almost squeeze it.

"How the heck should I know?" Nick retorted. "Do you want me to go out there and check?"

"Yes, why don't you? You're surely not helping any in here!"

"Oh, this is great! If you didn't drive like a pregnant hippo, we wouldn't be in this mess in the first place! Do you want me to drive?!"

"No, I want you to shut the fuck up!"

"Stupid ninny!"

"What was that?!"

"HEY!" Susan yelled. "Would you stop that? We got way bigger problems!"

"Yes we do!" Becky said grinding teeth. She was sitting by Susan with arms embracing her knees. "We got nothing but cowards in here!"

With furious eyes she looked at Frank, sitting across them. His tearful eyes could not return her punitive look.

"Asshole!" Becky said.

"Stop it!" Susan ordered her.

"Don't you dare to defend him! He killed Lucas!"

"He had to, can't you see? He got bitten!"

"We could've at least tried to think of something, maybe amputating his leg, I don't know!"

"He begged us not to do it! He didn't want to turn into one of these things, he wanted to die!"

"He wasn't thinking! He was scared! And you didn't even try to help him, none of you! All you could do was running scared!"

"Everything happened so fast, Becky. Please, I... I don't pretend to know how you feel..."

"Then don't! *'Cause* you're right! You have no idea how I feel! I loved Lucas!"

"Really?" Frank decided to join the conversation. "Well, I didn't see you being there for him! You ran away too, remember?"

"SHUT UP, SHUT UP, SHUT UP!" Becky jumped to Frank, angry teeth occupying most of her face. She slapped and kicked him with all she got. He raised hands to protect his head against such attack.

"Back off! BACK OFF!" Susan screamed, wrapping an arm around Becky's midsection, trying to pull her away from Frank.

"He was my best friend, okay!" Frank shouted. "It was very hard for me too! And yet, I was the one who had to put him out of his misery!"

"Enough!" Susan screamed her last ultimatum.

She managed to hold Becky down, and the girl burst into tears on Susan's right shoulder.

"This won't bring him back." Susan whispered.

"This won't bring Joyce back either." Frank murmured. "And she was only thirteen."

"Where we go now?" Becky asked, trying to get a grip on herself.

"Far from those dead bastards!" Nick said.

"Oh no, No, NO!" Paul suddenly shouted, hitting hard the steering wheel with his left hand.

"What...? What happened?" Nick mumbled.

"Right now, we're not going anywhere. We got a flat."

"Ah Jesus Christ, Jesus Christ, Jesus...!"

Paul was about to lose control of the vehicle. The van veered off harshly, almost overturning. A few yards from the main road, he finally brought the vehicle to a halt.

"Are you alright?" He asked everybody.

They all nodded a yes.

"This is great, this is just great!" Nick grunted. "What now?"

"Now, we run!" Paul said.

"What? Are you crazy? Those freaks will eat our guts, like they did to Joyce!"

"Not if we run."

"I say we stay here." Becky suggested. "Come on, they can't get in with all doors locked."

"And how long are you planning to stay in here?" Paul retorted "Until we starve to death? We have to try to make a run for it."

"Run where?" Nick intervened. "We are in the middle of fucking nowhere! As far as we know, those things can be everywhere!"

"My point exactly! We're not safe in here. They'll turn the car around, they'll break into here."

"Only if they see us."

"They will find us eventually. They can also smell us."

"But they can't get in!"

"Oh I think they can. Those fuckers are strong!"

"They are rotting corpses. They can't be stronger than a human being!"

"They seemed pretty strong to me." Frank opined. "Besides, there're too many of them. They might as well open up this truck like a tin can."

"Well, you pricks do what you want." Becky said. "I'm not moving from here."

"We can't stay here forever!" Paul spoke.

"Alright, then you go out there and see if those monsters listen to your bullshit!" Nick replied. "Maybe you're lucky and they don't eat sissies."

"Hey!" Susan protested, while Becky opened a very tiny smile.

Paul jumped to Nick and pushed him violently. They both crashed against the side of the van, shaking the vehicle and making a thunderous noise.

"Break it up, you're crazy?" Frank hopelessly tried to separate the two fighting men.

"Hey! Stop all of you!" Susan interrupted them loudly. "Look!"

Everybody looked out of the window, to the direction she was pointing at.

"That's beautiful!" Nick gasped "If we can make it there."

"The lights are on." Susan spoke. "There must be somebody inside. It's not that far. I think it's our best shot."

"Maybe our only shot" Frank agreed.

"Right on!" Paul said.

"I'm in the mood for a movie anyway." Nick spoke.

They turned to Becky. She hesitated, but finally said:

"Fine, let's go. At least a Cinemark is big enough so I don't have to look at your ugly faces all the time."

Very slowly and with extreme caution, Nick opened the van left door. He peeked outside. No sound. He waited.

"I guess we're good to go." He murmured to the others.

They stepped out of the vehicle one by one, as if such order was necessary. But they barely set foot on the floor and a symphony of snarls deafened their eardrums. Horridly deformed silhouettes grew bigger as they approached fast.

"Shit, RUN!"

They ran, trying not to trip on their own ankles.

"Did you close the doors of the car?" Nick asked.
"Of course not!" Paul replied. "I didn't exactly have the time!"
"Then we can't go back to the van anymore! Nice doing, genius!"
"Shut up and run you two!" Susan screamed.

Arguing in the middle of a run almost caused Susan to trip and fall down on the grass. But she managed to restore balance and kept on running.

They reached the movie theater and tried to open the door, to no avail.

"Hey! Open the door!"
"You guys, please, open the goddamn door!"
"They're going to kill us! Open the door please!" Their voices overlapped.

Only Susan didn't say a word. She frenetically waved arms and hands to a camera just above the heavy, thick gates. They heard a click sound. The doors unlocked and they ran inside. Frank had to kick one of the hungry beasts that kind of got caught on him.

Another click sound and the huge gates were locked again.

"Thank God for surveillance systems." Susan said breathless.

"Are you alright?" Paul asked Frank. "Have you got bitten... or scratched?"

"No, but that thing touched me!"

"It was a female dead." Nick noticed. "Guess she liked you."

"Yeah, maybe it was your sister!"

"Or your mommy!"

"Enough, you two!" Susan scolded them. "Damn it, you're such a bunch of kids!"

"And assholes too!" Becky seemed to agree, but her insult sounded general.

They walked around the lobby.

"Look at this place." Paul said. "Lights are on, everything's neatly organized, definitely not Hurricane Katrina torn apart and upside down like all other places we've been."

"We're surely not alone here, dude." Nick concluded. "Somebody's giving this place a lot of love."

"Maybe a movie fan" Frank proposed.

"And what are they showing tonight?" Paul queried.

"I hope it's not a zombie movie, we got plenty of that outside."

The men laughed boyishly.

"Shut up!" Becky said.

"Hello!" Susan shouted "Anybody here?"

"Hey, not so fast, sweetie" Nick interrupted her. "We don't know this people, or their intentions."

"That's right." Frank agreed. "What if folks here are into one of those apocalyptical cults in which mutants probe normal people's asses?"

"You're in the right place, dude." Paul spoke. "You have been seeing a lot of movies."

"Whoever they are, they opened the door and saved our lives." Susan replied. "Maybe they didn't show up because they are worried about *our* intentions." She raised her head and her voice again "Hello there! We mean you no harm, our car broke down! We just want shelter!" And, after a pause: "Thanks for letting us in!"

Only silence responded.

"Maybe they're just shy." Nick proposed. "I'm sure they'll come to us at their own convenience. In the meantime, let's eat!"

In less than ten minutes, they were all occupying the most comfortable seats in the biggest cinema of the theater, M&Ms, ruffles and pounds of popcorn all around them, not to mention gallons of soda pop distributed in five king-size plastic cups. They were feasting at will, but not watching anything in particular on the giant white screen.

"We could try to get into the projection booth." Frank suggested. "See if we can watch something."

"That'll be great to blow off some steam." Nick said.

"Only with the kind permission of our hosts, whoever they are" Susan replied. "We'd better get to know them first."

"They don't seem to have a problem with us devastating their food supply."

"Do you even know how to work a projector?" Becky asked.

"We figure it out. It can't be that hard. Today, everything's digital. It must only be a matter of pushing a couple of buttons and run some software."

"Like the movies you illegally download to your laptop?" Susan spoke.

"Precisely!"

"Maybe some other time" Susan decided. "Let's finish eating first."

"That'll take days!"

They all laughed, except for Becky.

"You got to eat something." Susan turned to her. "Come on, join the party."

"Unless there are vegetables in there, I pass."

"Popcorn comes from corn." Paul joked.

Becky just twisted her lips, and not to smile.

"You might as well put some weight now." Nick spoke to her. "It's not like the agencies are hiring too much these days."

"You might end up like those zombies out there if you don't put some flesh around your bones." Paul agreed.

"Yeah, thanks for reminding me that everything's hopeless now!" Becky complained. "As for the zombies, even their rotten dicks are bigger than yours!"

"Nice." Paul muttered.

"She got a point there though." Nick said.

"About their dicks being bigger than mine?" Paul asked.

"No, about everything being hopeless."

"Are you going all pessimistic on us now?" Susan queried.

"No, not pessimistic, just hopeless. See what we're doing now, hiding like rats, always running from one shelter to another. We'll probably have to run for the rest of our days, if we survive."

"Yes, it's tough not to be on top of the food chain anymore." Frank said.

"Right" Nick continued. "We're practically slaves of those dead fuckers. They appear, we run scared."

"They dilacerate our bodies if we don't." Susan spoke.

"My point exactly" Nick whispered. "They say jump, we ask how high. I'm sorry, but that feels pretty pointless to me."

"And to think that perhaps all we need to turn this tide is a hockey stick." Paul said.

Nick frowned "What are you talking about, dude?"

"Come on, man. We all watched that video together in the cafeteria, right before the campus was overrun."

"Oh, you mean the elementary school thing." Nick scoffed. "Jeez, I can't believe you fell for that one."

"Why? What do you mean?"

"It was obviously something cooked up by the press. It's just impossible that one girl could do all that."

"Don't you believe in girl power, Nick?" Susan turned to him. "Are you going sexist on me now?"

"I do believe in girl power. An army of powerful girls can take out hundreds of zombies. One single person, never mind if it's a girl or a boy, cannot."

"Why would the press stage such thing?" Paul asked. "Why going to all that trouble?"

"Maybe the government, wherever it is now, ordered the whole thing."

"Why?"

"I don't know, to keep our hopes up perhaps, to pretend that, after all the screw-ups they've done, there're still heroes among us."

"So, you don't believe in Apocalily?" Paul asked.

"Nope, I only believe in apocalypse, because there's one going on right now. That woman who so solemnly carried the crippled girl out of the school is nothing more than an actress or some daft top model they hired for the occasion."

"Hey!" Becky screamed.

"Oops! I mean, no offense, honey."

"And I bet they paid her in appetite suppressing drugs!" Frank joked. "Right, Bec?"

Paul and Nick grinned.

Becky practically jumped out of her seat "You know something, fuck you, fuck you all! I'm sick of this whole... I'm sick of you!"

And she walked away.

"Hey, don't wander around all alone!" Susan shouted, but the girl just kept on going until disappearing beyond the room exit.

"That was not nice!" Susan scolded the men.

"Let her go, the little prick." Nick said. "We all benefit from this. She surely can use some time alone and we can take a rest from her presence."

"That's cruel, you know?" Susan spoke. "She's our friend!"

"Stop defending her, Sue. Can't you see what you're doing?"

"She's been through a lot!"

"Yes, like all of us!" Nick talked real loud. "We all suffered, we all had losses since this whole mess started! She's just too selfish to see anything else other than her little pretty fairytales world!" He took a deep breath. "She's a spoilt little brat and you're making her worse! Damn it, everything's just a freaking giant mirror to her!"

Becky was in the restroom, looking in the mirror.

"Assholes!" She cursed.

Then, tears welled up in her eyes and she whispered "Lucas..."

She went back to the lobby and saw some protein bars in a vending machine. One might say she was really hungry. After making sure through the glass the bars were positively diet, she began to shake the machine real harshly, but it wasn't budging.

"You don't have to do that, darling." A very deep female voice startled Becky.

She turned around to yell at whomever that was, but froze speechless. A beautiful, slender, blonde woman was standing right by her.

"I'm sorry. I didn't mean to scare you." She said softly.

"No… No problem." Becky mumbled with a dumb expression. The penetrating blue eyes of the woman seemed to petrify her entire body, as if a simple look could wrap around a soul.

Becky felt a strange chill run down her spine. It was at same time uncomfortable and caressing. But who the heck was that woman?

"Who are you?" Becky then decided to just go ahead and ask.

"Call me Shane." The woman answered, opening a very white and sweet smile. "What about you, sweet pea?"

"My name is Rebecca, but people call me Becky."

"It's adorable anyway."

Becky was definitely enchanted.

"Oh, by the way…" Shane said sportively and went to the vending machine.

She simply pulled the door toward her.

"See, all you got to do is open it!"

Becky did not think twice and advanced to the protein bars. "Only one!" she magnanimously promised herself. In about thirty seconds, she had already devoured five bars. Shane looked at her motherly.

"There are more, honey." She said. "But you'd better take it easy. It's not a good idea to fill your stomach all at once. You clearly haven't eaten in a while. Give your stomach time to adapt."

Becky faced her with very childish eyes. Her mouth was too full to speak.

"Are you a top model or something?" Shane asked her.
"Trying to be" Becky responded a little suspicious. "Why?"

Shane laughed, as if reading the girl's mind.

"I'm asking because you're just too beautiful not to be a top model, honey!"
"Thanks!" Becky's face was illuminated by a smile, something she almost never did. "Too bad you're the only one who thinks so."
"I don't believe you!"

Becky never felt so comfortable and protected like in that moment. She didn't understand what was happening to her, but it was so good she just let herself go by such feelings.

"Do you run this place?" Becky asked, again with her mouth full.
"Can say that, yes" Shane replied. "Actually, I run a lot of places. Normally, I have more people helping me in here, but now I'm alone."
"You opened the door for us?"
"Of course!"

"My bubblehead friends are in cinema-one stuffing their bellies with all your snacks. They're actually making a hell of a mess in there. I hope you don't mind."

"Bubblehead friends!" Shane laughed aloud. "Oh, such a little rascal you are!"

Becky smiled again.

"And of course I don't mind." Shane continued. "That's why I opened the door for you! I want you to eat and have fun. Most of all, I want you to feel safe. Let's take a break from all the madness outside, what do you say?"

"I can live with that!"

"And nothing better than a movie theater to do so, huh? For most people, places like this represented everything that was good and glamorous and entertaining, bringing the best in each and every one of us, giving us a reason for living... I tell you what, I introduce myself to your friends and we all watch a movie together! And you get to choose it!"

Becky lowered her eyes all of a sudden.

"What's wrong?" Shane asked her.

Becky was usually as tightlipped as an oyster. But she caught herself yapping:

"You shouldn't talk like this! You shouldn't talk about how things used to be. You shouldn't talk about hope when there's none! There are no such things as *best in each and every one of us* and *reason for living*. This is a big pile of crap. Places like this sold fantasy, that's all. Two hours later, we had to be back on a shitty world, to a shitty reality!"

"You're in pain I can see."

"Damn right I am! Lucas... You know, my... he loved the theaters, he loved movies, but those jerks..." She started to sob.

"I can help you."

"What?"

"I can make all your pains go away."

"What the... What the heck are you talking about, Shane?"

However, Becky could no longer take her eyes off Shane, although she had lost the means to realize it. Her muscles paralyzed all at once, she could not move. And yet, Becky felt extremely good.

Shane said:

"The sunshine springs, happiness it brings.

Those eyes you should follow, to keep away sorrow.

Seek the giant bird you must, on her you shall blindly trust.

For the good science you will urge, from all impurities to purge."

Becky blinked a couple of times.

"Wow!" She said.

"It's amazing, isn't it?"

"Well, now we just have to find a way to beat boredom." Nick yawned.

"Try having your stomach pumped." Susan replied.

"You also ate a hell lot!"

"I know, but I like to nag." She smiled. So did the other three.

They lazily stood up, even having to put some efforts to do so.

"Man, I don't want to see food for at least a month." Frank said.

"I hope you don't have to swallow those words in a month." Paul spoke.

"I'm too full to swallow anything."

"We'd better try to find some weapons." Nick suggested. "We can't stay here forever."

"What kind of weapons can we find in a movie theater?" Frank asked.

"We can smash zombies' heads with movie reels." Paul replied.

"Very funny."

"Why don't we just stay here?" Frank suggested.

"Because we are still in the middle of nowhere" Nick answered. "If we eat every day as we did in the last fifteen minutes, we're going to run out of food real fast."

"Not to mention we still have loved ones to find." Susan said. "We can't just give up on them."

"But where we go from here, and with what vehicle? The good old van must be packed with walking corpses right now."

"That's a good point." Nick admitted. "Well, let's go find the creepo and then we see."

"Hey, you be nice to Becky!" Susan practically commanded him.

However, they didn't have to go very far. By the cinema exit the *creepo* was standing, together with Shane. And Becky was eating a large double cheeseburger, not exactly a veggie one.

"Hey guys." She said with her mouth full. "Sorry I left in such a hurry. This is Shane. She's the one who opened the door for us. She also runs this place."

"Hi..." Nick and Frank said insecure. Susan and Paul just nodded.

"Hi, everybody!" Shane replied with a bright, incredibly charming smile.

"Thanks for letting us in." Susan spoke.

The surprise of meeting their savior so suddenly was nothing compared to the astonishment of seeing Becky eating a carnivore, vein clogging meal.

"Oh, think nothing of it." Shane responded. "It was actually a selfish act. I was desperate for company. And I could never imagine I'd be visited by such nice folks. I should be the one thanking you."

"Um, guys..." Becky spoke. "I'm sorry I was mean to you before. What happened in the park was nobody's fault. If Joyce had obeyed Susan instead of chasing that freaking dog, she'd be alive now. Lucas was careless as usual and got himself bitten. There was nothing else you could've done. I was a jerk, I'm really sorry."

"Not at all!" Susan said emphatically. "Nobody's a jerk. It was a difficult situation, we all understand. Joyce and Lucas meant a lot to all of us."

"Thanks." Becky said very gently. Nick frowned.

"I'm so excited!" Shane continued. "I've never felt such positive energy like the one you bring. You'll fit in just fine. I can barely wait to show you around. Feel very much free to eat and drink all you want. Then, we meet back here for a movie. I got a pretty good selection of the cheesiest Hollywood trash of all times, just for you!"

"Alright!!!" Frank jumped.

ACT 6

Lily saw a rest-stop up yonder, with some fuel dispensers. She slowed down and stopped by one with *diesel* written on the side. It looked functional. There was also a convenience store sharing space with a restaurant called *Peace on Earth Diner*.

"Alright, boykie, this is it." She said. "Let's try to do this nice and easy.

"Are we expecting any trouble?" Clark asked. "This place looks so empty."

"Yes, that's what I thought when I stopped at this roadside bar to stretch my legs and perhaps have a drink, but some dead guys interrupted me in mid-moonshine."

"And I bet you took care of them Apocalily style, huh?"

"I took care of them so I could survive style."

Lily unlocked the doors.

"Empty your bag, please." She said.

Mate did as told.

They left the vehicle and closed the doors as smoothly as they could. The sound of the doors slamming shut was loud just the same.

"So, whatever you do, do it quietly." Lily advised him. "And if you have to go to the bathroom for number two, remember to fart low."

"I'll keep that in mind."

Lily looked at all sides. Instinctively, Clark did the same. She grabbed the fuel nozzle.

"It seems to be in order."

She anxiously turned to the vehicle and opened the tank cover a little too roughly, almost breaking it in the process.

"Hey, careful with that" Clark said. "This is not a motorized kangaroo!"

"Oh, this is nice!" Lily replied, a little more offended than Clark expected. "And I bet you think we also have chariots pulled by koalas, right?"

"Hey, I'm sorry! I was just kidding!"

"Then, let me tell you something, chap. Despite all labels you people like to plaster on foreigners' faces, all stereotypes you may say about Australia are powerfully inaccurate!"

Nevertheless, maybe because she accidently spoke a little too loud, or maybe due to a terrible twist of fate, ten morbidly deformed, snarling walking corpses appeared completely out of the blue, as if coming from the deepest catacombs of hell, advancing furiously toward them.

"Shit!" Clark cried in despair and started to scratch the side of the vehicle. "Open the door, Lily!"

However, as quickly as the wind, Lily drew a boomerang from somewhere inside her belt and tossed it. Armed with sharp razors on its concave side, the device sliced in half five skulls on its way up and another five skulls on its way back, to finally land safely back on Lily's hand. The beasts fell helpless on the floor.

She turned to Clark, who was staring directly at her.

"Well, maybe one or two stereotypes are accurate." She said.

"And I'm glad for that!" Clark took a deep breath. "Now I know what the fingerless gloves are for."

"It's never a good idea having your hand amputated by your faithful boomerang."

"So, do you have any more surprises in that utility belt of yours?"

"No, that's pretty much it, two little knives, a boomerang and the modular hockey stick on my back."

"Can I have the two knives?"

"No."

"What if I have to defend myself against zombies?"

"You just whistle and I come *quick*."

"Okay."

"Now seriously, we have to get something for you to defend yourself, only not my two knives. And, as I said before, those racquets of yours won't do it, unless some zombies play tennis."

"We can try to find something sharp in the convenience store."

Lily finished refueling her motorized kangaroo.

"Let's have a look." She agreed.

Lily opened the glass door to the convenience store and a bell attached to the doorframe jingled.

"Goddamn it!" Lily cursed as low as she could manage.

"Some people have no respect for sneaking in." Clark whispered back.

"Problem is folks who have those bells installed on doors never consider the possibility of a zombie attack."

"They just don't plan ahead."

Lily and Clark walked around real slow. They were cautious but heard no snarls.

"I guess the coast is clear." Lily spoke. "Anyway, keep your voice down. Those dead buckos are sneaky."

"You're telling me!"

"Alright, lad, try to find something you can use as a weapon, while I get some food and water."

"Perhaps I should try first on *zombie killing sportswear* section."

Lily smiled.

"Remember, be extra careful." She said. "If you see a zombie, don't engage, just call me."

"I appreciate your good advice, but believe me, it is utterly unnecessary. I won't engage a fly without calling you."

And they went to their respective errands. Mate Clarkson checked racks and shelves systematically, but couldn't find anything sharp or big enough to inflict damage. He found nail clippers, shoe buffers, nail files, head clips, one or two small pliers and a great variety of tennis racquets.

Another thing he found was a zombie walking like a drunk by the end of the long rack he was also standing by.

"Oh my God, Lily…" He tried to call her, but only peeps came out of his mouth.

That gave him a brilliant idea! Keep absolutely quiet and pray for the zombie to go away. And it was working, until the creature tripped on its own heels, turned around and saw him.

For somebody who seemed so unstable before, the living dead advanced to Clark surprisingly fast with wide open mouth.

"AHHHHH" He screamed, and in a desperate impetus snatched a pack containing a knitting scissor from a hook and hit the general direction from which the zombie was coming with it.

When he finally built the nerves to uncover his face, he saw the dead monster stretching lifeless on the floor with the scissor and the pack impaling its head.

"What happened?" Lily came from behind him.

She saw the zombie on the ground with its scalp pierced by the scissor.

"Yes, you can use this one." She said. "Just take it out of the pack next time."

"Wow! Did you see that? Very soon, people will be calling me *Apocaclark*!"

"Are you all right?"

"Sure! I saw ugly here coming and I knew exactly what to do."

"I heard a scream."

"It was the zombie."

"Oh."

But a very familiar choir of unmistakable growls echoed through the market. Clark took the scissor out of the dead skull and out of the pack.

"Ugh, this is gross!" He spoke.

Seven more cadavers found them. Lily drew her two knives.

"You know what to do, lad." She said.

And Clark needed to hear nothing more. Boosted by a courageous surge of stamina, he jumped to one of the growlers and thrust his new weapon right in its left eye.

"This is great!" He cheered himself.

And that was it. In a matter of minutes, Lily and Clark finished all attackers. Clark bravely killed the already mentioned zombie, while Lily killed the other six.

"Nice teamwork, partner!" He said.
"Right on!"
"I'm getting the hang of it."
"Good, that may come in handy. Now, we'd better go. I've already got everything we need for the moment. We're making too much noise and I don't want to start another party."

They went to the counter. Lily grabbed the tennis bag full with supplies and headed toward the glass door. But she retreated and turned to her partner.

"Hey Clark, we may have a little problem."

The man looked outside through the glass.

"I see." He spoke. "It seems the party already started.
"And we are the main course."

At least fifty rotting corpses were walking around Lily's truck, like drifting boats.

"What we do now?" Clark asked.
"We open our way through them."
"Okay." He said, but not so self assured.
"Take this." She gave him the tennis bag and he strapped it to his back.

Clark raised his knitting scissor.

"Just one thing," Lily said "take this matter seriously, never underestimate those dead psychos."
"I won't." Clark mumbled.

She opened the door and they left. It didn't take long for the living dead to notice them. Lily just walked toward the hungry enemies with Mate right behind her, getting nervous at every step. The beasts were inches from them and coming fast. Finally, the Australian woman decided to grab the hockey stick to mount it.

But Clark didn't have to do anything actually. With big shining eyes, he gazed with admiration at the elegant ballet performed by Lily, while she swung and twirled the hockey stick like the most skillful of swashbucklers, cutting heads as she went.

One by one, two by two, three by three, the hungry beasts tumbled down inert and nullified. She cleared their way enough so they could get to truck. But once they were inside, more corpses came.

Very soon, a horde of zombies completely surrounded the vehicle, pounding and climbing, shaking the truck real hard.

"Alright" Lily said behind the wheel. "The secret to safely deal with those creatures can be summarized in a single word, velocity. The faster you kill them, the better. Always look around you. They may be slow, but they can surprise you. They may come from behind you, from above you, or even crawling on the floor, they may come from everywhere. You have to be prepared all the time."

"Yes, I appreciate you taking the time to teach me and all, but I really think we should do something about those monsters on the verge of turning the car around!"

"You're right." Lily pulled a lever right below the dashboard.

Several pointy spikes shaped like cones projected out from all sides of the truck, impaling a good deal of the zombies. Lily pushed the lever back to its original position and the spikes retreated back inside the vehicle, dropping perforated creatures on the ground.

The falling of the zombies directly connected to the truck gave Lily enough room to start the engine and speed away from the rest of the horde.

"Spikes that come out of the hull..." Clark divagated aloud.
"Yep."
"Let me guess, daddy did this too."
"He had a problem with strangers messing with his property."
"And a very subtle way to show it, I can see."
"Daddy had a delightful way to handle matters, don't you think?"
"That's for sure. Is there anything else this *Apocamobile* of yours can do?"
"It takes you to places."
"It also takes you *out* of places, thank God."
"It's amazing what you can do with just a few gallons of diesel."
"Well, I'm just glad we got out of there. Damn, we were shaking more than Elvis' hips in that Ed Sullivan Show."
"Who's...?"
"Oh please! Don't tell me you're going to ask who Elvis is!"

"I was going to ask who Ed Sullivan is. Of course I know who Elvis is! You're talking about Elvis Presley, right, not Elvis Costello?"

"Who's Elvis Costello?"

"Never mind. Anyway, I do know who Elvis Presley is."

"Oh yeah?! Prove it!"

"Wop bop a loomba blop blop boom boom, tutti frutti, au rutti, tutti frutti, au rutti, tutti frutti, au rutti, tutti frutti, au rutti, tutti frutti, au rutti, wop bomb a boom bam blah blah, bang bang..."

"All right, stop that! You made your point! Jesus!"

"Elvis is the king."

"Oh yeah, he is."

"Do you wanna know what else I'm kinda partial to?"

"Hit me."

"Pink Floyd!"

ACT 7

Hector woke up with a cockroach in his mouth. He coughed it out, almost choking on it. He was confused, his head hurt. He tried to wipe sweat off his forehead. That was when he noticed he was in chains, attached to a makeshift bed with a torn mattress.

Hector looked around frightened, he could barely move. His eyes found Vince lying on a similar bed beside him.

"Vince! Hey Vince! Wake up, man! VINCE! WAKE UP!"

His brother moved, but couldn't open his eyes. Drool came out of his mouth.

"Come on, Vince, fight it man! Snap out of it!"

Slowly, Vince got a grip of reality, a terrible new one.

"What? What?" He mumbled scared, trying to move, but shackles strangled his wrists and ankles.
"Are you alright, bro?"
"Do I look alright to you? Damn it!"
"I know what you mean."
"Where are we? What is this place?" Vincent asked with a very fainting voice.

Suddenly, they shook real harshly.

"We are moving, goddamn it!"
"It looks that way." Hector agreed.

He saw another man lying in front of them, with thick beard and sidelocks, also in chains. He looked barely awake.

"Hey partner…" Hector called him.

"Yes…" He replied with an equally fainting voice.

"I don't suppose you know what this is all about, right?"

"No, my friend, I don't. All I know is I was participating in this rally, me and my colleagues, when some men in black suits came. That's the last thing I remember before waking up in here."

"Yes, pretty much like us. What's your name?"

"Aaron. What's yours?"

"I'm Hector, this is Vince. We are brothers."

"Nice meeting you, my friends."

"Likewise."

Then, a strange smell invaded the place and they passed out again.

Hector and Vincent walked with arms and legs shackled together, escorted by two men in military outfits. The brothers were numb and drowsy, as if on drugs. They were forced to stop in front of a room, where a third man carrying a club was waiting.

"All right, boys, strip." He ordered, tapping his hand with the club.

"W-what?"

"To your bare asses, scumbag, if I have to say it again, I break your ugly face!"

The brothers did not have a clear idea of what was going on. Their vision was blurred. Very slowly, they took off all their clothes, a terrible headache stabbing their skulls. In an instinctive gesture of shame, they covered their genitals with the hands.

The two men in uniforms pushed them into the room, causing them to crash against a tiled wall. They fell on the cold floor. All of a sudden, a strong jet of even colder water whipped each and every one of their pores, making them roll to the wall again. The brothers screamed in despair and pain, the water was drowning them, they couldn't breathe.

"It's cleaning time, boys!" The man holding the thick hose said.

"Too bad we can't wash this black skin off their bodies, huh?" The other man spoke.

"We can try and paint them!"

They laughed.

"So, did you have fun with the Jew boy?" The man with the club asked.

"Oh yeah, he cried like a girl when I shaved every single part of his disgusting body, you should've seen it, man!"

"I'm sorry I missed that one. But at least I'm having some fun with the wet niggers over there!"

And they laughed, laughed and laughed.

After being given shirts, pants and shoes without socks, Hector and Vince, again in shackles, were escorted by the two uniformed men to a huge, clean and air conditioned room. A distinguished man in a lustrous grey suit stood before them.

"Ah, they are much better now!" He said. "Well, at least within possibilities. Good morning, gentlemen. I'm the Minister and that's all you need to know for the moment."

"I don't care who you are, alright?!" Hector blew up very loudly. "This is a total absurd! We are American citizens who are supposed to start a new job here! Nobody's going to treat me like a prisoner anymore, you hear! I demand to speak with your superior right now!!!"

One of the thugs clubbed Hector right below his nape, causing him to fall down on his knees in pain. The other hit Vincent on the back of his legs to make him kneel down as well.

"Oh, and you will start your new jobs very soon." The man calmly said. "You're just not going to get paid for this one. Um, by the way, as I'm sure you've already realized, in here you only speak when spoken to. However, now that you mentioned, it's important to say that I'm the only superior you got for now, and you will respectfully refer to me as Minister. That being said, you'll be transferred to the power plant shortly, where you shall begin your new functions."

"Power plant?" Vince mumbled. "But we know nothing of..."

He was brutally interrupted by a harsh blow on his shoulder.

"What did I just say?" The Minister reminded him. "Now, before you go, you'll be allowed to spend some quality time in the patio to get some sun, not that you need it. It's my policy to always let my employees enjoy some good moments of relaxation before starting the hard work. After all, we wouldn't want anybody accusing us of being cruel, now would we?" He turned to the guards. "Gentlemen, if you please..."

And Hector and Victor were pushed out of the Minister's office.

Once in the big patio, the brothers walked under a melting sun burning their faces. The large field they were in was a vast piece of flatland that stretched all the way to mountains on the horizon.

In the vicinities constructions stood, some new, others run-down, but what really dominated the environment was a monumental dish antenna on top of a small building. They could see barbed wire fences surrounding the whole perimeter.

"Jesus, Hec, what is this, Hec?" Vincent spoke with a shaky voice.
"Hey, get a grip man!" Hector replied.
"What's going on, Hec? What's all this...?"
"HEY! Quiet you, let me think! There must be something we can do about this mess. I don't know what the hell is going on, but no way I'll just stand here and take this shit!"

A morbidly skinny and pale man passed by them, carrying recently cut wood.

"Hey, you there!" Hector stopped him.

The man might as well have been taken for a zombie if it wasn't for the fact he spoke intelligibly.

"Yes."
"Look, we need some help here." Hector said. "Something is terribly wrong. We don't belong in this place. Is there somebody we could talk to, you know..."
"Something is terribly wrong with this world and the people who run it!" The skinny man retorted. "And if I were you, I'll shut the hell up right now for the sake of your health. Believe me, if you think this is bad, you have no idea."

ACT 8

"Wow, this place is amazing!" Paul gasped.

"Welcome to Heavensville!" Shane said full of pride. "And our humble city is not named like this just by chance. This is the place you can live your life to the fullest."

"Like things used to be before this pandemic exploded right in our faces, I suppose." Susan said.

"Even better" Shane replied. "This pandemic, as you called it, helped us growing aware of the real important things, to never let such terrible events ever happen again. You won't find sick people or flesh-eating monsters in here. I guarantee we are totally protected."

"Like an oasis." Frank spoke.

"Or a sanctuary, like some of you might like to call it." Shane responded.

"This place is everything but humble, I can tell you that." Nick said.

Shane smiled "I'll take this as a compliment."

Becky walked alongside Shane, looking at the top of the imposing, shining houses with a serene expression.

"And what do you do in here?" Susan asked Shane. "Are you a community leader of some sort? Who built this place?"

"Ah questions..." Shane whispered "...so typical of the intelligent. I'm really lucky I bumped into you. I do believe we can talk better over lunch, what do you say?"

The maitre d' of Blue Ribbons looked dreadfully serious and awfully focused on his greeting high society's customers work, but his face surely smoothed a lot when he saw Shane coming with her new best buddies.

"Miss Shane!" He said with the regular labored courtesy.

"Hi Bob." She replied. "I'm bringing some friends from out of town to enjoy the delights of Mister Perrin's cuisine."

"Oh, and you shall have nothing but the best!"

"And make a note, Bob, put everything on my tab."

"Hey!" Susan protested. "You don't have to do that!"

"But if she insists..." Paul said.

"Shut up!" Susan retorted.

The maitre d' twisted his nose to such demonstrations of roughness, but Shane laughed deliciously.

"Consider this my welcoming present." She said. "Please, don't hurt my feelings by turning me down."

"We'd never do such thing." Nick responded. "Lead the way, Bob!"

"Nick!" Susan protested again.

"You heard the man!" Shane spoke sportively to the maitre d'.

The man in tuxedo lifted an offended nose and took the group to the best table in the place. A pompous, starched waiter immediately came with the menus.

"Man, I didn't know they made restaurants like this!" Paul observed. "This table alone is bigger than my dorm."

"On weekends, this place is also converted in a disco." Shane proudly informed. "And you are more than invited to join us in a little dance."

Frank frowned at the menu "Man, how can I order anything in here? It's all in French!"

"Be careful not to end up eating snails!" Paul joked.

"What?"

Both Susan and the waiter looked at them with very reproaching eyes.

"Hey, mister penguin," Frank turned to the waiter "can't we just have cheeseburgers, chicken wings, you know, the stuff?"

"Can you please find more ways to embarrass me?" Susan complained.

"Give the boys a break." Nick intervened. "We've never been rich before."

"And by the looks of it, you never will." Susan spoke.

Once again, Shane seemed to be having a lot of fun with all that.

"I tell you what!" She announced. "Georgiou, see if you can bring us the biggest, the spiciest, the juiciest and the greasiest six cheeseburgers you can get your hands on, together with three plates full of your best chicken wings. And don't be stingy on the ketchup!"

"Oh yeah!" Frank and Paul said almost in unison, exchanging high fives. "And bring some milkshakes to wet it all down!"

Nick grinned and Susan shook her head negatively.

Becky just kept watching everything with an expressionless face.

"But madam..." The waiter mumbled with a powerfully French accent. "This is highly unorthodox. I don't think we can..."

Shane turned darkly serious all of a sudden "Georgiou, will you please take our order?"

"Tres bien mademoiselle."

"Good." She sweetened her face again.

"And tout de suite!" Paul said.

The waiter left.

"What do you do in here anyway?" Susan asked Shane. "I mean, what's your work, your job, you know, your occupation...?"

"Oh yes, the conversation we started. I'm a kind of public relations in this place. I run my share of things, have access to this or that privilege, some of which you'll soon be enjoying."

"Alright, that's it, what's the angle, Shane?" Nick queried in a very suspicious tone.

"Stop it!" Susan scolded him again. "I guess we had enough!"

"Not this time, Sue. Come on, am I the only one here who thinks this whole thing is at least a bit peculiar? We simply jumped from hell to paradise just like that, Becky turns nice all of a sudden; yesterday, we were about to be eaten by zombies, but today we're eating in a fancy restaurant!"

"I just saw the wrongs of my ways." Becky finally spoke something. "I thought you were going to like the new me."

"Alright, Shane" Nick continued "amenities time is over. What're you up to?"

"Nick!" Susan faced him. "I can take these two little friends of yours acting like animals in a elegant place, even being assholes about things none of us ever had, things we're now having totally for free, but what I really can't take is you spitting on the plate from which you ate!" She turned to Shane. "Look, I really apologize for my friends..."

Shane immediately placed a hand on Susan's hand. Such unexpected touch caused Susan to feel something she had never felt before, a very bizarre sensation, yet extremely soothing and pleasant.

"No apologies are necessary whatsoever." She spoke to Sue in a sweet tone of reconciliation, like a mother trying to educate her little girl. "Nick is right to be suspicious. He reminds me of me when I first came to this place. As for your friends, they've been through a lot, Sue. May I call you Sue? It's just fair to cut them loose, at least a little bit, so they can blow off some steam, don't you think?"

Susan didn't answer. She had listened to each and every word spoken by Shane, but she was still trying to come to terms with those sensations massaging her soul. Shane let go of her hand and the sensations were gone.

"You can call me Sue."
"Thanks."

Then, Shane fixed eyes on Nick. A strange chill ran down his back. Somehow he knew how abnormal that was, but something in his mind told him to just enjoy it. Such chill was awfully comforting.

"Nick," Shane said "I was once as lost and confused as you are now. I had lost everything I cherished the most to this epidemic, pandemic, pretty much the story of most of us. But then, Mister Hedgiest found me and brought me here."

"Mister Hedgiest?" Nick murmured the question, his eyes lost on Shane's.

"Yes." She continued. "He's the industrious force who came to a city devastated by this strange disease, packed with sick souls who didn't know any better than destroying healthy humans, and he turned this entire community into what it is now."

"He kicked all zombies out of the city?" Paul asked.

"Yes, with the help of other people willing to follow his leadership." Shane replied. "We don't like to call them zombies, for they used to be like you and me. We'd rather call them *drifters*. And this wonderful man found me, a frightened little lamb ready to succumb to the idiosyncrasies of this new terrible reality. He gave me hope, a reason for living. And do you know what reason is that?"

The group of youngsters shook their heads.

"You!" She answered emphatically. "You and others like you. Mister Hedgiest did wonders for me, and I just think that helping others who were once like me is the least I can do to repay him. Believe me, what I'm doing for you, I did for many others, and I'll keep bringing people in for as long as I live!"

"And we appreciate you taking us in very much." Susan said.

"As I said, there's no need to thank me." Shane smiled. "This is my mission in life and I enjoy doing it."

"And you built those walls we saw to keep the zomb... the drifters away?" Frank asked.

"The community did." Shane responded. "The whole town helped."

"Speaking which, you seem very important around here." Nick observed still suspicious, but it was like he had to fight to bring the words to mouth. "Care to explain that?"

"Nothing to it, really" Shane calmly replied. "Since my rebirth in here, I've been working hard to bring as many people as I can to Heavensville. Then, I guess I kind of grew on Mister Hedgiest's concept and he made me his *director*, so to speak."

"And what this Mister Hedgiest is to all of you, a kind of mayor?" Paul queried.

"Yes, we can say that." Shane answered with a smile. "But we prefer to call him the *Minister*."

The waiter returned with their food and drinks.

ACT 9

"All right, Pink Floyd girl, I've been postponing this discussion because I know it's not your favorite topic, but I guess this is as good a time as any to bring the subject to the table. We've been on this road for quite a while now, sleeping in motels, stopping by gas stations, rest stops and small cities to get supplies and all. Now it's time to bring new balls to the court, as we say in tennis."

"When you finally get to the point, you know where you can find me. I'll be the girl behind the wheel."

"Where are we going anyway? What's the limit? Are we ever going to stop?"

"Ahead, sky, not for the moment" Lily yawned. "I believe that answers your three questions."

"Right. You are aware of course that, at a certain point, we'll run out of land and there'll be nothing but ocean in front of us."

"I considered that."

"And don't tell me this contraption can also turn into a boat!"

"I've never tried, but I don't think so. But, perhaps, it floats. Daddy was full of surprises. I just didn't try each and every button and lever in this thing because I'm afraid the seats can be ejected."

"Do me a favor, please, don't try each and every button and lever in this thing."

Lily smiled.

However, an exaggerated billboard by the side of the road could definitely not escape their attention. It read *your destination is here, so is your destiny. Come to us and suffer never more.*

"A nice promise" Clark commented, gazing at the gigantic sign.

"And surely in big letters."

"Yes."

"It's a little overdone considering the overall situation."

As they drove, smaller signs appeared along the road, practically at every mile - *keep on going, we'll take care of you; we can give you food, we can give you dignity; you are close, don't stop now; you are almost there, be more than welcome.*

"They believe in signs." Clark observed.

"I don't like it, too much publicity."

Lily had to stop. The road ended in two huge gates, so tall it was not possible to see beyond them. Equally big walls extended from both sides of such entrance as far as the eyes could see.

"What do you make of it, Lily?"

"I don't know, mate. I mean, Clark."

"It looks protected though."

"Too protected."

Loud noises resembling gears moving echoed through the air all around. The gigantic gates started to move backwards from Lily's truck and some seconds later, they were wide open, revealing what seemed to be a nice, civilized village behind the walls.

"They're inviting us in." Clark realized. "It looks cozy."

"I definitely don't like it, too good to be true. What do you think?"

"I believe we'd better give this issue some thoughts before stepping in."

"I agree."

Lily turned the vehicle around and sped away from the gates.

"Driving around this thing may take hours." Clark said. "Whatever is beyond those gates is goddamn big."

"We try to find some back roads."

"I hope there are gas stations on them."

"There will be. Besides, I trust my dad's wisdom. I wouldn't be surprised if this rig could also run on urine."

"Now that you mentioned…"

"We stop, don't worry. Let's just put some distance between us and those walls, whatever they are."

"Okay. A thought just hit me."

"What is it?"

"Maybe this rig can also run on alcohol, like those cars in Brazil."

"Then all I have to do is breathe on the tank."

Clark laughed boyishly at that comment. Lily couldn't resist and laughed too.

ACT 10

Nick, Paul, Susan, Frank and even Becky were doing quite well.

Susan had always dreamt of becoming a teacher; then, Shane got her a position in a prime elementary school, within a very prosperous district in town.

Nick and Paul leaned toward architecture and civil construction. Because of this, they were allocated on projects to maintain protection around the city, also participating in futuristic plans to build more houses and expand the village.

"Those are the layouts." Nick handled some papers to the chief engineer, a very nice, sportive boss by the way.

"Great!" He responded. "Perfect, that's exactly what we need. You and your friend Peter…"

"Paul."

"And Mary!" The boss joked. "Sorry about that. You and Paul will surely be a great addition to the team."

"We're happy to help."

"You'll fit in just fine. Now, take a break."

"Really?"

"Yes! You surely earned it."

"Thanks. Um, Mister Noble…"

"Yes, young man."

"The structures to improve security along the walls are ready for shipment. Just say the word and I deliver them to our field personnel."

"Oh, you just leave those on the patio, by the trucks. We have people to do that for us."

"Okay."

Frank became a competent system analyst. Computers, firmware and software were his passion. He did a very good job, between one videogame and another.

Becky was the fashion celebrity in town. Shane made her the main ad girl for a large variety of products, ranging from cosmetics to clothes, sometimes advertising even tools and general hardware. Pictures of her pretty face and sculptural body were all over town, on walls, public buildings and billboards. And she loved all attention received.

Like many other souls, in the middle of a growing hell, that small breakfast club seemed to have found their places in the sun.

After a hard and productive day in the office, even breaking some personal records on *Until Dawn* game, Frank came back to his apartment, way bigger than he needed, but he did not complain.

He was taking the t-shirt off when somebody knocked on his door.

"Great, just my luck!" He growled to himself, putting the t-shirt back on. "Better be important. They're about to show the *Texas Chainsaw Massacre*, director's cut, double gore version, on the local TV."

He opened the door. To his incredible surprise, Becky was standing by the doorway.

"Hi." She said.
"Um, hi" He mumbled the courtesy back.

And she didn't need any invitation to come right in.

"I need to talk to you." She said.

"Yeah, I mean... Okay. Why don't you come on in?"

"I'm already in." She spoke with a soft smile.

"Oh yes."

"You've always had a crush on me, right?"

She was close, her well built belly almost touching his. Obviously, her voluptuous breasts were already compressing his chest. Such proximity caused him to break in cold sweat.

"Um, I..." He stammered "kind of."

"You know, I've always liked you too."

"You have?"

"Right from the start."

"Jeez, I mean, you treating me like garbage since middle school really had me fooled."

"No, I was a fool."

She was nearly inside of him.

"Becky..." He stepped away from her. "Not that I don't want to live up the American dream, and every boy's dream for that matter, but are you alright?"

"Never better!"

She came to him again. He gave two steps back, but was almost touching the wall.

"Becky... What about Lucas?"

"He was a jerk."

"He was? I mean, hey, don't talk like this! He was my best friend!"

"He mocked you on your back."

"He did?"

"He called you *pool naked wiener*."

"Damn it! That only happened once and I was in my underpants! I wasn't even in the pool!"

"Are you in underpants now?"

She took off his t-shirt so fast it made his head spin, in both technical and figurative senses. A second more and her hand was into his pants, her mouth and tongue running along his chest and belly.

"That's right, let's skip foreplay..." He whispered, already engulfed by waves of extreme pleasure.

Frank woke up next morning feeling the king of the world. And better yet, he stretched one arm to his left and felt his companion still lying in bed with him.

"Great!" He thought. "She actually spent the night with me after we had sex! I guess I broke another record today."

And, to make his caldron of happiness overload even more, he soon found out she wasn't quite sleeping. Becky turned around and mounted on him, their bodies touching in aphrodisiac contemplation. She brought his right hand to her left breast, while she kept her other hand behind her back.

"Good morning!" He said all so happy.

"Good morning, my darling." She returned very softly.

"So, what else you got in your tool box just for me?"

"Now that I purified your inner side, time to work on your outer side."

"What?" He frowned.

Becky held a cloth soaked in chloroform right to his face. She firmly compressed it with both hands against the boy's nose and mouth. He struggled, desperately shaking legs and hands, trying to take the cloth off his face, but all in vain, her grip on him was just too strong.

He passed out under the gorgeous, perfect body of his night companion.

"I hope you enjoyed my so precious gift to you, honey dear." She spoke to the unconscious body. "Now sunshine will bring you redemption."

Nick was taking a coffee in one more moment of relaxation when Shane appeared in the break room.

"Hello Nick." She said. "How's work?"

"What work?" He answered. "I almost don't get to do anything, only the very easy part."

"You don't like it?" Shane frowned.

"Of course I like it! What's not to like? It's actually a dream work."

"Then, what's the problem?"

"It's just that... it doesn't feel right. I don't think Paul and I are contributing enough."

"Do you like this job?"

"Well, I don't think it's about..."

"Just answer my question, do you like what you do here?"

"Yes! My calling in life is civil engineering. That much I know."

"So, that's it."

"I don't understand."

"You're doing what you like the most, so to you this barely looks like work at all. Believe me, I talked to Mister Noble and he told me you and Paul are real hard workers, but you don't realize it because your job is also your hobby."

Nick pondered those words for a moment.

"Yes, you may get a point there." He finally agreed.

"Don't worry, Nick. I totally understand your scruples and I appreciate very much you having them. We walked a long hard road to make this place what it is now and we still have a lot of work to do. Believe me, we don't take bums in here."

"We'll help the best we can."

She smiled and went for some tea. Nick sipped a little more of his coffee.

"Um… Shane?"

"Yes?"

"Actually, I'm glad you stopped by, there's something I'd like to talk to you about."

"Sure, what is it?"

"How come I'm never allowed to visit the field personnel?"

"The field personnel?"

"Yes, you know, the guys who really get their hands dirty, the ones who actually raise the things I design."

"Yes, I know who they are. I'm asking why you want to meet them?"

"Just to get a better grip on the reality of things and how the stuff is really done, maybe even help them in whatever they need."

"Do you have any experience in field work?"

"No, but I didn't have any experience in design either, only some knowledge I got from high school and from my family business every time I helped dad. But your people taught me a lot and I just thought dealing with some hammers and nails for a change wouldn't hurt, also a great addition to my skills."

"You never get tired of surprising me, don't you?" She smiled again. "I know I said this before, but I'm sorry if I just repeat myself. I'm really lucky I'm bumped into you and your friends."

"Do I get to know the field guys?" He asked suspiciously and impatiently.

"I can't see why not! I'll arrange everything with Mister Noble."

"Thanks."

"You're welcome."

Shane made herself a chamomile tea. Nick finished his coffee, threw the paper cup in the garbage bin and headed to the door.

"Nick..." She called him.

"Yes." He turned back.

She walked to him with the cup of tea in her hands. She drank a little and fixed eyes on him. He could no longer take his eyes off hers, as if some strange force was holding his head completely still, like nails attaching it to the neck.

"Listen to this, my dear..."

Then, Shane said:

"The sunshine springs, happiness it brings.

Those eyes you should follow, to keep away sorrow.

Seek the giant bird you must, on her you shall blindly trust.

For the good science you will urge, from all impurities to purge."

All expression disappeared from the man's face. Shane spoke:

"You'll continue with your design work and let the little people fulfill their filthy; otherwise, so necessary duties. You're not going to get anywhere near the field personnel. It's better this way."

"It's better this way." He agreed like a robot.

"Great!"

At that very moment, Paul showed up in the break room.

"Hello chaps." He said. "What's up?"

"Hi Paul!" Shane walked to him.
"Hey Shane. Hi Nick!" He talked to his friend over her shoulder.

But Nick kept looking stupidly at nothing.

"Hey dumbass, I'm talking to you!" He insisted and turned to Shane. "What's with him?"
"Oh nothing" Shane replied. "He's fine, very fine. Now, I'm glad you're here, Paul. I've been meaning to talk to you."
"Shoot." He responded.

She fixed eyes on him and he hopelessly got lost in hers.

"Listen to this." Shane said.

ACT 11

"We don't need no education, we don't need no thought control..." Clark recited. "This is obviously a symbol against education. I just think they shouldn't do that..."

"No way!" Lily angrily retorted. "They got nothing against education! This is actually a statement to criticize the educational system in general, which sometimes smashes children instead of supporting them."

"But they clearly say *we don't need no education*."

"And they say even more clearly *we don't need no thought control*. That's what the song is all about. You educate children, you inform children, but you don't brainwash them with *dark sarcasm in the classroom*."

"Well, actually I can't argue very much with that. It's tough enough to be bullied by other kids, left alone by your teachers, who by the way should do something about it."

"Have you ever been bullied?"

Clark lowered his eyes. She glanced at him.

"So, have you ever been bullied?" She insisted.
"Yes!"
"Me too."

Mate looked at her.

"No way!" He said.

"My father was bullied too. I guess it's a little price you pay when you respect other's privacy, but they don't respect yours. If you are a quiet one, people get curious. If you don't satisfy their curiosity, they get cruel."

"There's also a matter of character involved, don't you think? Or, in this case, lack of it."

"I never said otherwise. Rapes happen based on the same principle."

Clark stared at his shoes again. He raised his head, hesitated a lot, and then his eyes were back on the shoes.

"No, I've never been raped." Lily said, as if reading his dilemma. "I was almost raped once."
"I'm sorry to hear that, but happy to know nothing happened after all."
Lily smiled "I love the way you don't know what to say, always knowing what to say."
"That's me." He replied, but frowning.

A silence followed, but a comfortable one, until...

"Hey, look that!" Clark suddenly jumped on his seat, pointing a finger ahead.
"Speaking on bullying..."

Lily turned the wheel harshly and the vehicle veered off abruptly. For a brief moment, two tires abandoned the floor. Like vultures, a pack of walking cadavers were about to devour a poor soul lying on the sand, who also looked like a corpse.

"Stay here." She spoke.
"Okay."

Lily stepped out of the car and finished the beasts. She carried the human being in deplorable state to the truck.

"Are you sure she's not one of them?" Clark asked. "Just take a look at her."
"She mumbled some words, or tried too. Besides, for some inexplicable reason, zombies don't eat each other."
"Can you blame them?"

"Anyway, she's devastated but not a corpse... yet."

"What the heck happened to her?"

"This is for a doctor to say. We need to take her to a hospital."

"So, I guess it's back to *multiple signs walled city*."

"We have no choice. In the meantime, we got a new mate in our bunch. Let's try to get to know her."

ACT 12

Hector and Vince were thrown on the floor like two sacks of cement. Some people working on stations around turned to them scared, surely disapproving the way those two men had just been treated. They've all had similar experiences.

"Back off!" A man in uniform screamed, pointing a semi-automatic machine gun to the general direction of the workers in that sector. "You know the drill, scumbag!"

"I told you we can't stay here!" Vince cried, still on the floor. "We know nothing of power stations!"

"Your problem, buddy."

Then, all armed thugs who escorted Hector and Vince left, closing heavy, thick metal doors behind them.

"I'm not your buddy, asshole!" Vince muttered.

Two workers came to help the brothers standing up.

"We also knew nothing of this business when those suckers dumped us here, *mano*." One of them said. "By the way, my name is Pedro and this is Raul."

"I'm Hector, this is Vince." He said breathlessly.

"Welcome aboard."

Once back on his feet, Hector went straight to the door and tried to force it open.

"Help me here, Vince."

And his brother joined him in the task.

"Don't bother mano." Pedro said. "Believe me, many of us already tried that many times over, even with some heavy tools we have at our disposal. It won't budge."

Hector and Vince were indeed sweating a lot. And the doors didn't move an inch.

"Yes." Hector panted. "Better rethink our strategy."

"Perhaps when they come back, we can jump them." Vince suggested.

"Good man."

"If they come back, it will be to give you hell." Raul warned. "And you can't fight them."

"Now, if you please follow me, mano, we got two free monitoring stations." Pedro spoke. "Guess they belong to you now. Don't worry, we teach you everything you need to know."

But Vince and Hector did not move.

"Except for one little problem, mano" Hector said. "We're not going to do a damn thing until somebody tells us what's going on here!"

"I tell you what's going on here." Raul said. "You've been selected to the distinguished basement of troublemakers. We keep water and power running for the riches, and in return they pretend we do not exist. And believe me, it's a blessing."

"And if you don't do what you're told, it's all our asses in a sling." Pedro completed with an anguished face.

"Is that so?"

"It is so, yes. You're not the first one who tries to do something about it and got others seriously screwed up."

Hector took some steps ahead and looked around. He estimated about thirty people working in that sector.

"And how do we survive in here?" He asked.

"They give us food and water, but just enough. We work business hours, then we are allowed to retire to some bunks, but we never leave this place. It's been long since I've last seen the sun. I show you where everything is, including our not so hygienic sanitary facilities."

"Those I could use." Vince said.

"Oh, but I don't work for a plate of food, my friend." Hector retorted dangerously loud. "I work to enrich my soul and make an honest buck. That's right, if I work, I demand to be paid in money! Mister Lincoln did a great job finishing slavery and I'm not willing to let it go to waste."

"Look, we are not lambs in here, mister!" Raul angrily spoke. "We know everything about civil rights! And we tried to make them count. But you got to listen to me! You still don't know what they are capable of. Consequences can be really disastrous."

"And who are they?" Hector queried.

"Powers that be, our bosses..."

"What happens if we refuse to work?" Vince asked.

"Then you die, or worse."

Hector and Vince turned around to find the owner of that new, deep voice. They found an old black man, with white hair surrounding a protruding bald head, also with a thick white beard. He spun on his chair to face the newcomers.

"This is Marcellus Malthus, our senior technician." Raul introduced the man.

"He's been here since forever, even when the world was not so crappy." Pedro complemented the information.

"And I saw my share of things." Marcellus said with a deep, low voice.

He lowered his thick white eyebrows, reached into his shirt pocket and took a picture. He handed it to the brothers and Hector was the one to take it.

"Wow, she's pretty!" Vince said, gazing at the gorgeous, elegant black lady in the photo.
"Indeed." Hector agreed.

They gave back the picture.

"Thanks." Marcellus spoke. "It's my daughter Michelle. She was just like you, brave and determined, the pride of every father. And I was proud of her."

He took a deep breath and continued.

"She also couldn't take the injustices of this cruel new world and she gathered around other folks who shared her views. They believed they could make the difference and we all believed them. And they did a good rebellion job, even managed to escape this place. But they came back."
"Dead?" Hector risked the question.
"Changed" Marcellus shook his head.
"I beg your pardon?"
"That girl who came back looked exactly like my daughter, only it was no longer her. She was too soft, adapted, accommodated, nothing like her."
"Are you saying they sent back somebody else pretending to be your daughter?" Vince asked.
"I'm telling you they sent my daughter back but she wasn't herself. I know my Michelle and that wasn't my girl. They did something to her, something to her mind. And the other rebels who helped her came back the same way."
"You're talking like they were brainwashed or something." Vincent spoke.

"I'm not saying anything. All I know is whatever voodoo they did to her was very powerful. After that, some men in suits came here, pointing guns to keep us quiet. They took everybody in this sector to the big courtyard outside, something they never did. We knew they were up to no good."

He lowered his eyebrows again and choked.

"They made us stood in formation." Marcellus proceeded. "And they made the rebels stood in formation right in front of us, including my daughter, facing us. Then they all pointed loaded guns right to their own heads... their faces sweet like cotton..." His hands started to shake and tears welled up in his eyes. "They pulled the trigger!" Marcellus burst into tears. "My baby, my Michelle... blew her head off! That wasn't her, she would never... God, my Michelle! They wanted us to see that! They wanted me to see it! Please, God, let me die!"

Pedro and Raul ran to comfort the old man, placing sympathetic hands on his shoulder.

"It's hopeless, can't you see?" Marcellus continued to cry. "We can't beat them! They own us!"

Hector and Vince looked shocked at the devastated old man.

"Damn, Hec! How come people just shoot their own heads like that?"

"They have powers." A short, skinny woman spun her chair from her station to face the brothers. She surely didn't belong in there as well.
"Powers?" Hector frowned.

"I heard stories." The woman continued. "Somehow, they enter your mind and control your will. They force you to do whatever they want."

"And you are..." Vince came to her rather anxious all of a sudden.

"My name is Maria and I used to run a hair parlor."

"And you will again." Hector assured her.

She smiled, but melancholically.

"Somehow, I still can't accept this whole deal." Hector whispered to his brother.

"I'd be surprised if you could, bro. But we'd better be extra careful in this one. It seems there's some dark magic going on."

The person working in the station beside Maria caught Vincent's eyes.

"Hey, I remember you..." He said.

But the man did not take his eyes off the monitors. Vince came closer.

"You look different, but... Oh yeah, it's you! Yo Hec, get a load of this! This guy... Aaron, it's it? He's our bunk mate in the truck! Man, I'm glad to see you! You survived, man!"

But Aaron was still not responsive. He looked distant, as if living another life.

"I mean..." Vince continued, a little more cautious. "I almost didn't recognize you without the..."

"Don't look at me, alright?" Aaron finally reacted. "I'm a monster! Look what they did to me!"

"You're shaved, that's all."

"They stole everything that was most precious to me!" He replied, nearly weeping.

Hector strode to him furiously and grabbed his arms, forcing the man to face him, lifting him from the chair.

"Hey!" Aaron tried to complain. "I have to pay attention to those monitors!"

"You pay attention to me now!" Hector retorted. "They may shave your head and even your face, but they cannot shave your spirit! That's what matters! Don't give the suckers the satisfaction to see you down!"

Aaron didn't answer and his eyes were on the floor.

"Look at me when I talk to you!" Hector ordered "Eyes, man, eyes!"

Very slowly, Aaron surrendered to the pressure and raised his eyes to meet Hector's.

"What do you do?" Hector asked.

"I'm in charge of sector C. If some alarm appears..."

"No, not what they want you to be! I'm asking what you really are!"

Aaron hesitated, but realized the big man standing before him would not let him be unless he answered his questions.

"I'm a doctor" He finally responded "a surgeon actually."

"This is great!" Hector said satisfied and let go of his arms. "And you'll be practicing medicine again in no time!"

"Don't make promises you can't keep, my friend."

ACT 13

Susan had just finished teaching her classes and watched the children leave the room. They walked away awfully slowly and orderly, almost bureaucratically. Well, she didn't give that many thoughts, she got other things on her mind.

When the last child was gone, she left the classroom and found the principal across the main hall, talking to some parents by the exit. Susan walked to them discreetly, not to disturb their conversation.

When they finished and the principal was left alone, Susan went to her.

"Missus Hildenbrandt, can I talk to you for a second?"
"Oh sure and please call me Agnes. How many times I have to tell you this, young lady?"
"Sorry, I was kind of accustomed like this."
"Oh, perfectly all right, but we're rather informal in here, as you've already noticed. Walk with me, please."

They went down the school corridor side by side. It was Agnes who spoke first:

"Oh, by the way, I just want you to know we are all very pleased with your work here, both me and the parents. The children love you."
"I'm glad to know that."
"Now, tell me dear, what can I do for you? Is there something wrong with one of the children?"
"Oh no, they're all adorable and I like them too. It's just that... well, you know, I'd like to ask you about how things work in here, I mean, in general."

Agnes laughed "And I'll answer your questions to the best of my knowledge, but I hope you don't get too technical. I'm just an elementary school principal, you know." And she laughed again.

"It's nothing that complicated really. It's just that everything seems so fine in this city, everybody has food, water, electricity, where do all these come from?"

"Mister Hedgiest, the Minister, got everything under control. We all heard about agriculture projects, but we are not totally self sustaining yet. The soils are still too contaminated by all this sickness plaguing the world, but cleaning is underway. Also, some courageous boys volunteer to go outside the walls in some errands for supplies, things we cannot grow in here for the moment. But very soon we'll have our own livestock."

"What about electricity and water supply?"

"Have you ever heard of the famous Gingerbread Dam?"

"Yes, sure."

"Well, such dam happens to be in our midst."

"Really? I didn't know that. I'm not originally from these parts, you know."

"Actually, this town grew around the banks of Gingerbread River, for the soil was very rich, but that was before the outbreak. Tons and tons of water were waiting to be put to a good use. The dam was built together with a power plant to provide residents with water and light."

"But then, the outbreak stroke."

"Oh yes, I pretty much witnessed everything – the horror, good souls getting sick to later become horrible creatures, healthy people running scared of the deranged..." She lowered her green eyes. "But some of us had no other place to go and were forced to stay and fight the drifters. I lost my beloved husband and son in the process."

"I'm sorry to hear that."

"But when all hopes seemed lost, Mister Hedgiest came. He led us to victory upon the monsters and initiated works to reactivate the power plant."

"And it's fully operational now?"

"Well, we don't receive that much information. The important thing is we get our water and power. I heard the dam area is not entirely safe, the walls don't go that far, but our workers are trying to fix this. Anyway, general population is not allowed to venture around those parts."

Susan left the school and on the way she waved to some parents walking home with some of her students. They were all nice and friendly.

She also went home. Everything there was within walking distance. Money was still a necessity, but surely not a problem. Susan earned way more than local cost of living. It was a dream life. And she was bored.

Susan came to her two stories house, which she had the privilege to enjoy all alone. After kicking her shoes out of her feet, she sat down on the brand new couch and turned on the plasma TV. And round and round all channels, then round and round again, there was nothing on local TV, only garbage. Certain things never change.

She looked at the wristwatch, four-fifteen in the afternoon.

"Gosh!"

Susan turned the TV off, put the shoes back on and decided to leave for a little stroll.

"I'll be with you in a few!" Becky said, apparently happy to see her friend. "Just a couple more pictures and I'll be right with you."

Susan waited about fifteen minutes, during which she entertained herself with some fashion magazines. But only two people appeared on most pages, Shane and Becky, the first giving interviews about how things were prospering and the latter selling such ideas with glamour.

"Publishers here surely wreck their brains to find scoops." She thought.

"Hey Sue!" Becky came back, hugging and kissing cheeks so effusively that her friend almost fell on the floor.

"Hi." Susan responded stunned by such displays of affection.

"Sorry to keep you waiting. You know how it is, there's always one more picture they want to take, for a better angle this, a different view of that, they won't just let me be."

"You don't seem very upset by that, though."

Becky smiled.

"It's been some days since we last talked." Susan continued. "How are you?"

"Posing for a lot of pictures, appearing in a thousand commercials, giving autographs, talking to fans, being the center of attention, can't complain."

"Uh-huh. What about Frank?"

"What about him?"

"Well, I haven't seen him in a while, either. Do you know what he's up to?"

"Frank... Oh yes. He's been relocated."

"Relocated?"

"Yeah, he's now working for a bigger IT company called *Stardust*. The boy's doing quite well."

"It's surely a good climbing, considering he spends most of his days playing games. Well, I'm not at liberty to talk. I'm not doing much with my working hours either."

"But that's not a surprise. Basically, Frank only acts when some device breaks. As equipment here almost never breaks, he needs to find something else to do with his time. The only difference is that now he's doing this in a much bigger office, earning the double of money."

"And with a much better play station I take."

"Yes!" Becky laughed a fake laughter.

"Why am I only learning this now?"

"Learning what?"

"About Frank changing jobs!" Susan raised her voice impatiently.

"You didn't ask."

Susan stared at Becky with not so friendly eyes.

"I'm just kidding!" Becky amended. "It's just that everything happened so fast! I myself got to know this only recently."

"And what's the address of this company, Stardust?"

"I don't know."

"You don't know?"

"Nobody told me."

"Alright, no problem, I got to go now."

"So soon?"

"Yes, I have some errands to do."

"Going for a shopping spree, huh?"

"Hardly" She whispered.

"What?"

"Nothing. Nice seeing you again."

"Likewise. Come visit me more often. Everybody wants a piece of me, but I'll always have time for you."

"Thanks, bye."

"Take care."

Susan left the set and the movie complex. She checked the watch, five-thirty. Time seemed to run backwards over there. Nick and Paul would still be at the office. She decided to also pay them a visit.

"Excuse me…" She called one of the trainees who seemed awfully busy.

"Yes?" However, he stopped immediately to give her a very enthusiastic attention.

"I'm looking for Nicolas and Paul…"

"Oh yeah, Nick the Brick and Paul the Sprawl, great guys. And you got to be Susan! They surely talk a lot about you!"

"You don't believe a word they say."

"Oh, now I believe! Wow. You're even more beautiful than they described you."

"Thanks."

The happy youngster kept smiling to her, congenial but pointless.

"Um, could you tell me where I can find them, you know, Nick and Paul?" Susan queried.

"Oh, alright, they are in the break room."

After getting directions to the mentioned place, she went there. And in fact she found her friends sitting on a table, enjoying coffee and some fruits from a big refrigerator on the corner.

"SUE!" They immediately stood up and walked to her.

"Please don't hug and kiss me." She said.

"Okay." They replied.

"So…" Susan started.

The two men faced her with anticipation.

"How you guys doing?"

"Fine, fine" Nick replied.

"Good." Susan spoke.

"Actually, this moment calls for a celebration!"

"It does?" Susan frowned.

"Oh yeah!" Paul answered. "Let's have dinner together!"

"When?"

"Now!"

And so they did.

"Have you guys heard from Frank lately?" Susan asked down at *The Happy Walnut Restaurant*, a nice place with a good Hawaiian cuisine.

"Oh yeah" Paul answered "The lucky son of a gun's been relocated."

"Where the hell have I been?" Susan grunted.

"Relax, Sue." Nick spoke. "No need to get all grumpy. You've also failed in contacting your friends to tell what's going on."

"True" She admitted "but that's because there's not much to tell, same old, same old."

"Yeah, like the rest of us." Nick agreed.

"It'd be much easier if we had cell phones." Sue pointed out.

"I asked around." Paul revealed. "People back at the office said infrastructure to support wireless communication is still not ready. Engineers are working on it."

"What about those antennas we see everywhere? Every house in town had one, including mine."

"Maybe it's for TV."

"We don't actually need cell phones." Nick spoke. "Everything is close-by in this city. If you need us, all you have to do is scream."

"Very funny."

"And I don't believe good old Frank is a matter of concern. He scored big this time!" Paul cheered. "The lucky bastard was transferred to that *Starfish* Company!"

Susan faced him "Shouldn't it be *Stardust*?"

"Oh yes, Stardust."

"Stardust, that's the one."

"It sounds like a big deal, right?" Susan said.

"It's an important firm around here."

"This is funny, because on the way to your office I asked five people about this company and nobody knew a damn thing about it."

"Maybe you should try asking for Starfish." Paul joked. He and Nick laughed.

"Do you know the address of this firm?" Susan asked in a not so amiable tone.

Both men shook heads negatively.

"Okay..." Susan spoke. "I hate to eat and leave, but I have to go."

"Come on, Sue!" Paul complained. "We got so much to catch up."

"You have to try the desserts in this place!" Nick suggested. "They make the most delicious *haupia shortbread bars*."

"I'm sure they do, but I still have a lot of work to do to prepare for my classes." Susan had to bite her tongue a couple of times for saying such big lie. "Thanks for a wonderful dinner."

Susan checked the time again, seven-forty six. At least she managed to kill some time. She walked the streets at random and they were awfully empty. But Susan didn't feel like calling it a night, not for a long shot.

Walking was not a problem for her. On the contrary, she did that a lot and loved backpacking trails, much better exercise than going to the gym, she thought, and healthier too.

And she walked, planning to walk until her legs faltered, which wouldn't happen so soon. Susan had a lot of free time, a dangerous thing sometimes. She used the main street, called *Happy Trails Boulevard*, as reference.

It was almost nine-thirty in the evening when she reached a way less suburban zone. There were a lot of trees and very few houses around. Susan was not sure where to go from there. She started to be afraid of getting lost. Even so, she continued straight ahead, following a narrow, but well maintained asphalt road.

That was when two men in police uniforms stood in front of her.

"Good evening, miss." One of them said in cordial tone.
"Good evening." She returned a little bashful.
"May I ask what you're doing here?"
"Just taking a walk to clear the ideas."
"Not through here you will not. It's dangerous. Where do you live?"
"1505 Cosgrove Street."
"This is right in the city center! You surely walked a great deal, miss!" The man spoke with genuine admiration.
"I did a lot of backpacking, you know, when the world was still standing."
"No wonder you're so slender and athletic." The other man said very nicely.
"Thanks."
"Don't let my wife hear you. She nags at me all the time to lose weight. I don't want her to have any more ideas!"
"With a bulge that big, we can't blame the lady." His partner joked.
"Hey! You're not in any shape to talk about my bulge, fat ass!"

And they both laughed sportively. Susan only smiled, but she couldn't help finding those two very nice fellows.

"Why is it dangerous to go further ahead?" She asked.

"There could be drifters, dead people, from this point on. It's no longer safe."

"And this road leads to some place in particular?"

"The industrial zone" The other man replied. "But the walls don't quite get there yet. We got people working on it."

"But we are safe back at the city, right?" Susan queried, faking fragility.

"Oh yeah, don't worry none. Our guys can deal with the critters. It's just their work would be greatly impaired if they had to also worry about civilians nosing around. I hope you understand."

"Oh sure."

"If you're looking for ways to blow off some steam and clear the ideas, I know very nice discos in town. Just don't tell my wife! I can give you their addresses."

"No, that won't be necessary. I know some places myself."

"Excellent. Do you want a ride? Our car is right behind that ridge over there."

"No thanks. I came here walking and now I consider a matter of honor to come back the same way, if you boys don't mind."

"Not at all. Gee, I wish I had that much energy!"

"You do. Believe me, you do. Bye guys! Thanks for the warnings."

"No problem. Bye."

"Take care."

Susan went back the same way she came, and she could feel the cops' four eyes watching her every move. Eventually, she disappeared from view.

It was ten-fifteen. Sitting on a rock, the two men kept doing their night-watch, or trying to. One of them was taking a nap. The other woke him up. They both stood up and went to the car. The vehicle headed toward the so called industrial zone, very strange, considering they deemed such direction dangerous to follow.

Very carefully, Susan opened the cover of the dumpster she was hiding in and peeked outside. The men were gone, coast was clear. She didn't exactly smell like Paco Rabanne when she jumped out of the container.

"Damn it, the things you won't do…"

She armed herself with a piece of pipeline she found in the dumpster and continued walking down the road, to whatever was waiting for her.

ACT 14

"So, did you talk to her?" Lily asked.

"Yes, I asked her name." Clark replied on the passenger seat. "She tried to say something, but keeps choking on her own drool. She needs help."

"We're almost at those gates again. I just hope they open the doors for us once more."

"Lily, I'm kind of worried here. What if she has the thing?"

"You mean the disease that turns people into zombies?"

"Yes."

"I don't think so. They don't act like this before turning."

"How can you be so sure? Have you ever witnessed people turning?"

"No, but I watched enough zombie movies to know I'm right."

"How many zombie movies you watched?"

"Only one, but it seemed to make sense."

"Right. And what do you think it happened to her then?"

"She looks poisoned to me."

"Poisoned? Do you believe somebody did all this to her, as in starving her nearly to death and all?"

"It's just a theory, mate. People find ways to survive, even in situations like this. Nobody would ever do such thing to oneself, not even to commit suicide."

"I still think she got the zombie fever. She's going to turn any minute."

"She needs to die first. And we won't let her die."

They arrived at the big gates. Lily began to blow the horn like mad. The devastated woman got really agitated on the back of the truck. She tried to say something, but the words didn't come.

"Clark, you have to go back there and calm her down."

"Alright, but keep your knives ready!"

The tennis player dragged himself to the woman, while Lily screamed and honked to the gates "Hey! We need a doctor! We got somebody seriously hurt in here!"

"Calm down, dear, everything's going to be fine." Clark tried to comfort the woman, caressing her head. "Please, don't bite me."

She mumbled something unintelligible.

The gates got open and Lily accelerated inside. They were immediately intercepted by a car with siren and red light. Lily stopped the truck. A man in police uniform came out of the car.

"Listen!" Lily said. "We have a woman here in serious need for a doctor."

The policeman peeked inside and saw the poor soul lying on Clark's knees.

"Oh my Gosh!" He said. "Follow me!"

The man ran back to his car and promptly led the truck to the best hospital in town.

"Is she going to be fine?" Clark asked the distinguished doctor, grayish on the temples, sitting on the hospital bed, examining the woman he and Lily brought.
"I still have to run some tests." He answered very sure of himself.
"What happened to her?" Lily queried.
"Too soon to say something, but the tests will tell us more." He stood up. "Anyway, if she survives, it's all thanks to

you. You did great bringing her here. You might have saved her life."

"Just do what you can for her." Lily whispered.

An extremely gorgeous, elegantly dressed woman came to the room and vehemently shook hands with Clark and Lily. The patient lying on the bed moved, but nobody noticed.

"We appreciate very much what you did for this poor woman." She said, holding and shaking Lily's hand with both hands. She did the same with Clark. "By the way, my name is Shane, very honored to meet you."

"Um, it was nothing." Lily responded. "We just happened to bump on her. This is Mate Clarkson and I'm... Leila."

Clark glanced at her.

"Nice meeting you both." Shane said. "Sheriff McBeattie, the guy who brought you here, has just a few questions for you before you can enjoy our facilities. Feel very free to do so when he's done. And, in the name of the city, you are more than welcome."

"Thanks." Clark said. "Are you the leader of this community?"

"Kind of. As a matter of fact, I work very closely to the leader, and he let me represent him."

"So, you even have a sheriff around here." Lily observed.

"Part of a task force we're building. Our village is finally flourishing after a great ordeal, as you can imagine, and it's important to have some law and order."

"For sure" The Australian woman agreed. "But tell me more about this town, how did you get all this?"

"I know you're curious, but all your questions will be answered in due time." Shane responded. "But for now, I really need you to talk with Mister McBeattie. It's important that we gather as much information as possible, to investigate what happened to the woman you brought."

"You're right."

"I promise I'll give the matter the due priority."

Everybody left the room, except for Shane, left alone with the patient. She closed the door, slowly walked to the bed and stared at the woman, who got agitated again.

"N-no... No!" The patient mumbled.

"Mission accomplished, sweetie." Shane said.

Lily and Clark followed Sheriff McBeattie. He led them to a waiting room. They entered.

"I just need to check on something and I'll be right back." The policeman spoke.

He left and closed the door, leaving the two road friends alone.

Clark turned to Lily.

"Leila?" He asked.

"People here seem to have facilitated access to information. I don't want anybody making any more fuss about my name."

"I really don't think you should be so ashamed of..." He stopped in mid sentence and sniffed. "Do you smell that?"

"Yes, and it's strong."

They looked around and realized a white smoke coming out of the ventilation system. Clark's eyes goggled toward Lily.

"It's a trap!" She shouted.

Clark ran to the door.

"It's locked!"

"No problem." She said and rushed to break the lock with one of her weapons.

But there was no time. The gas dominated their senses and they collapsed unconscious on the hard ground.

The grids of the ventilation system sucked the fog back inside. After a few minutes, the door opened and Shane went into the waiting room, accompanied by two men in suits.

"Down with freckled face here?" One of them asked, nodding at Clark.

"Yes. Take this abomination out of my sight." Shane replied.

The men carried him away.

Shane got down on her knees by the feminine sleeping body. She gently rubbed a hand on Lily's temple.

"Leila…" Shane whispered. "Nice try, dear. Welcome to my town, Apocalily. I was waiting for you."

ACT 15

Susan had been walking for about two hours and asking for more. She could continue like that, keeping the same pace, for two, three hours more, whatever, only with the food from dinner.

And nothing had happened. She saw no zombies around whatsoever, no cops nor soldiers fighting any enemy. Everything was calm and peaceful, except for the usual animal talk from the woods.

At a certain point, she heard loud noises coming from some trees. She stopped and raised her pipe. It was just a raccoon. But at least such unexpected surge of adrenaline broke boredom for a while.

Anyway, she was sure those cops had lied to her. Why?

There were light poles illuminating her way on both sides and the road was paved, everything very civilized. However, she did notice the asphalt began to lack maintenance as she went.

And up a cloudy draw, she visualized definite signs of civilization. A whole city rose before her eyes - the Industrial Zone, perhaps? It looked way bigger than just a zone. She picked up the pace.

As she got closer, she realized that town wasn't anything like the one she had been living in. Constructions over there had surely seen better days. Some roughly built houses stretched like slums, along with wastelands and buildings that seemed abandoned.

Everything was poor and dirty. Was it a ghost town? Zombies lived in there? What such city was doing in there anyway?"

Susan kept on walking, but she started to get a little thirsty. Absolutely nothing happened and boredom settled again. The pipe in her hand felt heavy and unnecessary. She decided to throw it in the nearest trash can she found.

Eventually, Susan reached a part of the town that looked a little less mournful. City lights cheered up the place a bit. Such view would be romantic if the neighborhood in general didn't smell so bad.

However, there was a population living in there and not a zombie one. Suddenly, it felt like she was on some suburban area in Chicago, one of those places she and her parents avoided in a not so distant past, but it looked like another life to her.

And the signs of population didn't seem to like her very much. As she walked, unfriendly eyes turned to her. She began to fear for her safety and considered getting the pipe back. But it was too late. Susan calculated that turning back would just get potential hoodlums even more curious about her. She decided to go into a bar.

And the regulars in there weren't exactly prime society either, but they looked distracted and harmless enough. Susan sat down by the counter.

"Good evening." Bartender said. "What are we having tonight?"
"Beer" She replied.
"Beer it is."

Some minutes later, he came back with the bottle. Susan drank a little too much from it all at once. She was thirstier than she thought. "Better take it easy, I can afford losing senses in a place like this."

As if reading her mind, a muscular man with a cap and tattoos on his biceps, who until then was sitting a few stools from her, came closer.

"Hey there lady" He said.
"Hey" She answered, trying not to show how scared she was.

As per previous experiences, his attitude didn't suggest he was there to make a pass on her; nevertheless, his whisky loaded breath could tell a different story later on. Anyway, she knew that ignoring him would just make things worse.

"You're not from around here, right?" The guy asked with a raucous voice.

Susan was hoping such fact wasn't so obvious, but it seemed she was wrong.

"Why do you ask?" She said trying to be polite, but not as nice as to give her new interlocutor any wrong ideas about her intentions.
"Never saw you before." He drank from a little bottle he brought with him. Naturally, that didn't improve his breath any. "You came with the refugees?"

Susan hesitated. She knew she couldn't afford hesitating.

"That's right." She managed to say.
"Pretty messed up out there, huh?"
"Too many drifters around, yes."

The man grinned *"Drifter* is a word used in Uptown. Over here, we call them *lamebrains."*

"Shit!" Susan thought. "Of all the stupid things..."

"Are you from Uptown?" He hardened his tone. *"Cause* we don't take kindly to those folks roaming around these parts."

Susan needed to get a grip. Once again, she was taking too long to say something. She hid her shaking hands behind the counter. Other customers began to look at her as well. Their expressions were everything but sweet.

Finally, she raised her eyes and stared at the man with the best poker face she could manage.

"How do *you* know they are called drifters in Uptown?" Susan asked him in a threatening tone.

The guy faced her. She firmly kept defying eyes on him.

"She got a point there, Buckner." The bartender came to the rescue. "Care to explain that?"
"Fuck this. I have to wake up early in the morning." He finished his drink, stood up and threw some money on the counter. "Keep the change." He said to the bartender before turning his back on him.
"There's no change due." The bartender spoke, but Buckner was already gone.

"Model citizen" Susan thought while breathing in relief.

The other customers also lost interest and came back to their businesses.

"But you are new in the neighborhood, right?" The bartender queried.

Susan realized she wasn't out of the woods yet.

"Yes." She choked a little bit.

"Then, welcome to *Hellsville*." He said. "Or, like the *Uptowners* say, Industrial Zone. But we prefer to call it Downtown."

"Thanks. It looks like a cozy place."

"If you don't mind the cozy reeks around here" The bartender laughed. "Where do you work?"

"I'm kind of in between jobs right now." Susan replied.

"Yep, the Center of Refugees, if that's what they really are, can be very slow, good for nothing most of the time."

"Those jerks" Susan emphasized, not knowing who she was insulting.

The bartender smiled "I need some help around here, in case you got nothing. Pay stinks, but tips are good, occasionally. Anyway, it's a living."

"Thanks." She returned the smile. "I'll give the, um, Center of Refugees one more chance. If they keep stalling me, I come back here."

"It works for me."

Susan considered it was a good idea to leave before she had to answer more questions on topics she didn't have the slightest idea about.

She paid for the beer and asked where the restrooms were. She needed to take a lick badly. Walking a lot can be very diuretic.

After using the facilities, Susan left the bar and walked the streets. Two prostitutes passed by her giggling and waving little purses. Despite of the overall roughness of the place, strangely she felt better there than in Uptown, her new home.

The streets got empty all of a sudden. She kept on walking. Two large silhouettes came into view. Illumination was not so good in that area. But she could clearly distinguish a shine coming from badges on their uniforms.

"Hey you!" One of the figures said.

Susan was at a loss as to what to do next. Then, she ran. And they chased her.

Being in much better shape than her persecutors, she managed to put some distance between them, but she didn't know the area as much as they did, and that made all the difference. Susan was faster; however, she couldn't lose the pursuers and they eventually cornered her in an alley behind a restaurant.

The men approached her, but still could not see her face. Two strong hands seized her from behind, one covering her mouth, violently pulling her among garbage bins to a back door. From the policemen's point of view, she simply vanished in thin air. They took off their caps and scratched heads almost at the same time.

At the entrance of the restaurant by the main street, somebody locked the door and turned around the sign hanging on it from *open* to *close*. But the cops came and knocked on the glass, almost to the point of breaking it.

"Hey, calm down, suggy!" A big man wearing a shirt unbuttoned at the top opened the door and spoke. "Do you want to wake up the rats?"

"No fooling around, Marion!" One of the policemen harshly said. "Did you happen to see somebody hiding by your back door?"

"No, and my name is Mario!"

"Are you sure there was nobody there, Marion?"

"I'm positive! Why are you even asking, darling? Didn't you boys know there's a curfew going on?" He said sarcastically.

"Hey, you are this close to get arrested for disrespecting an officer!"

"Really? Oh, I can barely wait! Are you going to search me too, perhaps both of you?"

"Ah, forget it, Joe!" The other cop grunted.

"I really hope you're not hiding any outcast in there." Joe spoke in a threatening tone. "I don't suppose you want to disappear like many others of your kind."

"If that makes you feel any better, you can come right in and take a look." Mario said caressing his exposed hairy chest. "And don't forget to bring the handcuffs. My friends dig men in uniform."

"Let's just go, Joe! We still have a lot of ground to cover tonight. I'm hungry!"

"You stay out of trouble!" Joe spoke pointing a finger at Mario.

"Oh, I hope not." He closed the door and locked it.

"I hate those fags." One cop commented to the other while walking away.

After making sure through the glass the cops were gone, Mario came back inside.

"Don't fret, folks! I took care of them... as usual!" He said to the tall man in Tuxedo, sharing a couch with Susan, who was drinking a cup of coffee.

"Sorry about the way we brought you here." The man spoke to Susan. "We had to think fast."

"You might've saved my life out there. I won't question your methods. Thanks for taking me in, and for the coffee."

"Oh, don't mention it, dear. It's always a pleasure to meet new people and screw with those guards in the process."

"You run this place?"

"Oh yeah! And welcome to *Fleur du Soir*! Actually, our cuisine is not French, but the name is pretty catchy. Make yourself at home, dear."

"Thanks. What's your name?"

"You can call me Tess."

"I'm Susan, but please call me Sue."

"Very well, Sue. What a beautiful girl from Uptown is doing in a place like this?"

"Um..." Susan stuttered. "I came with the refugees, actually."

"Oh no," Tess opened a small grin. "You can fool those saps out there, but not me, honey. You're from Uptown. It's written all over you. But don't freak out, you're safe in here. It would be very hypocritical of me to label other people. We're all decent folks. This is a restaurant, not a bordello."

"But... what's the deal with this place and this whole Uptown, Downtown thing? What's going on?"

"First, you tell me what you're doing here. Believe me. This is so utterly unconceivable that curiosity is killing me."

"Well, let's say I sneaked in here..."

"Yes..."

"...partially because life was too boring..."

"Dangerous, dangerous reason..."

"...and partially because a friend of mine, who was supposed to be in Uptown, disappeared. His name is Frank and I was kind of hoping to find him here."

"What's his name?"

"I told you, Frank."

"No, darling, I mean his family name."

"Oh, it's Frank Herrera."

"He's here alright."

"What? Where? How do you know this?"

"I don't precisely know where he is, but his days in Uptown were counted anyway. They have ways to know our origins and they are very particular in their selection."

"I don't understand."

"You see, they don't allow in their precious little paradise anyone who doesn't meet their high standards of purity. And the pariahs end up here, either doing the hard work, or surviving whichever way we can."

Susan needed some moments to digest all that.

"This is absurd!" She said, almost dropping the coffee. "This can't be right!"

"It is, honey."

"Then you have to do something about it!"

"Oh, many people tried. They all vanished in thin air."

Susan frowned.

"They want the town to grow, so they search for new people outside the walls." Tess continued. "And the privileged ones are taken to Uptown and the unprivileged unlucky bastards are loaded into trucks as refugees and presented to the so called Center of Refugees, another name for temporary incarceration. And in most cases, the lucky ones don't know about the destitute ones."

"Surely not!" Susan agreed totally outraged. "But it seems the destitute ones know about the privileged ones."

"Some of us do. Anyhow, you got the picture, I guess. Folks in Uptown live like queens, while people in Downtown work hard and even supply them with everything they need."

Susan's eyes sparkled by hearing that.

"Then, that's it!" She said. "Stop working for them. They depend on you, right? Go on a strike, make them sweat, fight for your rights!"

Tess lowered his neatly trimmed eyebrows and shook his head.

"What?" Susan asked.
"I fear for you, honey."
"Why?"
"Because I like you. And it's people like you that vanish in the haze."
"What do you mean vanish? It's right about time for you to elaborate on that."
"It's pretty much self explanatory. Those who make trouble disappear, simple as that."
"Disappear how?"
"I'm not sure and it's dangerous to talk about it, even in private. Rumor says they are downgraded from employees to slaves. The Gingerbread Dam and the power plant are off-limits. Nobody knows what goes on in there. It's still better to work like a dog for a salary than for loaf and water. They have dreadful ways to keep us on a tight leash. Those who vanished never came back."

Tess shifted position near Susan and tenderly held her hand between his.

"Why you did this, Sue?" He asked. "You're in terrible danger now!"
"I don't think so. Nobody up there knows I'm down here."
"Those two uniformed nincompoops who chased you almost found out."
"Yes and I think I met them before."
"Really? When?"

"About three hours ago, still in Uptown. I was on my way here."

"Be extremely careful with those types, my dear. They're our local Gestapo or KGB, depending on what side of the border you are."

"They stopped me alright, even tried to be nice and all. They also told me this zone was not safe, still plagued by drifters, lamebrains, zombies, whatever."

"Well, they would say that of course, to keep you from coming here. But I can see you're too brave for your own good."

"So, this area is secure, right?"

"Oh, even more secure than Uptown. Actually, this perimeter and the one around Gingerbread were the first areas they walled. They depend on the power plant to have electricity and on us to have the rest. It'd be stupid to let such important places unprotected. Don't worry. You won't see lamebrains in here, not dead ones at least."

"I got to go now." Susan announced.

"Oh no! I'm not letting you take any more chances! There's a curfew going on, and in this very little time we've been together, I grew fond of you."

"I appreciate very much all you did for me, but I still got things to do."

"No, you don't! You're going back to Uptown, forget you've ever been here and live a good life."

"I can't, especially after everything you told me! Besides, life up there is not for me. I need excitement, do something with my life. I can't just be an angel playing harps on some cloud."

"It's better than becoming a drumstick in some hell."

"I told you I'm not in danger! Nobody there knows I'm here."

"Then let's use this to our advantage. Tonight, you're sleeping in the restaurant. I have a room on the back. It's the only place to be. There're a couple of hotels around, but you're not going to like them, unless you don't mind sharing the bathroom with cockroaches."

"Thanks! Tomorrow first light, I'll be out of your hair."

"That's for sure, only not in the way you think. I serve two restaurants in Uptown. Six o'clock sharp, two of my trucks will go there with supplies, and you'll be in one of them. When they arrive, my men will find a way to sneak you out safely, and that'll be the last you'll ever hear from us and this place."

"I appreciate you trying to protect me, but sorry, no can do. I can't live like this."

"Like what?"

"Having to choose between a Stalinist brainwashed bullshit fairy tale and a Nazi labor camp."

"You sleep over it. And don't bother locking the door. Believe me, nobody here is a threat to you."

"Maybe, I'm the threat."

"Smarty pants!" Tess said pinching her nose.

Six o'clock in the morning, but Susan rejected each and every proposal to be in any delivery truck.

"Sorry, I still have some errands to do in Downtown."

"I'm begging you, darling!" Tess spoke with hands together like an angel. "You're such a good girl. Please, tell me you won't do anything stupid."

"Acting stupid makes life worth living."

"You have no idea who you're dealing with. Listen, you got a good thing going on up there. And the world is changed now. Don't ruin everything only for nostalgic notions of conscience."

"Nothing can ever be good without freedom."

"There will be cops patrolling the boundaries between Downtown and Uptown. If you just waltz in there, you'll be in serious trouble."

"I can take care of myself."

"I really doubt that."

Susan tenderly involved Tess' hands in hers.

"Thanks for everything you've done for me." Sue spoke. "I'll repay you as soon as I can."

"There's nothing to repay, dear. I just don't want anything bad happening to you. Please be good."

"I will."

Tess embraced Susan in a very tight hug, followed by an affectionate kiss on her cheek. By seeing Susan disappearing on a corner, the owner of the restaurant frowned and shook his head.

"Poor butterfly."

The town wasn't so big and things were way easier to find during daylight hours. Susan could also have a much better picture of how devastated the city was.

Susan had been raised in a family not quite rich, but surely well positioned in high society. The reality of that place was kind of new to her. However, after experiencing the hollowed manners of a real sumptuous life, she was beginning to enjoy such neighborhood.

She calculated that everything there worked like in any small village. News of a newcomer like Frank would surely be in everybody's mouths and ears in a matter of hours.

There were some shops in town, but only with the necessary stuff, no leisure places, not many chances to have fun, other than nightlife. The only movie theater she found was closed and heading for demolition. Good movies were probably an Uptown privilege.

But at least during the day, people looked more civilized, hard workers trying to make a living, very different from those who roamed the streets at night.

Susan asked for a certain Frank Herrera on a gas station, some hardware stores and a construction site. Over there, a guy named Phil said yes, they had heard of a newcomer, a new "refugee", but he didn't know where he was allocated.

Finally, a woman carrying a malnourished kid directed Susan to a car repair workshop and took that chance to ask for a little change. Why the hell not? Susan thought and gave the lady more money than she could have possibly dreamt of. The poor woman walked away practically dancing, her kid was most likely going to be sick.

Susan went to the mentioned workshop, but she didn't find Frank. He found her.

"Susan!" He screamed and ran to her.

And Susan was involved in another tender hug.

"Am I glad to see you!" Frank said nearly crying. "What are you doing here?"
"Jeez, I could ask you the very same! What happened?"

Frank felt eyes and ears on them. He asked one of his colleagues to cover for him and took Susan to talk outside the shop.

"It was Becky." He said, nervously looking all around.
"What? What do you mean Becky?"
"Well, she walked into my room one night... You wouldn't believe. And she knocked me out cold. She put a rag on my face. I guess it got chloroform or something. I passed out. Next thing I

knew some men in suits dragged me here and I was a mechanic all of a sudden."

"Becky did that to you? I can't believe it!"

"She hasn't been herself, Sue. Come on, she's been acting weird since we took shelter in that Cinemark."

"Yes, I noticed."

"It was that Shane woman. She was alone with Becky for a while. She did something to her."

"This is a little far-fetched, don't you think?" Susan shook her head.

"It got to be her, Sue! The way we feel when she looks straight at us, when she touches us, don't tell me you didn't notice!"

"Yes, I did notice something, but it might've been an impression caused by the first friendly contact we had in days."

"It's more than that. You can't trust her."

"But I got no choice. There's something fishy going on here and I can't figure it out all by myself. I need the help of somebody important and Shane's the only authority I know." She took a deep breath. "Now, let's get out of here."

"What?"

"Come on. We got a job to do."

"Um… I can't leave this place."

"What? Why not? Just quit this job and let's go."

"It's not that simple. The police, they told me… they won't let me leave."

"They can't keep you here against your will!"

"That's not what I heard. My coworkers said I might even get shot if I try to come back to… the place I've been before."

"This is not possible."

"What if they are right, Sue?"

Susan did not answer and remained silent for a few seconds.

"What the heck is going on here?" She sighed. "Okay then. You just stay put and I'll see what I can do."

"You got to get me out of here, Sue!" He practically begged her.

"I promise I won't let you down."

"Just don't trust Shane."

"Maybe she's not even aware of all this. Perhaps that minister she mentioned has some secret agenda she doesn't know of."

"You can't take this chance."

"Just trust me on this one, okay! We're going to be seeing each other soon."

She said goodbye to him with another hug and walked away.

"Don't trust Shane!" Frank shouted again.

Susan went to the convenience store at the gas station and bought three power bars and two small bottles of mineral water. That was all she needed to walk back to Uptown.

But she didn't go very far. After only one hour walk, a police car stopped right by her, blocking the way. And two well known figures left the vehicle, this time not so nice.

"I want to see some hands!" Joe commanded, pointing a gun at her.

"I'm carrying nothing but food and water." Susan assured them after swallowing hard.

"Bring her, Tony."

The other cop pushed her against the car and cuffed her. Then, he threw her in the backseat, without many regards for her head. They wore badges and uniforms, but clearly did not have any training at all in police work.

"I want to talk to Shane." Susan requested on the way.

"You want nothing." Joe answered coldly.

The road got less bumpy as they went, until the asphalt became smooth as a baby's face. And the houses quality and size improved a lot, starting by their flowery, well taken care façades; they were approaching Uptown all right. It was amazing how that same distance looked so short by car, Susan pondered.

However, a group of cars resembling limousines was blocking the road on the unofficial border to the fancy town. Men in suits were leaning against them, looking very confident.

Joe had to bring the car to a harsh halt, burning some rubber on the way. "What the f..."

He and his partner got out of the car, stepping heavy on the floor, their faces fuming in anger. Susan just watched, handcuffed in the backseat.

"What's the meaning of this?" Joe asked angrily to one of the men in suit, who by the way didn't seem to care. "We're taking a prisoner here!"

"And I thought it was protocol to check with me first." Shane said, as if coming from nowhere.

Joe's attitude changed from lion to kitty in a matter of seconds, same as Tony, his partner.

"Take this woman out of the car and uncuff her, gently please."

"But..."

"Now!"

Joe obeyed her with his head low.

"This woman happens to be my friend!" Shane revealed outraged.

Susan couldn't help looking at the cops with a mild smirk.

"W-we didn't know that, ma'am." Joe stammered. "But she was caught in the forbidden zone!"

"Because of your incompetence, yes" Shane retorted. "Now, stop wasting my time, do something right for a change and check if the perimeter is secured now!"

"Yes, ma'am."

And, like two school boys lectured by the teacher, they got into the car and drove away.

Shane strode to Susan.

"Are you alright, my dear?" She asked.

"Yes." Susan replied. "Listen, Shane, we need to talk. It's very urgent."

"I couldn't agree more! Naughty, naughty, Sue. You should've known better than venturing into those woods. It's still a hot zone in there."

"Look, I'm really sorry for what I did, but this is one of the things I have to talk to you about."

"Sure. Did you eat? Did you sleep? Can you work today?"

"Yes to all three."

"Then I walk you to school. You tell me everything on the way."

And, as they went, Susan told Shane all about her last night adventures, not skipping any sordid detail.

When they arrived at the school, Susan considered Shane's reaction a very promising one.

"I'm shocked." She said. "It's not possible that so many things are happening without my knowledge." Shane took a deep breath. "I guess I'm not exactly the brightest cook in the jar, am I?"

"Don't worry, Shane." Sue comforted her. "The important thing is you have all the facts now."

"Only knowing facts won't fix anything! Alright, you go ahead and give your classes while I take all this to Mister Hedgiest. He got a lot of explaining to do. We meet back here by the end of the working day."

Before Susan could respond, Shane was gone. The place was already packed with children and the bells rang, announcing the beginning of classes.

And the hours went by without further excitement. When the bells rang again, bringing the school day to an end, all children left in their usual, strange orderly manner.

"Time to call in a day!" The principal talked cheerfully in the lobby. "Are you coming, Sue? Maybe we can take a coffee or a tea at *Mary Jane's.*"

"Sorry, I can't today. I agreed to meet with Shane after classes."

"Oh! We're getting important, aren't we?"

"Nah" Susan said flushing.

"See you tomorrow then."

"See you."

Susan was all alone in the school entrance, nobody to talk to except for her mind, plagued by concerns. A chill crept through her skin. Nevertheless, Shane didn't take long to show up.

"Let's talk inside." She said.

Susan hesitated before asking the capital question, she very much feared the answer.

"Did you get something, I mean, with the minister?" She finally built her nerves.
"Even better!" was Shane's surprising answer.

Susan frowned, but the other quickly took her to one of the classrooms.

Frank was waiting in there, sitting on a student desk.

"Susan!" He screamed again, only this time relieved and not anguished.
"F-Frank! Jesus!" She couldn't believe her eyes. "Come here you!"

Not surprisingly, they hugged again, both breathless and gasping in relief. With a new wave of energy powering up her soul, Susan spoke firmly:

"Now, Becky is next on my list. Don't worry Frank, she and I will have a serious talk."
"I'll do that." Shane said. "It seems I'm not that inefficient after all."

Feeling they had forsaken their so diligent savior, Frank and Susan immediately turned to their host.

"I don't know how to thank you enough, Shane!" Susan said.
"Right on sister!" Frank spoke as well "And to think that I doubted you."
"Don't worry, folks. It's always a pleasure to be of assistance."

Then, Shane drew a gun from her back pocket, pointed it at Frank's head and pulled the trigger.

A deafening sound roared through the empty corridors, while blood spilled on Susan's face. The already dead young man crashed against the cold floor.

"AHHHH!!!" Susan screamed in despair and confusion, a rainfall of tears flooding her eyes.

But Shane was not in the mood for scenes. She dropped the gun on a table and with a powerful grip seized Susan by her hair and throat, forcing the desperate woman to face her.

"Didn't I give you everything you could possibly want?" Shane asked her with a voice deeper than usual. "What was missing, huh? What was missing? And you simply sneak into the impure zone! Oh, you disappointed me, Sue."

With unbelievable strength, Shane pushed Susan's body down to bring her eyes very close to Frank's destroyed head. But Susan could not stand the horrible sight and closed her tearful eyes.

"See what you did?" Shane spoke. "This is on you, sweetie! Your smugness killed your friend!"

She pulled Susan up again, still holding her hair and neck.

"Amidst all hell outside, I took you and your stupid friends in." Shane continued, her voice slowly coming back to her usual tone. "I gave you things you couldn't possibly imagine, not even in your wildest dreams. And that's how you repay me?" She took a deep breath. "You're such a hypocrite. Lecture your friends again about spitting on the plate from which you ate."

She forced Susan to look her in the eyes and she paralyzed. Tears were still running down her face, but Susan was too defeated and nullified to utter anything else other than weep.

"Do you know how easily I can control your archaic weak mind, like I did to Paul, Nick and Becky?" Shane asked the rhetorical question. "I could make you bark and roll over, but I got other plans for you, a chance to redeem yourself. I'm giving you a very special mission, one I'm sure you'll accomplish. For the moment, just sleep."

Susan's eyelids fell upon her eyes like shutters hitting a window in a hurricane. And she went into deep sleep.

She was able to wake up, but barely, still feeling drowsy. Her head was spinning. The fact it was completely dark in the place she was didn't help her senses to regain balance. Susan was felling terribly sick. She bent her body to throw up. That was when she realized her arms and legs were tied up to the chair she was sitting on by very thick straps, strangling her wrists and ankles.

"H-h-help..." She tried to mumble.

Suddenly, bright lights came to life, almost blinding her eyes, which got used to darkness. While she struggled to adapt to clarity, two men entered the room with syringes.

"Disgusting!" One of them said after seeing the pool of vomit on the floor.
"Let's get this over with." The other said "Time for a refill, honey."

"No, no, please! Don't do this, please!" Susan begged with the last drops of her strength, but in vain.

They stuck needles in unhealed holes already existing on both her arms, suggesting those were not the first injections she had been given in a very short period. And the entire content of the syringes was poured right into her system.

Susan convulsed on the chair as if having a seizure, drooling all over her shirt, while the two men simply left the room, killing the lights on the way out.

She was barely conscious when they tossed her into a reclusion cell. Her body twitched and shook a lot.

"So, we give her full package?" The grey-haired man wearing green apron asked Shane beside him.

"You may go easy on the drugs, but cut solid food this time." She answered. "Give her only water. She's already skinny, but we can always improve her figure."

"Better give her some protein complements and caffeine too. We don't want her to lose consciousness so soon, right?"

"Nice thinking, doc."

"And how long are we keeping her that way?"

"Till I say so."

And they left, closing and locking the heavy door, not that such measure was necessary. Susan tried to stand up at times, but her legs faltered and she was down on her knees again.

She lay down on her back, sharing space with rats and some insects, while looking at the small window with bars at the ceiling.

"Frank...!" She sometimes whispered. "It's all my fault..."

Every time she heard steps, she tried to scream, but nothing came out. She was very weak. Susan could only bring herself to drink the little water they gave her.

Shane stopped by her cell every now and then to check on her general state and make sure her prisoner was only getting worse.

After days in reclusion, taking shots twice a day and deprived of solid food, Susan was visited by Shane again, but this time she came accompanied by Sheriff McBeattie.

Susan was nothing more than skin and bones, her state of mind an enigma. If she could talk, she would probably ask them to kill her. Susan had been reduced to a zombie, only not technically.

"Is she ready?" McBeattie asked.
"Pretty much, I'd say."
"To the hot zone with her?"
"Yes. Take her to the latest coordinates of the truck, according to the satellite feed."
"You got it."

Susan was loaded into a van like a piece of meat. The sheriff drove the vehicle out of the walls, into the unprotected zone.

After reaching the due satellite coordinates, McBeattie stopped the van, got out, opened the side door, lifted Susan on his shoulder and dropped her on the sandy terrain. He came back inside and honked twice to attract zombies.

When he saw a reasonable number of them coming, he closed the door, started the engine and sped away back to the city gates.

Dead rotting humans approached Susan almost in circles, like vultures.

Lily turned the wheel harshly and the vehicle veered off abruptly. For a brief moment, two tires abandoned the floor.

"Stay here." She spoke.
"Okay."

Lily stepped out of the car and finished the beasts. She carried the human being in deplorable state to the truck.

"Are you sure she's not one of them?" Clark asked. "Just take a look at her."
"She mumbled some words, or tried too. Besides, for some inexplicable reason, zombies don't eat each other.
"Can you blame them?"
"Anyway, she's devastated but not a corpse... yet."
"What the heck happened to her?"
"This is for a doctor to say. We need to take her to a hospital."
"So, I guess it's back to *multiple signs walled city*."
"We got no choice. In the meantime, we got a new mate in our bunch. Let's try to get to know her."

ACT 16

Two guards took Mate Clarkson to the shower room and threw him on the hard floor. One of them grabbed him and pushed him against a short wall between showers.

"I bet you like this, huh fun boy?" He said leaning on Clark's bent body from behind, his hands strongly compressing the young man's face against cold tiles. "Are we having fun yet, party boy?"

He then threw Clark on the floor again and kicked him right in the stomach. "What about some foreplay, what do you say?" And he kicked him once more, this time on the face. "You people make me sick!"

"Easy there, Drake!" Another guard said with a smirk. "You don't even know if he's a tutti-frutti."
"He looks like a tutti-frutti to me! He got a knitting scissor on him. You like to knit, boy? Anyway, even if he's not a fag, I guess mommy's boy here needs to man up a little. And I got just the thing!"

And Mate was hit by a powerful jet of water, after they stripped him of all his clothes.

"Hey, he got those spots all over his body!" One guard observed.
"Too bad they don't come out with water!"
"Well, we can always try!"

And they kept on whipping Clark's body with the jet of water. He screamed in despair. They finally closed the spigot and took him out of the shower booth. Then, they spanked him for a while.

"Toughening up already, huh?" Drake said.

Even from his station, Pedro could hear the unmistakable click sound of the heavy door being unlocked from the outside. As the sector was ample and awfully silent most of the time, each and every little noise in there resounded through the walls like a thunder.

"This is it!" Hector said to Vince.
"Just say the word, bro."
"Hey, don't do anything stupid!" Raul warned them. "It's all our asses in a sling."

While the two brothers got ready to make their move, Marcellus shook his head negatively on his chair.

The door was opened, but before Hector and Vince could jump whoever was coming, they saw the punished figure of Mate Clarkson getting tossed inside. Two men with machine guns entered the room.

"Hey, look what they did to this guy!" Vince said in horror. "This is a not a way to treat a human being!"
"Damn right it's not!" Hector replied grinding teeth.

He advanced to one of the guards with furious anger. The man pointed the machine gun at his chest.

"Don't do it, man!" Pedro begged.

Hector stopped but didn't take his flaming eyes off the armed man.

"Back off, coon boy!" The guard said.

"Care to call me that without the piece?" Hector defied him.

"Easy there, monkey! Or you'll know how a Swiss cheese feels like."

"What about just the two of us, man to man?"

"Come back to the jungle where you belong."

He slowly walked backwards, still pointing the weapon at Hector. The other man aimed his machine gun to the general direction of everybody else in the sector. They left the room and locked the door.

"Racist chicken!" Hector grunted.

"This man needs help." Vince screamed holding Clark in his arms. "They beat him up real bad."

"Sure." His brother said.

They carried the young tennis player to a chair.

ACT 17

"You can imagine how disappointed I was when you just turned your back on us the first time you reached our gates." Shane said.

"Where's the guy who was with me?" Lily asked in a demanding tone. Her wrists and ankles were chained to the wall behind her. There was also a metal strap around her neck, bolted to the wall.

"This is irrelevant now. But I assure you his permanence among the living also depends on how much you cooperate."

"If you wanted us here, why didn't you just ask? You didn't have to torture that poor woman!"

"Oh, it was necessary to prove a point."

"Yes, that you are a big son of a bitch!"

Shane frowned at Lily. She was surely not used to any other approach other than flatters, adulation and worshipping.

"I should expect this kind of language from you."

"Now that you got me, you can undo whatever you did to that woman." Lily said.

"I'm afraid this is no longer possible."

"Who are you anyway?"

"Like I said, Shane is my name, very nice to make your acquaintance. And don't bother telling me your name. Obviously, I already know who you are."

"I wasn't going to. We're not friends, stupid."

Shane got serious again.

"Well, you told me at the hospital all my questions would be answered in due time." Lily recalled. "And it seems I'm not going anywhere now." She waved her shackles.

"Why the hell not? I was looking forward to talking to you."

"Okay, I'm listening."

"I'm a crucial element in an extremely important project brought about by very special people, a joint venture that involves some countries concerned with the future of the planet."

"And I can see torturing innocents and putting people in chains are also a key element in this thing."

"No, those are just accessories for a greater cause."

"So, basically there're a bunch of other guys pulling your strings."

"Au contraire. Without me, there is no project. I was conceived, built, modeled, perfected to lead, to dominate, to execute, ultimately to make sure everything works as flawlessly as it can possibly be."

"I don't understand. You talk like you're some kind of robot."

"Oh no, I'm human indeed, only improved, enhanced by the wonderful domains of science."

"Are you saying you're some sort of test tube experiment from a lab or something?"

Shane shook her head but remained firmly composed.

"Such a shallow description for something that's way beyond anything your small mind could possibly conceive." The elegant woman retorted.

"That means I'm right. You came from a test tube and a toaster probably, and now everybody has to pay for that."

Shane came near Lily in a threatening way. She fixed eyes on the Australian girl.

"They selected me right from birth because I presented the highest ESP among the babies. This is *extrasensory perception*."

"I heard about it. So, they picked you because you were the most lunatic baby they got."

"In a way, yes. But along the years, they gave me more. My brain wound up becoming a very sophisticated broadcast system." Shane tapped her head with a forefinger.

"I don't quite follow."

"I didn't expect you would. It suffices to say I'm able to transmit and receive radio waves together with my ESP. Thanks to this, among other amazing things I can also control regular minds as easily as you tie your shoelaces."

"And that's what you're going to do now, control my mind?"

"Oh no, it won't be necessary in your case, honey. I prepared something very special just for you. They filled up my brain with much more than just domination capabilities."

"They only forgot to add some common sense to the mix, not to mention intelligence."

"Joke while you can. Believe me, I do admire your spirit, but it's worthless."

"What's this project, this venture you mentioned, all about?"

"I'm very glad you asked. You see, the world was getting too crowded and Mother Nature can only take so much. Unfortunately, not so bright human samples insist on breeding like rabbits and our resources were running scarce."

"You got me in a loss again." It was Lily's turn to frown.

"It's a Malthusian thing. I trust that even an uneducated person like you knows what I'm referring to, right?"

"Yes."

"Well, Earth's population needed to be drastically reduced before the rabbles drank and ate everything we got. And a very exclusive group of people took matters into their hands."

Lily opened her eyes real wide, pondering about the implications of such words.

"Don't tell me you and your idiots are responsible for…"

"Oh, the spreading of the virus created by our scientists was very successful indeed!" Shane proudly interrupted her. "The majority of population turned into flesh-eating living dead and they did some cleaning on their own, pretty ingenious huh?"

Lily shook her head as much as she could; however, the metal strap strangled her neck.

"Why?" The Australian woman asked. "What do you gain by destroying the world and its people? Why are you doing this?"

"Ah, the million dollars question! The zombie plague is just the beginning. Now, it's time to repopulate the planet, but only with those who really count. And the defective ones can work and serve us, as it should have always been, under control and in the quantities predetermined by us. Now, what do you think of the plan?"

"I think you're nothing more than a psycho byproduct who likes to play God!"

"Just a matter of reference, God can be whoever people want Him to be."

Lily faced Shane with angry eyes.

"And how do I fit in all this?" The Australian queried.

"I was getting to that. Considering the current situation, people eventually have to come to us for protection. That's when we make the due selection. Or at least that was the general idea. And we were doing rather well, but something happened, something that turned the tide a little bit."

"What was that?"

"The elementary school event, the one you so actively participated in."

"What's that got to do with anything?"

"Your little prowess brought new hopes to people, gave them reasons to live. They started to believe life can be more than

141

just plague and suffering. The press worked against us in that one, those fools. They would do anything for a scoop. Now, a great deal of survivors only wants to find you, copy you, be just like you, fending for themselves while helping others, instead of seeking my protection."

Lily's eyes changed from angry to incredulous.

"You didn't know that, did you?" Shane realized. "A myth was created and this is bad for business. And now, the myth shall die."

Shane pulled a lever on the wall. The chains holding Lily's wrists went up, forcing her to raise arms above her head.

"So that's it?" The Australian girl asked. "Are you going to kill me?"
"That would only make a martyr out of you."
"Then what? You've already tied me up dungeon style, very unoriginal by the way. What's next, some kind of torture, perhaps electricity through my body, a hot wire to my head, you telling me how your day was?"
"I got a better idea."

Shane walked away and disappeared from view. Suddenly, a semi-putrefied, horridly deformed dead man ran straight to Lily. Instinctively, she held her body against the wall behind her, also turning her head to the left.

The zombie stopped only inches from Lily's right ear, his protruding exposed jawbone trying to bite her. The creature was detained by a long chain tying his skull to the opposite wall.

Lily panted heavily, the terrible dead breath of the gnarling beast all over her nostrils. One single move and the creature's twisted teeth would reach some part of her body. He seemed to have a preference for her face. His dreadful mouth jiggled up and down.

Shane came back into the room and stood beside the zombie.

"I believe that you, of all people, should know what this is, right?" She asked, drumming fingers on the monster's skull.

"Looks like your clone." Lily still managed to say.

"Very funny, darling. You must have noticed, of course, he's not coming after me."

"Can't blame the lad, you're distasteful even to him."

Shane smiled "I can control him as well. But now, I'm letting his guts dictate his actions. You can actually see them." She laughed. "Sooner or later you'll have to twitch and that'll be enough for him to bite you."

"Only bite me, not killing me?"

"That's right."

"Why?"

"I want you to turn into a zombie. Then, I'll arrange for a little accident to happen. You'll eat and dilacerate three children to pieces, with lots of cameras filming and reporters taking pictures. And the press will have yet another field day, the great Apocalily biting children to death as a zombie! That's a way to kill a myth."

"You're going to have children killed just to foul my image?"

"That's the idea."

"You don't have to do that. I do anything you want. Just put me on the air, I pledge allegiance to you. You don't have to kill anybody!"

"Very noble, but I'm afraid that won't be enough. You have to fall into disgrace before the judgmental eyes of public opinion. People will again need a shoulder to cry on and I'll be more than happy to offer them mine. This world doesn't need any more heroes, left alone a daddy's little girl from overseas who thinks she's Captain America."

Lily didn't answer.

Shane came closer to her "What, no snap come back to this one?"

She took two steps back.

"Well, I leave you two lovers alone." The blonde woman concluded "Time for the general public to return to old habits, by which I mean living pointless lives, so they have to live the life of celebrities to make up for empty existences. The difference is there'll be only one celebrity to worship, and that'll be me!"

Shane winked at Lily and turned around, leaving the Australian woman with the zombie trying to eat her.

"Too bad those scientists of yours never gave you a soul." Lily still said. "All they had was an endless supply of ego and they used it all on you!"
"A necessary evil" Shane decided to answer that. "People give too much credit to appearances, they always did. Now, if you excuse me, I have other pressing matters to attend to. When I come back, you'd better be snarling. Bye!"

And she left.

The zombie's head was dangerously close to Lily's ear. His growls were almost deafening her.

"Man, I'm in a pickle here!" Lily mentally assessed her overall situation. "Think, girl, think! What daddy would do? What daddy would do? Help me, daddy!"

From that new angle, she could see all her gear sitting on a corner, but far out of reach.

Then she remembered "Oh my God, Clark! The lad might be in trouble, I need to do something!"

However, muscle fatigue was settling fast and painful cramps seized her limbs. Lily was about to be betrayed by her own biology. Some part of her body could move involuntarily at any second, making her reachable to the zombie's teeth.

ACT 18

At the power plant, Aaron tried to patch up Clark's wounds as best as he could, using the few bandages at his disposal, with the help of Maria. The young man told them his sad experiences with the guards beating him up. Everybody in there had similar stories to tell.

"After they spanked me for the second time, I understood they were volunteering me for something." Clark was finishing his tale. "Then they took me to some starched guy in suit who liked to be called minister and he kept on calling me *rusty boy*. Finally, they tossed me here."

"Yes, it seems we can't even have freckles around here." Aaron commented.

"It's clear they're not exactly the liberal types." Vince observed.

"What do you do?" Hector asked Mate, noticing the young man was a little down. "And if you answer with the word *sector* followed by a letter, I'll kill you!"

Mate opened a sad smile.

"I used to play tennis."

"And I used to roll the dice for money with some other kids in the neighborhood back in the day. Come on, buddy, I need more details! Are you a pro?"

"Yeah, sort of."

"Oh man!" Vince cheered. "You mean you played for a living, like those guys we saw on TV sports classics, Connors, Borg, Federer and the Spanish guy what's his name?"

"Nadal?"

"That one!"

"What do you mean *sort of*?" Hector talked to Clark again.

146

"I wish I was anything like those guys you mentioned. Actually, I wasn't doing so well. Maybe I can do better in the power supply business."

"Hey, this is loser talk and while I'm here, I don't want to know about this stuff!"

"It's just that sometimes it's not so easy to reach the flag on top of the Empire State Building."

"Well, nothing is easy in life, that's what makes it thrilling. And what the heck are you talking about?"

"It's just an analogy she, I mean, my traveling companion... Ah, never mind."

"No, no, tell me!" Hector pressed. "We're making good conversation here!"

"Oh, I sense there's a miss tennis player somewhere, hein buddy?" Vince said.

"I'm jealous already!" Maria smiled.

"Nah, far from that" Clark lamented.

"You do know this is also up to you, right?" Hector spoke. "She's only lost if you let her go without even trying. What's her name?"

Mate shook his head, looking embarrassed all of a sudden.

"Come on." Vince insisted. "He just asked her name, not her erogenous zones."

"You won't believe it, but here it goes. Her name's Lily Master."

"And so?"

"Lily as in Apocalily."

As the sound reverberated a lot in that environment, about thirty heads took their eyes off monitors to look straight at Clark.

"No way!" Pedro said.

"Yes, way" Mate replied.

"My God!" Another voice shouted. "So, she really exists!"

"She was captured as well!" Clark rushed to inform before somebody else gasped.

"Oh."

"She was with me and we both got caught. I don't know where they took her."

"They must be doing awful things to her." Maria speculated.

"How come Apocalily was taken that easily?" Raul queried.

"We were betrayed." Clark whispered. "We came here to help a woman we had rescued from the living dead outside, and they knocked us out with some gas."

"Yeah, there's no way to protect ourselves against treason." Vince pondered. "We know that very well, right bro?"

Hector nodded in agreement.

"Damn it!" Vince said. "One more hope that goes down the drain. Easy comes, easy goes."

As quickly as they turned around, thirty faces lost interest and came back to their respective monitoring stations.

"I don't care." Maria spoke and turned to Clark. "How is she?"

"Oh, she's everything they say and more."

"That good, huh?"

"Yes. I don't even know what she was doing with a guy like me. I guess she only took me in her truck out of charity or something."

"Man, why you people insist on busting my balls?" Hector angrily retorted. "Now, you listen to me, kid! I know why your tennis career wasn't flying. Because you suffer from a serious case of self-pity! They only get you down if you let them."

"You'd better listen to the man!" Vince emphasized.

"Wait a minute…" Mate suddenly frowned. "I've seen you guys before…"

"I'm sure you have!" Hector opened his large white smile.

"Oh boy, here we go again…" Vince whispered, rolling eyes around the sockets.

Hector came near his brother and held his chin up so to face Clark.

"Take a good look!" His smile seemed to become perennial.

"Times Magazine, Forbes…" Clark divagated. "…was it Times or Newsweek?" Then, his eyes shone *"Hector and Vince, Routers and Since*! It's you, right?"

"The very same!" Hector said with pride.

"It's a stupid rhyme that makes no sense, but he insisted on calling our company like that." Vince complained.

"Mamma loved it!"

"But sister hated it!"

"We are surrounded by celebrities all of a sudden." Marcellus commented. "Too bad Miles Davis couldn't make it."

"Man, you were the fastest growing company in the country, according to The Economist!" Clark pointed out.

"Fifty departments in the headquarters alone, more than eight-hundred employees countrywide and counting!" Hector informed.

"We did business in all states, even abroad, and going further." Vince completed.

"Yes, I read that Cisco and Juniper were getting really worried." Mate said.

"As they should be!" Hector spoke. "Our product is much better, and that's because we made it like this. I can tell you, we didn't make a fortune from scratch by sitting our asses down, waiting for the fairy godmother of money to pay us a visit."

"Yes, but now you're here, like the rest of us slobs." Pedro said.

"And with this attitude, I'm starting to think you really belong in here." Hector retorted. "It's in your power to do something, but you choose to conform and accommodate, always in the path of least resistance."

"Fuck this shit." Pedro whispered turning to his screen.

"What's that?" Hector spoke walking to Pedro with heavy steps.

"Easy bro" Vince tried to hold him. "It's not a good time to start another world war."

"I want to know what he said." Hector insisted and turned to Pedro. "Say that again looking at me!"

"You'll get us all killed, okay!" Pedro shouted back, standing up and facing Hector "Or worse! Didn't you hear what Marcellus said? You and your little uprising babble bullshit will get us all in a world of hurt! Probably you're here because you talked like this outside, can't you see? They heard you, they hear everything! And you dragged your brother to the mud with you!"

"I'd be with him no matter what!" Vince responded.

"They're just a bunch of white folks doing a lot of shit and you're taking it!" Hector argued.

"Hey Mister *Norma Rae*" Raul intervened. "Has it ever occurred to you they might be listening to you right now? Cause if they are, they'll be ready for whatever we could possibly try here."

"I don't see any cameras!"

"It doesn't mean they're not there." Maria said. "They do have surveillance in the corridors outside the sectors."

"They might have planted mikes in strategic places we can't see." Another worker suggested.

"I'm sorry, man." Pedro said in a moderate tone. "Really, I meant no offense, I'm sorry for everything I said. But you have to wake up, man. If things are bad now, they can still get a lot worse. Accept reality, it's good for you, it's good for us, we all live longer. It's not the best of the worlds, but it's a living. We've been doing this for some time now."

"And how long is that?"

"It varies. Some came two weeks ago, some are newcomers like you. Raul and I have been here for six months now, and Marcellus over there has been in this racket for thirty-two years."

"Thirty-three next week" Marcellus informed. "Thirty-three long years…"

Hector took a deep breath and walked around. Everybody came back to work, except for Vince and Mate, who kept looking at Hector.

The big rotund man walked to Clark.

"Mate's your name, right?" Hector asked him.

"Yes, Mate Clarkson. But Lily called me Clark, you see, mate's a too common word in Australia and all… It's a thing between us."

Hector pondered those words for a while and said "Let me ask you something…"

"Sure."

"Is Lily human?"

"What? I don't think I got it."

"Just answer my question. Is Lily human?"

"Yes."

Hector nodded and walked around again.

"So, she wasn't an alien or any kind of super being." Hector divagated aloud, his voice echoing through the indoor environment.

"What difference does it make?" Raul spoke. "She's most likely dead now."

"But she surely left us something, didn't she?" Hector continued. "I want your attention, all of you. May I have your attention, please?"

"We are so dead!" Pedro grunted.

Vince grinned "When he starts with the thing, nobody can stop him, believe me."

"I'm not stopping until I have your undivided attention!" Hector raised his volume even more. "I can be a real pain in the neck!"

"That's for sure." His brother whispered.

Workers lazily turned their heads to look at him, hoping he would eventually calm down and leave them alone. One man didn't move. His eyes remained stuck on the monitors.

"Hey you!" Hector walked to him. "I'm talking to you!"

He turned his chair around to make the man face him. And Hector found out half his face was horridly burned, with an inexistent right eye, replaced by pieces of dead skin. But Hector didn't seem shaken by such sight.

"What's your name?" Hector asked.

"Prashant."

"Nice meeting you, Prashant."

"Likewise."

"The guards did this to you?"

"When they dragged me out of my house, they separated me from my wife and daughter. I didn't take kindly to it. In that little audience we all had with this minister guy, I spat on his right eye. It seems they didn't like it."

"Are you willing to fight to be with your wife and daughter again and, who knows, maybe get some justice in the process?"

"We need more people, much more people."

Hector shook his head in agreement and walked back to the center of the giant sector.

"Then, it seems Apocalily was just human." Hector said looking at Clark, who nodded. "And yet, she fought and killed more than a hundred zombies and saved lots of children, all by herself. This is an example of what will and determination can do when one sets his or her mind on something!"

He took a deep breath and continued "Ladies and gentlemen, we are also humans and we are way more than just one. I guess it's clear what's missing here. But that can be fixed. Those pricks out there are not super humans! We can fight them if we're all together in this one!"

"What about their power, the thing that happened to Michelle and the other rebels?" Maria asked.

"Well, we got an advantage Michelle didn't have." Hector replied. "We know they got some kind of power. All we have to do is be careful about it. Come on, who's with me?"

People around him only scratched heads.

Hector walked to Aaron.

"What about you, my man? They shaved you, now we shave them, how about some payback?"

"I'm sorry, I cannot help you."

"Why not?"

"Because I'm not like you! I just can't do it, I'd probably ruin everything."

"It's not a matter of being like me or anybody else. It's a matter of being the best Aaron you can possibly be!"

"Nobody believed that my brother and I could possibly make a business work, especially considering where we came from." Vince spoke. "We got a lot of naysayers, but our mamma always believed in us and that made all the difference."

"I'm not your mamma," Hector said to Aaron "but I believe in you."

Maria stood up "I'm with you!"

"I'm with you!" Raul said as well.

Pedro looked at him.

"Come on, man." Raul spoke. "What we got to lose?"

"Yeah, what the heck, everybody dies one day." Pedro concluded. "Alright, I'm in."

"I'm in!" Clark jumped "For Lily!"

"It'll never work." Marcellus said.

Hector turned to him with disappointed eyes.

"Not without me!" The old man completed and Hector's eyes sparkled. "I've been around more than anyone of you by far and a good deal of that time was in these premises. I know people in other sectors that can help us. They're also motivated, only waiting for the right people to come. And you boys look right enough to me."

Hector went to him "Are you sure?"

"Those men out there owe me big for what they did to my Michelle." He stood up with difficulties, Hector had to help him.

"Come on, you lazy bums, get your sorry asses out of those chairs and let's kick some white trash ass!"

Some minutes of a dreadful silence followed.

"I'm in!" Prashant said.
"I'm in!"
"Count me in!"
"I'm in!"

One by one, at their own pace, the workers stood up to confirm allegiance.

Hector walked to Aaron "What about you?"
"Do you have a shaving kit?"
"Oh, I get you one!" He smiled again.
"Then I'm in."
"Well, bro, it seems you got yourself an insurrection." Vince said.
"I confess I wasn't quite expecting that."
"You do realize, of course, our friends outside might have watched and listened to every word you said and they may know what we're up to."
"Maybe not, maybe they don't care to watch us, because they trust too much those alleged powers of theirs. Anyway, it's a chance we have to take, there's no turning back now."
"By the way, do you have a plan?"
"No. Do you?"
"Not quite."
"I do." Marcellus said "Something I've been cooking up in my mind since Michelle died."

ACT 19

Susan's replacement was teaching her class when Principal Hildenbrandt knocked on the open door and entered.

"Good morning, Missus Hildenbrandt." The children said in choir, as best as they could pronounce that name.
"Good Morning, children!" She smiled.

The principal went to the teacher and they whispered a brief conversation. The teacher seemed to like what she heard.

"Missus Hildenbrandt has something very important to say." She announced.

The children quieted down like little statues. The principal took the floor.

"Oh, I'm so proud to tell you that we have a very illustrious visitor today! The most important man in town, also responsible for our so long lasting prosperity, is honoring us with a surprise visit! Oh yes, I'm talking about the Minister himself!"

Mister Hedgiest made his glorious entrance into the classroom. All children stood up in respect, while the two adult women smiled and applauded like little girls.

"Good morning, Mister Minister!" The children's choir resounded again.
"Very good morning, my dear little ones and also my lovely educators..." He turned to the women, who had to put some efforts not to pass out due to so much panting. "You make me look like some kind of priest. You put me on the spot here!"

Teacher and principal laughed at the joke sounding like chicken clucking, while the children didn't acknowledge it so much.

"Now, getting to business" The Minister continued "I have a very special announcement to make! Today, we're starting a very big and, why not saying, ambitious project, one we expect to be both fun and educational. And, get this, due to your impeccable record and excellence in teaching methods, three students of this very school will be picked up to participate in this so important project to our future, one from this class and two from other classes, to be decided in a later time, but still today!"

Children and adults clapped their beloved leader, speaking on a project they knew nothing about until then.

ACT 20

It was late at night. The north district in Heavensville went dark all of a sudden. Power was out in a region comprising four blocks, and residents were lost and bewildered for such event was extremely rare in that town.

In the power plant, the transmission sector was in an uproar, with workers running up and down.

A furious man with machine gun thundered into the monitoring section, his face red in anger. Another armed man stood guard by the doorway. Maria came to him.

"I don't feel so good." She said.
"What's the problem, sweet heart, you're in your period?" He grinned.
"My head hurt! Do you have aspirins? I think I'm going to be sick!"
"Fine! Just don't get this hall all dirty!" He got distracted for a fraction of seconds reaching into his shirt pocket. Maria slid nimble fingers through the doorframe behind him.

"What you incompetent scums are doing in here?" The other guard yelled at everybody. "The north district got no power for the last half hour! Transmission said they only knew about the problem now! What kind of shitty monitoring are you doing here?"
"You see, man, we just had…" Vince said standing in front of the guard.
"Out of my way, maggot!" He pushed Vince to the side, dropping him on the floor. He stopped in front of a station. "All red alarms are flashing like a freaking Christmas tree in this panel! How come you took so long to engage Transmission?"

"Like the man was about to say before you interrupted him," Marcellus spoke "We had a little communication problem. Our phone lines went down and only now they came back online. If you guys maintained this place a little better or gave us radios, this sort of event wouldn't happen."

"This is not an excuse!" The man said a little insecure, taken by surprise before such convincing explanation. "Considering all your years, old timer, I expected more from you."

Marcellus glanced at his wristwatch without the guard realizing it. Precisely that moment, power sprung to life again on the north district and residents breathed in relief. Intrusive local internet and garbage TV prime time were back to their homes.

"See, everybody happy!" Vince said, standing up.

"Not thanks to you!" The guard stood his ground. "The rations for this entire sector will be reduced to half portion!" He waved his weapon as if it was a baseball bat.

"With the food they serve in here, it's actually a favor." Maria whispered in an almost inaudible voice.

He and the other guard left with furious steps, locking the door.

Hector, who until then pretended he was working, turned his chair around from a station and said:

"Did you see how they acted? They don't have the slightest idea what we're up to!"

"It's possible." Marcellus agreed. "I've just been on the phone with Bill, my guy in Transmission who shut down the north district, and he told me guards over there also don't suspect a thing."

"They think we're just a bunch of dogs they can say roll over and play dead every time they want." Vince concluded.

"We were exactly like this for a long time." Pedro whispered.

"By the way, are you all right?" Hector asked his brother.

"I'm fine. That guy was pretty rough on me, but he left me a little compensation." Vincent proudly swung a walkie-talkie "Right from his *undies*." He gave it to Hector.

"You still know how to do that. Mamma never approved."

"Too bad, because sister taught me."

"Anyway, did you also get the key to the door?"

"It crossed my mind, but the guard would've realized it the second he tried to lock that door. Still, no worries, *'cause* I got the next best thing."

Vince walked to one of the heavy doors and simply slid it open. Everybody gazed at him. Then, Vincent took a small piece of bandage out of the slot on the doorframe where the lock bolt should be.

"Man, those guys are so full of air they fall for the oldest tricks in the street book. Maria blocked the slot with some rags. When they lock the door, it does the same click sound, only the lock bolt goes nowhere. Good work, honey!"

Maria nodded.

"Alright, now close that door before they realize it." Hector ordered.

"Sooner or later, that moron will notice his radio is missing." Raul reminded him.

"Right, we have to do this fast." Hector went to Marcellus. "Okay, this is for you." He gave him the walkie-talkie. "Now, what do you got for us?"

"Gather around everybody." Marcellus requested.

All workers, including Mate Clarkson, surrounded the old man as best as they could, to see the large layout papers spreading all over his station.

"I know this place like the back of my hand, but you don't, so pay attention." Marcellus started. "You see this place here?" He pointed a finger to a spot on the paper.

"Yes" was the general consensus.

"This used to be a games room, surely big enough for that. But it was converted into a warehouse back in the nineteen-nineties, because bosses at the time thought it was too much of a distraction."

"We can never have any fun!" Vince commented and Maria smiled.

Marcellus continued:

"Some friends of mine who work in *Supply and Logistic* told me they saw a lot of guards and men in suits going in and out this place, but nobody other than them is allowed to go anywhere near there."

"They are probably using the warehouse to keep weapons, ammunition and perhaps radios!" Hector spoke.

"My very thought exactly." Marcellus agreed. "Ultimately, that's your objective, ladies and gentlemen. Once you get armed, you can see there's a free path to Prescott Road, right behind Gingerbread Dam."

"And we just have to take this corridor here straight to the warehouse." Hector said, sliding a forefinger along the paper."

"You can't go through there." Marcellus disappointed him. "It's too obvious. There will be guards at every square foot on the way."

"But it'll be dark everywhere."

"It's still too risky. And don't forget that darkness works both ways. I don't have flashlights to all of you."

161

"Then, what do you suggest?"

"This aisle here, it used to be a conveyor belt shaft."

"It's a little too narrow, don't you think?" Hector frowned. "And look at those distances. It'll add at least twenty more minutes to our crossing. Not to mention we'll only fit one at a time, going in a single line. This is strategically dangerous."

"That's why I believe there'll be no guards in there. Don't forget they underestimate us badly."

"The warehouse will be heavily guarded too." Aaron spoke.

"We create a diversion to cover our entrance." Hector replied. "And I was thinking of you and Mate over there."

"I can be very diverting." Clark said.

"That's it." Marcellus concluded. "It's a lousy plan, but it's the only one we got. And remember that we're mostly counting on our captor's sloppiness. They may prove to be better than we think."

"Then, we'll have to improvise." Hector said. "Now, listen up all of you!" He took advantage that everybody was already around him. "We'll try to do this quietly, but if they shoot at us, we'll have to shoot back. We might have to kill people, the same way some of us won't get out of here alive. If any of you doesn't want to go through with it, I totally understand, there'll be no hard feelings or consequences."

But each and every worker stood his and her ground.

"Many folks here have been waiting for this moment." Prashant said. "We either get the hell out of here or die trying."

"Good." Hector said. He looked at Maria. "We know this people might have some kind of power. It may be brainwashing, hypnotism, we don't know. So, whatever you do, don't listen to any bullshit they may say to you. If some song or anything else starts to play on the PA system, just cover your ears and sing your own tune aloud. Do not interact with anybody else other than ourselves."

A choir of "Got it" was heard.

"Great! Now, take your positions and pray."

All workers dispersed, ready for the fight.

"This is so exciting!" Maria said to Vince.

"Have you ever handled a gun?"

"Well, I handled several kinds of hair-dryers. The principle must be the same."

Alone again, Hector turned to Marcellus and said:

"Are you sure you're not coming?"

"I can barely stand up, left alone walk. I'd just slow you down. Prison breaks are young people game."

"You know they'll come here. And they will find you. And you know what they're going to do."

"I lived enough years and they've already taken from me everything I got."

"They'll do the same with Bill, over at Transmission."

"It's hard to believe, but he's even older than me. And we've been talking a lot in the past weeks. He also lost a hell lot to these people and he knows the odds."

"I'll try to get my hands on a walkie-talkie as soon as I can. Then, I'll tune to your frequency."

"And I'll be your eyes while you're out there for as long as they let me live. You'd better be quick, son."

Hector stretched his hand and Marcellus accepted it in a firm handshake.

"Do me a favor, will you?" The old man requested. "Don't let us die in vain. Get out of this place and tell the world what's happening here. You'll find somebody who cares. Those racists can't be everywhere."

"You got it."

"I'll be praying for your soul."

"And I'll pray for yours."

Hector turned around again and screamed with a powerfully loud voice:

"Alright everybody, time has come! Let's do this for our way of life, our freedom, for Michelle…" He looked at Clark. "…and for Apocalily! May her heart and soul grow within each and every one of us!"

"YEAH!" They all shouted with fists in the air.

"Vince, go to the door."

"Got it, bro."

Hector turned back to Marcellus and said "Kick ass!"

Marcellus grabbed the landline phone. After a couple of rings "Hey Bill, it's me." He looked straight at Hector. "Get this dump back to the Stone Age!"

"With pleasure!" The voice on the other end replied. "Good luck to your boys."

Hearts pounded so loud they could even be heard. Anticipation and expectation seized everybody's minds.

Seconds passed and nothing happened. Anxiety grew. Knots spread around stomachs and breathings were getting heavy.

"Why is it taking so long?" A woman named Natasha whispered anguished.

Suddenly, all lights and systems went down, including surveillance. Flashlights came to life. Vincent opened the door.

"Follow me!" Hector shouted.

More than thirty workers left the sector. Marcellus stayed, appreciating tranquility and darkness.

"Through here! No, wait! To the left!"
"Are you sure?"
"Not quite."

The fugitives kept on moving fast along dark, eerie corridors. Only the front squad had flashlights. Voices overlapped.

"I can't see a thing!" One man in the back squad complained."
"Just follow the guys on the front."
"Keep your voice down!"
"Are you still there?"
"Are you talking to me?"
"Stop pushing!"
"Don't bunch up!"
"Hey, get your hands out of there!" One woman whispered.
"It was an accident!"
"Shut up you all! They'll hear us!"
"Boy, we're not ready for this. We're just simple technicians. Well, what can we do?"

And they continued. Hector brought the entire group to a halt. And they were quite a lot.

"Where to now, bro?" Vince queried.
"This way."

"Are you sure this is the shaft? Man, these flashlights don't help much!"

Sounds of heavy steps grew louder in the near distance.

"Better make up your mind, bro. We're about to have some company."

"I recognize this metallic reek. Some heavy stuff went through here before, most likely on a conveyor belt. Follow me."

"Right on." Vince signaled to the rest of the group, and one by one the message went through.

They were on the move again. And the shaft was even narrower than they thought.

"Damn it!" Hector cursed. "I might consider losing some weight when we're out of here." He spoke, sucking his bellybutton as much as he could.

"You might also consider becoming a little gentler."

"This is beyond me."

The deeper they went into the aisle, the hotter it got. The power shut down brought about by Transmission also turned off the ventilation system.

"Man, this is starting to look a lot like Palm Beach." Vincent observed.

"Do not stop everybody!" Hector ordered the group. He then whispered to his brother "We still have a long way to go." They were both sweating a lot.

Breathable air was running thin. An older man in the rear fell on his knees. Mate came to his aide.

"Are you alright?"

"Yes, I just need a second to catch my breath."

He managed to stand up, with the help of Clark and Natasha.

"Thanks guys. I'm good to go."

However, loud steps other than theirs echoed again through the awfully closed environment.

"Stop, stop, stop!" Hector commanded, trying to keep his voice low but audible.

That sudden halt of the front squad almost caused the entire group to fall on each other like a domino.

"It sounds like those steps are all over us!" Hector noticed. "Where are they? Did they find us?"
"Not yet, but we might have a little problem." Vince carefully directed his flashlight beam upwards.

There was a grid on the ceiling through which it was possible to see the boots of the guards running on the upper floor. Obviously, the soldiers would also be able to see the fugitives downstairs, if they pointed their flashlights at the grids by their feet.

"Don't anybody make a sound..." Hector said.

But the heat was unbearable, not to mention the excess of carbon dioxide produced by their own respiratory systems. And they were all panting hardly.

The steps silenced on the upper floor. One man coughed.

"Damn it!"

They waited a little more.

"I guess we're good to go now." Vince suggested.
"Not yet."
"Man, it's really hot in here."
"There might still be one or two of them up there."
"Our brains are too deprived of oxygen already." Aaron alerted, wiping sweat off his forehead with the back of his hand. "We need to go now."
"Alright" Hector gasped. "We should have used the main corridors."
"Those men upstairs are the proof we did the right thing by coming through here."

And they walked and walked as best as they could, but most of the group was tired and dizzy. The shaft seemed to never end.

"Hey bro, look at that." Vince gasped with all breath he had left.

There were natural light visible from a curve up ahead.

"Man, I'm glad to see this!" Hector cheered. "I think we made it."

He ordered the group to stop again. He and Vince went to the curve and took a peek.

"It's an exit, yes!" Hector breathed in relief. "And it seems the coast is clear. Let's go real slow."

One by one, the whole group left the narrow shaft, finding ways to squeeze in that new section of the plant. Nobody knew how long they had been walking. The crossing took a lot longer than expected. The first sunlight of morning was already invading the place.

Some workers gazed at the big glass windows above, like children in an amusement park. It had been long since they last saw the world outside.

"Alright, let's take five. The air is way fresher in here."

They all sat down on the floor, sweating and panting a lot.

"Do you know where to go from here, bro?"
"I have an idea. We're close. If I remember those layouts, we have to follow those windows... that way."
"Cool."

Five minutes later, they continued with Hector taking the lead. They found the warehouse, former game room, currently weapons shop. Two men in suits with machine guns were guarding the door.

"What we do now?"
"We wait".

After ten minutes or so, a man in military outfit came. The ones in suits made room for him. He unlocked the door.

"Alright" Hector whispered. "Mate, Aaron, commence operation *old ladies' yak*."

Aaron and Clark started yelling at each other as loud as they could manage:

"You let them escape, you blundering incompetent!"
"No, you let them escape, you bumbling fool!"
"You called me what?"

"No, you called me what?"

"What the heck!" The men in suits went to their position, to be easily subdued by twenty-three workers.

The lonely soldier also came out of the room with pistol in hand, but was also overwhelmed by the remaining twelve.

The fugitives entered the warehouse. There was more than enough room for everybody.

"Sweet!" Vince said. "Yo Hec, get a load of this! Arnold Schwarzenegger would reach sexual climax in here!"
"Good. Arm yourselves and grab all explosives and ammunition you can carry."

"Here you go, milady, some hair-dryers for you." Vince handed two guns to Maria, together with magazines.
"Thanks." She loaded them with impressive ability.
"You do know your way around hair-dryers!"
"Some customers got a little rough sometimes."

Hector took a semiautomatic machine gun and loaded it. He also found a shelf full of walkie-talkies.

"Let's see, frequency, frequency... Hey Marcellus, are you still with us, over?"
"Hector, my man!" came the voice over the radio. "I'm glad you made it, over!"
"Don't pop the champagne just yet. We know they're looking for us and they are pissed. Now, if you could please tell us how we get out of here..."

But he was interrupted by heavy machine gun fire. Bullets crossed the air all around.

"Oh God!" Hector screamed.

"They found us!"

"Get down, get down!"

"Return fire, goddamn it!"

Soldiers came into the room firing weapons and splitting in smaller details to flank the group. The fugitives tried to return fire, but most of them didn't know how to shoot. Some workers were hit and fell on the floor dead.

Vincent, Hector and Maria took cover behind a wooden crate. Others tried to do the same.

"What the hell is going on there, over?" The old man shouted on the radio.

"Marcellus, Marcellus... Oh God!"

"Don't stop shooting, bro!"

"Marcellus, they pinned us down! You got to get us out of here, man... over!"

"The only way out is through a..." Marcellus's voice faded.

"What? I can't here you!"

"... up... you... have..."

"You're breaking up!"

The deafening roar of the weapons continued to break into their eardrums.

"...attic, the only way out is through an attic, over." Marcellus came back.

"And where's this attic, over?"

"Right above the place where the pool table used to be, over."

"Great!" Hector grunted. "Now, all we have to do is go back in time before the nineteen-nineties! Hang on." He turned to Vince. "Cover me, bro."

"What?"

Hector tried to stand up, but a bullet grazed his shoulder.

"Get down and shoot, you fool! Are you crazy?"
"HEY!" Hector screamed to whoever might listen. "Somebody back there find an attic!"
"Are you alright? You're bleeding."
"I'll live. Let's try to give our guys back there some cover."
"An attic, huh?"
"That's right."

The brothers shot all they got, together with Maria. Nevertheless, more experienced soldiers made their way into the warehouse and they were about to put an end to the rebellion.

"Over here!" Natasha shouted pulling some ropes that brought a ladder down.

"Time to go!" Hector said.
"Yes, but let's try to crawl this time, what do you say?"
"I hear you."

The fugitives covered their escape with all ammunition they had. One by one, they climbed the ladder. The first ones who got to the attic found a door to the roof. It was locked by a padlock. They shoot it open.

Hector, Vince, Aaron, Pedro, Raul, Prashant, Natasha and Maria waited for the others to come. Only six more survivors made it to the roof, four men and two women. Most of them had to cover faces until their eyes readapted to the intense sunlight.

"Hey you!" Hector called the last one who climbed. "What about the others? There're still many of us down there."

"I don't know." He gasped, sweating and bleeding. "Only soldiers were coming up last time I looked back. And they almost killed me!"

"Oh God!" Maria cried. "Where's Mate?"

"He's not here!" Vince said.

"I guess he's still down there."

"We can't leave him!"

A worker named Harper, former Fourth Brigade sergeant, came with four hand-grenades.

"We're running out of time." He said. "I have to blow this thing to Kingdom Come!"

"But we still have people down there!" Maria wept helplessly.

"And their sacrifice won't be in vain!" Hector said firmly. "I promise you that!"

"Are you sure, bro?"

"We got no choice."

Hector nodded at Harper. The former sergeant removed four pins and threw the grenades into the attic, and down the ladder.

"Fire in the hole!"

The group ran to the roof edge and covered their ears.

They could see fire balls shattering windows, while the structure shook under their knees. Desperate screams were heard. Maria burst into tears on Vince's shoulder.

"We had no choice." He whispered, but his hands were trembling.

"I need to take a look at your shoulder." Aaron spoke to Hector.

"It's just a scratch." He answered and grabbed the radio "Marcellus, you there, over?" His voice faltered.

"I heard an explosion!" The old man replied. "Was that you, over?"

"Yes. We're on top of the warehouse, now what? And it'd better be good. We lost good people here, over!"

"You have to jump to the roof of the cafeteria. It's quite close, over."

Hector stretched his neck "I see it, over."

"You go down the fire escape and you'll see some bunkhouses on the right, over."

"Hang on."

Hector led his reduced group to the places indicated by Marcellus. The warehouse roof collapsed down in shambles the second the last one of them made the jump to the cafeteria.

Once at the bottom of the fire stairs, Hector brought the walkie-talkie to his mouth again.

"I see the bunkhouses, over."

"You're almost there. Behind them, there's a gravel path. Follow it for about two hundred yards and you'll find the perimeter fences. You jump them and you're out of this hell. Careful with the barbed wire, over."

"We can deal with the barbed wire, but two hundred yards! Over."

"You'd better rush, young man, over."

"Alright, we jump the fences, then what, over?"

"Then it's no-man's land. You go north and you'll reach Prescott Road. And I hope you got a lot of weapons. There'll be flesh-eating walking corpses coming your way."

All lights and systems came back to life in the power plant.

A couple of men with machine guns entered the Monitoring Sector and walked straight to Marcellus. The soles of their shining shoes hitting the hard ground echoed loudly in the almost empty room.

One of the men pointed his weapon at the old man's head, while the other took his radio and turned it off.

"Good morning Jolt, Cooper." Marcellus said calmly. "What can I do for you gentlemen today?"

"Your little escape plan has failed, old timer." Jolt replied. "All your people were killed by our soldiers."

"Well, not all of them. I've just talked to some friends of mine who used to work here, and they seemed just fine."

The man put the radio aside and slowly walked to Marcellus.

"And where are they?" He asked the old man.

"Halfway to Shangri-la, last time I checked."

"You dirty old coot!" He also pointed his machine gun straight at the man's head.

Marcellus just looked at him with a mild grin.

"When we captured your daughter," Jolt continued "an entire army detail banged her. And she liked it a lot! You should've seen her moaning. No wonder she was smiling when she blew her head off at the patio."

"That wasn't my child." The old man responded. "Anyway, I know she was above you and the rest of your filthy crooks. And you'd better watch your back from now on."

"Why is that?"

"Because you are a sinner. You did a lot of bad things and our Lord Jesus Christ is watching. And reckoning will be upon you, perhaps even sooner than you think."

"Maybe, but in the meantime, say hello to your floozy daughter!"

The two men unloaded their machine guns on Marcellus' body.

Down at Transmission, under the protests of friends and workmates, Bill insisted on taking all the blame, and he was also gunned down several times.

INTERMISSION

Take a little time off to rest your eyes. Take a walk,
have some coffee or tea.
Just don't watch TV; otherwise, your eyes won't rest.
And don't worry, all zombies will be waiting to eat
you when you're back!

ACT 21

"An upheaval took place down at the power plant!" Mister Hedgiest informed by the big window, with urgency in his voice.

"Yes, I read the papers." Shane replied. "It was more like an attempt to escape actually."

"Whatever, I just hope you realize the unprecedented component of this incident. We're having trouble keeping the population calm. Rumors are already flying all over town and people are worried."

"I'm aware of that." Shane yawned.

"I hope you're still calm when this whole thing blows up in our faces!"

"I can deal with the situation, Robert. I've been through worse. I just don't think panicking and hyperventilating will help matters. You suits love to freak out every time there's a problem."

He turned to face her "I'm happy you're so confident. Because I think your measures are a total disgrace!"

"I'll get everything back to normal in no time, but only if you don't interfere. Just go back to your platform, deliver your little speeches and pretend you lead something."

"You won't talk to me like this!"

Shane turned and faced him as well. Her eyes caused him to retreat.

"Don't forget who actually calls the shots around here." She said.

"Don't forget who made you."

A couple of guys in uniforms knocked on the already open door and entered the room.

"Don't worry, Robert." Shane spoke smoothly. "It's a setback. I'll deal with it properly, as long as you and your bureaucrats stay the hell out of my way."

She turned her back on him and walked to the men, completely ignoring the minister's furious look.

"Colonel Hartford and Major Talbot reporting, ma'am" One of them said.

"I love how you boys brag about complimentary ranks." Shane spoke. "Now, I believe you have a report to deliver, colonel."

"Yes, ma'am. The insurrection in the power plant is fully contained."

"Really? Can I have some figures?"

"Um... s-sure" He stuttered. "Thirty-five workers broke out of the monitoring sector, but we took care of them."

"Would you kindly tell me how? And please, stop waiting for me to ask you questions before telling me everything."

"Yes, ma'am" He mumbled. "Thirty-five tried to leave the premises, twenty were killed, but... fourteen escaped."

"What about our casualties?"

"We lost twenty-seven soldiers in the explosion."

"Oh yes, the same explosion that blew our dear weapons room to smithereens, is that right?" She asked.

"Y-yes, but we took care of it."

"And I suppose I should sleep better because of that. A group of disorganized machine operators puts together an escape plan and nearly succeeds. Fourteen of them in fact escape and our arsenal is destroyed. I hardly call this *contained*. Do you, colonel?"

Hartford hesitated. "No, ma'am."

"We had a similar incident before, but we controlled it so easily." Shane continued. "What happened this time?"

"They had help from the inside."

"Not exactly a surprise, considering that nobody in there is allowed to go outside. Can you please elaborate?"

"Two senior workers helped the rebels from two different sectors. But we took care of them as well."

"You seem to take care of a lot of things, except for what really matters, perhaps."

Hartford swallowed hard. Talbot remained mute.

"You said twenty were killed, fourteen ran away." She continued. "If my math doesn't fail me, that's thirty-four."

"Oh yes, I almost forgot! We captured one."

"Can you make it with an *I.D.*?"

"It's that freckled guy who came with Apocalily."

"Excellent, finally something good came out of all this, not thanks to you, of course. And I assume you know what to do."

"Yes ma'am, *procedure 39* is being applied as we speak. Further punitive actions are also in place to provide the population with the customary example. Everything is under control."

"Nice" Shane sighed. "And I apologize if I was a little rough on you, colonel."

"No problem, ma'am, we're all under great stress, I totally understand."

"Thank you."

Then, Shane looked him right in the eyes. He was forced to return the look. A couple of seconds later, Hartford fell on the floor, his body twisting in a strange manner.

"Robert, call a doctor!" She ordered.

"Me?"

"Yes you. And quick, this man is having a stroke!"

"How do you know that?"

"Because I caused it."

Very reluctantly, the minister grabbed the phone.

Shane stood face to face with Talbot. He froze in cold sweat.

"So…" She said. "It seems our beloved Hartford will have to be discharged for medical reasons. But don't worry. I have this feeling only his brain is permanently damaged."

Talbot glanced at his former superior officer.

"And I believe congratulations are in order!" Shane continued. "You've just been promoted to colonel and you're the new squad leader. I trust you'll put an end to this whole mess and recapture the fourteen escapees. Then, you'll help me making an example out of them."
"Sure, ma'am."
"Dismissed."

Colonel Talbot turned around in a labored military fashion and walked out the door.

"The doctors are on the way." Mister Hedgiest informed.

Shane approached him.

"See that man over there?" She nodded at Hartford drooling on the Persian rug.
"Yes."
"Don't forget we all can have strokes, especially at your age. Now, if you excuse me, I have a dinner to attend to, one that involves three lovely children and hopefully an Australian zombie."

Shane opened a half smile, turned her back on him and gone she was.

After making sure she had left the building, the minister grabbed the phone again.

"Hello... Yes, good morning Harland, this is Robert Hedgiest. I'm doing fine, thanks, and you? Glad to know it. Listen, I need the codes for Termination Factor. Oh no, not immediately, but I'm afraid we are indeed in a Delta Status." After a brief pause "Yes, by all means, I have the authorization numbers right here, let me check..."

At the local school, six parents were nervously waiting for the principal in her office. Two fathers walked back and forth while one mother poured coffee from a pot into a paper cup.

The remaining father and the other two mothers were sitting down, trying to entertain themselves with magazines. But they only showed Shane and Becky, much more of the first and less of the latter.

They all knew each other, even had a little chat when they arrived, to cope with the waiting, but gave up at a certain point, choosing to silently worry in the privacy of their thoughts.

Why had the principal asked them to come to the school at those strange hours, and only that specific group? Was it some kind of extraordinary and private *PTA* meeting?"

Missus Hildenbrandt came into the room with a very dismal face, looking way older than she really was. All eyes turned to her.

"Good day to you all." She said. "Sorry to keep you waiting, thank you very much for coming on such short notice. I apologize for that too, I surely appreciate your efforts. As you can imagine, a matter of the utmost urgency has arisen."

"What's wrong?" One mother asked.

"I'll go straight to the point. I'm afraid something very bad happened, and your children are involved."

ACT 22

Once again, the pale and freckled body of Mate Clarkson was violently pushed to a wall.

"Alright, rusty boy, time for a little walk in the park." Sheriff McBeattie said. "Load him up, boys!"

Two deputies dragged him to a police car and put him in the trunk.

"What are you going to do?" Mate asked in panic.
"You'll see." The sheriff replied and slammed the boot lid shut.

He drove beyond the city gates before bringing the vehicle to a halt. McBeattie drew his gun from the holster, popped the trunk open and pulled the tennis player out. He slammed the lid shut again and hit the young man twice with the handle of his pistol, making him tumble on the barren terrain, still conscious though.

"Here's the deal, friend." The sheriff said. "You broke the law and now you must pay your debts with society."

He kicked Clark's stomach with his huge right boot and continued:

"And in order to do so, there's nothing better than some good, healthy and outdoors community service." He cleared his throat. "Some walking corpses will come to you and reduce you to pieces. You'll be wide awake to enjoy it all, part of your sentence, you know. In ten minutes I'll come back here to pick up your pieces and spread them around the Industrious Zone, to show folks there what happens to criminals around here. Well, court is adjourned."

McBeattie holstered his gun, jumped to the police car, honked twice and sped away.

"Come back, don't do this, please! COME BACK!" Mate Clarkson screamed and cried, but there was no one else to hear him other than zombies.

And they came fast, lots of them, snarling, growling, a huge circle of dead people surrounded the poor man. And this time, who was there to save him?

Creatures in all degrees of putrefaction had their filthy hands all over Clark. Exposed muscles and flesh mixed in a pool of reanimated dead organs, mouths and teeth about to tear his entire body apart.

The young man could already visualize his guts all over the place, with him still alive to feel the pain. Mate thought of his family, daddy, mommy and baby sister "Sorry I couldn't reach you!" He sobbed.

Clark still had a few seconds to get a glimpse of his horrible death, but what he saw was something else entirely. A boomerang cut the air, together with several heads, causing a lot of creatures to collapse on the ground around him harmless and defeated.

And the device flew round and round, destroying beasts as it went, until finally landing on a fingerless glove, wrapping up an Australian hand.

"You seem to have a knack for this sort of thing." Lily said in a mild laughter.

By using her two little knives, she opened way through the zombies to reach her friend.

"LILY!!!" He screamed with eyes flooding in tears.
"Good guess, partner!"

She was a brunette, short, skinny girl, but to him she looked more like Beyoncé, Charlize Theron and Jennifer Lawrence, all rolled into one, that moment.

"Sorry I'm late." Lily said, stretching a hand to help Clark standing up. "I had some trouble escaping captivity, a kind of peculiar one I might add."

However, a lot more dead people kept on coming, slow but steady.

The Australian woman reached into her sheath, took the hockey stick and began to assemble it. The creatures were closing on them fast.

"Why you always wait till the last possible second to mount your hockey stick?" Mate asked her.
"It's an exercise of concentration." She answered.
"It's alright. We also need that in tennis."

And that was all she wrote. When the stick was ready, there was no much the poor, defenseless zombies could do. Clark snatched the two small knives from Lily's belt and did some killing on his own.

"Are you sure about that?" She asked.
"Yes! I'm tired of being your comic relief."
"Alright, let's give them hell!"

"Um, by the way, we'd better do it in less than ten minutes. The stupid sheriff who brought me here will be back soon."

"Okay, let's wrap this up in nine minutes, what do you say?"

Eight minutes and forty-seven seconds later, McBeattie drove to the same spot he dropped Clark.

"Very well, pretty boy, time to pick up the garbage!" He said while leaving the car. "I want to see some guts. And I mean it literally, hahahahaha!"

But the only guts he found belonged to zombies. And none of them looked like Mate, not even remotely.

"*Whaaa*?!" The sheriff opened his jaw in a dumb face.

And before he could even consider thinking of the possibility to react somehow, Lily was already compressing the blades of her boomerang against his neck. He immediately raised hands right to the air.

"Clark, get his gun and point at him."
"With pleasure" The tennis player did as told.

McBeattie's eyes goggled and his lips trembled in weep mode.

"I usually don't kill non-zombies," Lily said "unless they make me. And you don't strike me as someone willing to die for Shane. Well, are you?"
"Shane?" Clark whispered.

The sheriff was too petrified in fear to speak. He wanted to shake his head to say *no*, but if he did, his throat would be cut by the blades.

"You're a little too quiet, aren't you?" The Australian woman spoke. "Just blink once for *yes* and twice for *no*."

He blinked twice to answer her previous question.

"I didn't think so." She said. "Then, you're not coerced to do what you do?"

McBeattie blinked twice again.

"So, being a neo-nazi fuck is your calling." Clark observed.

"It's not that, alright?" The sheriff finally spoke. "I have a family, okay? I have to think of them! It's hell out here! But in there, we got security, privilege, a chance to be how we used to!"

"And in return, you only have to torture and kill once in a while, right?" Clark said.

"It's not my fault, okay?" The sheriff started to sob. "Shane is not one to be messed with."

"How Shane controls minds?" Lily asked.

Now, Clark definitely frowned at her.

"I'll tell you later, lad." She turned to him.
"Okay."

Then, she faced McBeattie again to wait for an answer.

"It's a rhyme." The sheriff mumbled.
"A rhyme?"

"Yes, I don't remember the exact words. It's like a poem or something. She says it to a person and the bastard obeys her all along."

"Some kind of hypnotism, perhaps" Clark divagated.

"Could be" Lily agreed.

"That's how things work over there." McBeattie continued. "If you behave, she takes you in and treats you right. If you don't, she says the rhymes and you follow her every command."

"So, you got all the breaks without having to lift a finger of your hand." Mate said.

The cop didn't answer.

"In other words, you go there and become a politician." Lily concluded.

"And whoever's not good enough to live in paradise is sent to your Auschwitz-like power plant!"

It was Lily's turn to frown at him.

"I'll tell you later, lass." Clark spoke.

"Okay."

Problem was, while they talked, more walking corpses approached. Never mind how many of them were killed, replacements always came. Lucky they announced their presence with a lot of growls.

"Um, Lily, we might have to go now." The tennis player pointed out. "Our hungry friends will be joining us soon."

"No worries, we just throw this guy here to them. While they're busy feasting on him, we just waltz to the car and get out of here."

"Please, please, don't do this, please!" The sheriff burst into tears.

"Yes, that's exactly what I said when you did the same to me." Clark reminded him. "You didn't seem to care."

"I'm sorry, okay, I'm sorry!" McBeattie wept. "It's not my fault... not my fault... Please, don't kill me! I got wife and kids!"

"Yes. And such a lousy role model you are!" Lily grunted.

They pushed the sheriff to the police vehicle and forced him on the driver's seat. Living dead were slowly surrounding the car.

"Where are we going, Lily?" Clark asked.

"To the town hospital" She replied. "We have to rescue that woman we rescued from the zombies. I got a feeling she's not being treated properly in there."

"Got it."

She turned to McBeattie and said:

"You'll take us there smoothly and anonymously. If you even wink funny, I'll either slit your throat and feed you to the zombies, or just feed you to the zombies." She grabbed the walkie-talkie from his belt.

"Okay!" The sheriff said, wiping tears off with his hands.

"Now drive."

"But those rotting things are blocking the way!"

"Then run over them." Lily suggested. "Don't worry; they're not going to sue you."

ACT 23

Shane lifted the garage door that led to the hangar. It was very heavy, but such fact wasn't a problem to her. Even so, she found it too easy to open. She checked chains and pulleys of the mechanism and verified they were all ruined.

She remained composed, but some feelings she wasn't quite familiar with took possession of her senses.

The elegant woman walked, her high heels producing loud tap dancing noises. She froze all of a sudden, her heart for the first time assaulted by two sensations very foreign to her - surprise and dread.

"No, this can't be right. This can't be right!"

"What happened to our kids?" One mother asked Missus Hildenbrandt with anguish and fear corroding her face of terrible expectation. Her husband was wrapping an arm around her.

"Oh, they are fine." The principal clarified. "They are in the toy room with one of my teachers."

"Damn you!" One father exploded. "You could have said that in the first place! Jesus Christ!"

"You're right, I'm sorry. It's just that I'm too nervous. Something very unprecedented took place and I confess I don't know how to deal with the situation."

"Why don't we all calm down, take a coffee, have a seat, and then you tell us what's going on?" Another mother suggested with gentle, understanding eyes.

ACT 24

"Cuff yourself." Lily ordered the sheriff.

"Are you locking me up in the bathroom?" McBeattie complained. "This is a hospital, for crying out loud! There could be all sorts of bacteria in here!"

"If they are disgusted by you like I am, you got nothing to worry." Lily answered.

"Besides," Clark said "you're in a good position here. If nature calls, you're already in the right place."

"And I suggest you resist the temptation to scream for help, because *we* might respond to it." Lily spoke. "And those zombies outside still have their appetites."

"Fine!" The sheriff muttered and cuffed himself to a pipe.

"Court is adjourned." Clark said to McBeattie.

The grey-haired doctor left the break room, looking satisfied. He nodded at some beautiful nurses on his way to the elevator. He pushed the button. When the doors opened, he went inside.

"Wow, those girls are getting better." The doctor couldn't help whispering once the doors closed again.

"And perhaps you are not!" Lily stood up behind him, with Clark by her side, pointing the sheriff's gun to the doctor's hip. "You do remember us, right?"

The Australian girl pushed the emergency button and the elevator stopped between floors.

"Yes." The man answered insecure. "Please don't hurt me. I do whatever you want."

"What's your name?" Lily asked.

"Doctor Blake."

"I'll call you Blake, because you're hardly a doctor." She said. "You should be treating that woman we brought here. Well, we've just been to her room and she doesn't seem to be doing any better. What are you giving her in those IV bags?"

The doctor hesitated. Clark pressed the gun against his back.

"She's under *Luviximil*, okay!" Blake finally replied. "She also took some shots of it. But believe me, it's basically a soporific for the muscles, she's not in any danger!"

"It looks way more than that." Clark said.

"I can bring her back!" The doctor assured. "Just say the word!"

"Not you, doc" Lily determined. "I don't trust you. We need to find ourselves a real doctor."

"What are you going to do to me?" Blake asked.

"What's the name of the woman we brought, do you know?"

"It's Susan."

"Great." Lily continued. "You'll accompany us to Susan's room and you'll help us getting her out of this dump. But first, we need to blend in."

Doctor Blake was walking the hospital hallways toward Susan's room. Clark and Lily were following him on both sides, dressed like nurses. The tennis player was hiding the gun in his apron pocket, still pointing at Blake.

They entered Susan's room and Lily closed the door. Clark could now expose his weapon to the doctor.

"Alright," The Australian girl said "you know what to do, *doctor death*. Start disconnecting her."

"Judge me as much as you want." Blake muttered while detaching the patient from monitors and tubes. "I suffered serious losses before they found me. I saved lives in this hospital, okay! I was given a chance to continue practicing medicine. I'm useless out there like everybody else. At least in here I can do something!"

"Yes, as long as you oversee one or two atrocities, right?" Clark spoke.

"And flush your Hippocratic Oath down the toilet." Lily completed.

Blake finished disconnecting Susan.

"I guarantee everything that was done to her can be undone." He said. "I didn't break my oath!"

"Then get a taste." Lily spoke.

"What?"

"You heard me, doc. Stick a needle in that bag, fill it up with some of the goo and inject yourself with it."

"I... I can't!"

"Oh come on! If the substance is as harmless as you said, what is the problem?"

"But..."

"It's always better than the alternative." Clark cocked the gun hammer.

"Alright, alright!"

Doctor Blake did as Lily told him and got a taste of his own medicine. He fell on the floor, convulsed for some seconds, then held still, but it was clear he was awake.

"Now he's practicing medicine." Mate commented.

Lily and Clark pulled the gurney with Susan on it, covered with a sheet, only her head was exposed. When they left the elevator down the main lobby, a security guard stopped them.

"Hey, where are you taking this patient?"
"She's been transferred." Lily replied.
"Transferred where?"
"She can't stay in this hospital!" Clark said with urgency in his voice. "She's got the plague! It's not safe in here! She'll turn into a flesh-eating living dead! And she bit me! Oh my God, I'm turning! Aargh, aargh!"

The man ran to the nearest corridor.

"Good one, partner!" Lily praised him.
"I can't believe he fell for that one."

But he came back with five more guards.

"They didn't all fall for this one." Lily observed.

Clark drew the sheriff's gun and shot twice at the ceiling. People in the lobby screamed in fear, covering their heads. The guards also froze in their places.

"All right, this is, um... a kidnapping!" Mate shouted, waving the pistol back and forth. "We are taking this patient here to later, you know, ask for a ransom and everything!"
"And get the money from the vending machines ready!" Lily talked. "That will be the ransom... possibly!"
"Everybody on the floor!" Clark screamed and the whole floor complied. "And stay that way for fifteen..."
"Twenty."
"Twenty minutes, yes!"

Then, he and Lily left the hospital pulling the gurney.

"Those people are kind of idiots, aren't they?" Mate said.
"Don't be so hard on them."

They got to an ambulance and carefully placed Susan in it through the rear doors.

"Hey!" Two other men left the front of the vehicle. "What do you think you're doing? You can't just load an ambulance like this! I want to see your permits!"

"Sorry, we had no time to get them." Clark said. "This is very urgent, this patient got the disease!"

"The disease, you mean, the one who turns people into dead beasts?"

"The very same" Lily confirmed. "And she got the airborne strain."

"Airborne strain?"

"That's right. And we have to... we need to... ACHOO!!! Sorry. We need to evacuate her immediately before the virus spread like water!"

But before she finished the sentence, both men were already far in the distance.

"They are kind of idiots." Lily wound up agreeing.

They finished securing the gurney firmly into the ambulance, got into the front seats with Lily on the wheel, and sped away.

However, they didn't go very far. A great number of limousines quickly came from all streets around and blocked the ambulance. Lily had to step harshly on the brakes not to hit one of them. Men in black suits got out of the cars, fire-weapons in hands.

"Step out of the vehicle!" One man commanded.

"News spread fast around here." Lily observed.
"No worries!" Mate said smiling. "I got an idea."

He pushed buttons in the dashboard until finally finding the one that activated the sirens.

The annoying blare caused most of the men to cover their ears, but none of the limousines actually cleared the way.

Disappointed, Clark turned the sirens off.

"They don't respect sirens around here." He sighed.
"No problem." Lily said. "Let's do this *Death Race* style."
"And what is *Death Race* sty... AHHHHH!!!"

Lily stepped on the gas pedal with everything she got and the ambulance dashed forward like mad, forcing several men to jump out of the way, limousines violently thrown to the sides after being crashed by the heavier vehicle.

Some soldiers fired machine guns at the ambulance, but it accelerated out of range.

"See that, mate?" Lily spoke. "I've always suspected that an ambulance could open way through limos."
"I'm glad we found that out." Clark responded pulling himself together and checking if everything was okay with Susan. "And next time you want to corroborate a thesis, let me know first."
"Sure. I'm just not comfortable driving on the left side, you know."

However, they passed by another police car hiding behind a billboard.

"Oh no, not again!" Tony cried "More trespassers! This place is starting to look like the Fifth Avenue!"

"Darn it!" Joe cursed. "Well, let's go."

The police car pursued the ambulance. Lily saw it coming in the rear-view mirror, red lights blinking like Las Vegas, a deafening sound blaring.

"Shall we respect their sirens?" Clark queried.

"I got an idea." Lily answered.

She stopped the ambulance. The police car parked right behind it. The two cops left their car and adjusted their clubs on the belts.

"Step out of the vehicle!" They heard that order again.

But Lily and Clark came out from the back. The policemen stood still and brought hands to their guns.

"We need your help!" The Australian woman spoke.

"Fast please!" Her partner emphasized.

The cops ran to the ambulance.

"What's going on here?" Joe asked.

"Are these working?" Clark frowned at the two defibrillator pads in his hands. He decided to try them on the two men standing before him.

The surge of electricity caused the policemen to fly backwards and collide against the police car windshield.

"Guess they are." The tennis player concluded.

"They're fine." Lily said after realizing they were still moving. "Let's go."

And the ambulance sped away again, disappearing into the woods.

"I hate this job!" Tony cried massaging his hips.
"Shut up!" Joe said.

"We need to get a doctor to Susan back there." Lily said, noticing the woman was moving uncomfortably on the gurney.
"Let's follow this road. It got to take us somewhere."
"I didn't know you knew how to handle a gun."
"Well, it's not a tennis racquet, but it also hits balls."

And they took that time to tell each other about their respective adventures from the moment they were separated.

"Jesus!" Clark spoke astonished. "You mean the freaking zombie was almost biting you?"
"And he smelled worse than my armpits in those hot Australian days."
"How did you get out of that one?"
"Well, it's kind of complicated."
"Complicated?"
"A little embarrassing too."
"Oh."
"Anyhow, I escaped. After I broke out of there, I crossed path with this woman. She was bringing the three children I was supposed to kill as a zombie. Good thing she was ahead of schedule. She said reporters were coming to document some important educational event local leaders must have invented. But everything was cancelled when I told her what really happened in there."
"How did she react?"

"She was shocked, a very good sign. Her mind wasn't under control, only misinformed. I asked her to tell people the truth about Shane."

"Do you think she's going to do it?"

"We'll find out."

"What about that starched guy I told you about, the one who calls himself the minister? He looked more like a pigeon in suits."

"We take a look into it."

"So, that means we're not leaving this place just yet."

"No. Let's finish this."

Clark turned to her and said with a grin:

"So, the great Apocalily is back in another crusade, to save the world for democracy and the highest values!"

"I'm just doing this because this Shane character pisses me off!"

"I don't believe you."

"I don't care what you believe."

"I think you do."

"Then I do."

Some signs of civilization became visible on the roadside.

But Lily had to fiercely step on the brakes, causing some rubber to stain the pavement. In the unofficial border to Downtown, a group of about fifteen guerrilla-looking men stood in front of the ambulance, blocking the way and pointing machine guns.

ACT 25

Shane was about to enter the gigantic complex that comprised several TV studios, when a strident voice calling her name made her stop. She turned around to see what the fuss was all about.

"You!" The middle aged woman said grinding teeth and pointing a forefinger at Shane. "You!"

"Yes, I guess we all realized you're addressing me." Shane replied serenely.

"You awful, evil woman! How could you? How could you?"

"I gather you and your small group have something to speak with me about. What can I do for you, Principal Hildenbrandt?"

The educator stood right in front of the elegant woman, with a mob of angry men and women behind her.

"You lied to us all!" The principal said. "You're nothing more than a fraud under loads of make-up!"

"Lovely. What seems to be the problem, Missus Hildenbrandt?"

"That educational event you and your minister so much bragged about is a farce! You just wanted to kill innocent children to maculate the image of a great woman."

Naturally, lots of people stopped what they were doing and gathered around the scene, hoping to become bystanders for a very promising spectacle based on somebody else's disgrace.

"Great woman..." Shane whispered. "I really wish I knew what you're talking about."

"I bet you do! I was taking those innocent children to your so called event when this woman, Lily, stopped me right on time. And she told me what you actually wanted to do to them."

"Which was...?"

"Oh please! You had arranged for Lily to turn into a flesh-eating monster, so she would later kill the poor children!"

Voices started to buzz all around.

"And why would I do such thing?" Shane asked calmly.

"To discredit the great Apocalily!"

The buzz turned into loud and surprised conversations.

"I see." Shane responded placidly. "These are very serious accusations, Agnes. Are you prepared to substantiate them with something more than just the words of a possible renegade?"

Agnes Hildenbrandt kept her eyes on the woman, but couldn't argue back. Taking advantage of that favorable momentum, Shane said:

"Anyway, thank you very much for bringing such important matters to my attention. I'll check into all your concerns and rest assured I'll come back to you."

But the crowd of parents following the principal started to scream and protest. Sensing the situation was about to aggravate, the circle of bystanders closed on them, anticipating more tumults for their amusement.

"Oh no!" Hildenbrandt finally spoke. "You're not going to talk your way out of this!"

"All right" Shane replied. "What do you want me to do? I'm all ears."

The principal hesitated again "Well, I..." She cleared her throat. "As a citizen of this city, also a representative of the parents whose children study in my school, many of them with me today, I demand that you are arrested under the accusations I just brought upon you."

"That's right!" Somebody in her group screamed.

"Okay." Shane said. "Let's suppose I'm arrested. Then, who's going to take care of things? You, Missus Hildenbrandt, perhaps some of the ladies and gentlemen you dragged to this thing, or maybe one of you folks, who interrupted your works to gift us with your so meaningful attention?" She raised her voice to address everybody.

All of a sudden, a huge number of men wearing riot police gear, armed with shields, clubs and tear gas came out of the TV station complex. They didn't seem to be there to arrest Shane. Most people in the crowd retreated. Even curious bystanders get scared when situation changes from spectacle to threat.

"Or perhaps I should open the gates and invite the drifters in," Shane continued "and everything I built just for you will go down the drain. Do you still remember how life was before I took you in and gave you a home?"

She advanced to the principal, who took two steps back.

"Like I said, thanks for bringing me your concerns, Principal Hildenbrandt. I'll look into them, I'll take them to the minister and we'll surely get back to you."

Then, addressing everybody again, Shane said "Now, you may all return to your wonderful jobs, sophisticated lifestyles, with all possible fringe benefits you seem to enjoy so much. And this time, try to show a little gratitude for a change!"

The principal lowered her eyes. Most parents in her group scratched the back of their heads. Bystanders lost interest, many of them disappointed with the peaceful outcome of the standoff. Everybody slowly came back to their businesses.

"Good." Shane spoke. "I appreciate it." She turned her back on the mass and walked proudly into the complex, followed by her entourage of riot policemen.

Once inside, Colonel Talbot ran to her.

"I need to talk to you, madam."
"Yes colonel."
"Well, first, I saw what just happened out there. This can be a matter of concern."
"Not at all, as you can see, I handled things."
"Sure, and you excelled in it as usual!"
"Thanks. Now you can stop kissing my ass and get to the point."
"Yes ma'am. It's just that I'm kind of worried about the whole Lily situation. She's on the loose now, and things can still run out of control."
"Hardly. Have you and your men been to the Industrial Zone and got the package?"
"Oh yes madam, the flock is being gathered in the hangar as we speak."
"Good. Then don't lose any sleep over it. There's more than one way to kill a myth. Now, if you excuse me, I have a speech to deliver on national TV."

ACT 26

"Friends of yours?" Lily asked Clark.

"Yes!" The man replied, narrowing his eyes.

"Really?" She asked surprised. "You do know the question was meant to pull your leg, right?"

"And it did. But I know those two guys on the front row. Stay here."

Clark jumped out of the ambulance, but so did Lily.

"Hey Pedro, Raul, what the heck are you up to?" Clark spoke, "Put down the weapons, man!"

"Mate!" They ran and hugged him. "Jesus, man, you made it out!" Pedro said. "I can't believe it! You got *cojones*, *mano*!"

"You're tougher than you look, *hombre*!" Raul spoke.

"Well, I had help." Clark nodded at Lily.

"I can see that." Pedro said.

Lily shook hands with Pedro and Raul.

"This is Lily." Clark introduced her.

"Yep, we figured as much," Raul spoke, "Honored to finally meet the Apocalily."

"The honor is mine," Lily nodded, "And all this Apocalily fuss is overrated."

"I hope not." Raul said.

"So, what's with the road block?" Clark queried.

"We've been attacked." Pedro replied.

"Really?"

"Yes, I guess we suffered a little payback for the rebellion at the power plant. You can't stay here. You have to join the others."

"We got a sick woman in the ambulance. She needs medical attention badly. But it's not the zombie fever, or whatever they call it."

"*Si, tu tranquilo*. You and Lily go to a place called *Fleur du Soir*. It's a restaurant that's sheltering us. You just follow this road and take a right at the only gas station in town, can't miss it. Once there, you look for a guy named Tess. Tell him you're with the group who escaped the power plant."

"Got it."

"You'd better run, man. There're some bad people looking for you and the *chica*."

"Okay, be seeing you guys."

"Godspeed, *amigo*!"

They hugged again. Lily and Clark climbed back to the vehicle.

"So, it seems you're growing in the ranks of the revolutionaries!" Lily said. "This is kind of cool. You're the bad ass warrior now."

"Not yet, but I'm working on it." He responded humbly.

The men cleared the path for the ambulance.

"Only one gas station in town?" Lily said.

"Just follow my lead, chica."

They found the restaurant and pulled over by its glass door. Two sentries walked to both sides of the vehicle, also pointing weapons.

"I want to see some hands!"

"We need to talk to Tess." Clark said.

"For the moment, you need what we tell you to need."

"There's a sick woman in the back" Lily spoke. "She needs help."

"This is your problem."

"Fine" Mate said. "Just tell Hector, Vince, Maria and the rest of the bunch that you denied help to Mate Clarkson and Apocalily."

"Jesus, man! What's with you and going straight to the point? Get this thing to the parking lot while I open the backdoor."

"Hey, nice seeing you again!" Vince said.

"Glad you made it!" Hector spoke, with a bandage covering part of his shoulder.

"They dragged me out of there before I even knew what was happening." Mate recalled. "Last thing I remember is a big ball of fire where the warehouse should be. A little after that, they knocked me out."

Clark exchanged compliments and high fives with the ones he got to know so well, and was even graced with a tender hug from Maria. He recognized some, but most men and women in that huge lobby were strangers to him. Tess, their gentle host, wasn't in there.

At least forty people were gathering in the room. Nevertheless, Tess' place was big enough to hold way more than that.

"Why are there so many people in here?" Mate asked.

"It's a kind of an emergency meeting." Vince responded.

"We've met with Pedro on the way here." Clark said. "He told me you've been attacked."

"Yes. Some heavily armed soldiers came to the Industrial Zone, beat up a lot of residents and even kidnapped some others, men, women and children."

"That's why we set up that road block you met." Hector spoke. "Pedro and Raul volunteered for it."

"There's no way to know where they took the ones they abducted." Maria whispered.

"We rescued a woman, but she needs medical attention." Lily said.

"I can help you with that." Aaron offered while he finished patching up a shred wound on Maria's leg. "How bad is this woman hurt?"

"Well, she's more like poisoned. It's something called luxomol, luxavil..."

"Luviximil" Aaron corrected her. "I know the drug. It's a heavy stuff. I can deal with it, but I need to take her to a hospital."

"Yes, we have one." A young man named Ahmed spoke. "It's not exactly the cleanest place on Earth, but we can arrange everything you need. I take you there."

"She's in an ambulance back in the parking lot." Lily informed. "Door is open, key is in the ignition."

"Let's go." Aaron said and he left with Ahmed.

"And you are Lily Master, I presume." Hector came to her. "It's surely an honor and a privilege to make your acquaintance!"

"Thanks." She shook hands with him. "The honor is all mine. Clark told me about you and your group. What you did took a lot of courage."

"And a little temporary insanity" Vince completed, also shaking hands with her.

Clark introduced her to the ones he knew.

"Oh my God!" Natasha screamed hysterically, moving fists up and down. "You're Apocalily, right? God, you're alive! We're saved!!!"

"Whoa, whoa, whoa!" Tess said, getting into the room. "Let's not get ahead of ourselves in here." By using a remote control, he turned on a big TV attached to the wall and increased volume. "We'd better listen to this."

Shane was on the screen, beautiful and glamorous as ever.

"...most of you know me, but some of you don't. Then, let me introduce myself..."

"This is probably being broadcasted from coast to coast," Prashant said "which in this case means from one edge of the town to the other edge of the town."
"She doesn't speak to both Uptown and Downtown very often." Tess informed. "Normally, she only speaks to the worthy ones. This can't be good."

Shane on TV:
"...there's a reason why I'm coming to your homes today. Sorry to interrupt your regular programs, but what I have to say is of the utmost importance. I know many of you have been hearing rumors carelessly spread. I'm here to tell you exactly what happened in the same clear and straightforward way I always conduct myself, hoping to address all your concerns and put your minds at ease."

Population could see her on giant screens located at strategic points along Uptown. In Downtown, people saw her in bars, restaurants, hospitals, or at home. She could also be heard by means of a powerful loudspeaker attached to a tall pole in the center of the city.

Shane continued on TV:
"Some time ago, a group of lowlifes, renegade terrorists invaded our power plant, coming from the back roads around Gingerbread Dam, in a treacherous attack. Their plan was to

211

deprive you of running water and electricity to make us weak and exposed to a wider attack. That's why the North District was temporarily out of power. But you have nothing to worry about. The invader's coward attempt to ruin our lifestyle has been foiled by the courageous efforts of our troops, restoring electricity and water to sustain our families."

"But I'm afraid we're not out of the woods just yet. Most of the thugs were captured, but some of them are still at large. Actions and measures are in place to find and arrest those evil characters, but we need your help."

At that moment, a picture of Lily, not a very flattering one, appeared on the screen, a serious face staring at the viewers.

"I told you this wasn't good." Tess spoke.
"Yes." Lily agreed. "I look fat in this picture."
"You look pissed in this picture, sis." Vince realized.
"Maybe they did some reverse Photoshop." Clark said.

Shane on TV (voice over):
"...Believe me, this woman is not what you think she is. As I'm sure most of you know, her name is Lily Master, but what you don't know is that she's actually a con-artist who took advantage of a tragic event in an elementary school to build herself the image of a saint, taking credit for the brave work of several police officers, the real heroes. There's no such thing as Apocalily, it's just a media invention blown out of proportions."

"And there's a reason why I'm mentioning her. She was part of the group that invaded and terrorized the power plant. And she's one of those who escaped. Oh yes, this horrible woman is among you now. Recently, Lily used a very important educational event announced all over town to spread a lie through our community, saying it was all a plot to assassinate children to discredit her."

Clark glanced at Lily "She's smart."

Lily nodded.

Shane continued on TV:

"It's such an absurd, huh? But some people believed it. Well, let's show this vicious, intemperate girl we're not fools. Lily Master is nothing more than a scoundrel and a looter, who just wants to infiltrate your homes and steal everything you hold dear."

"Yep, she means business." Clark commented.

"It's okay." The Australian woman replied. "I've been called worse."

Shane was done talking about Lily, which became obvious when a picture of Hector, also not a pretty one, appeared on the screen.

Shane on TV (voice over):

"According to our intelligence, the leader of the terrorists is this man. His name is Hector Dryland, convicted of murder and sentenced to life prior to the plague. He was in prison, but we believe he found a way to escape incarceration when the pandemic broke loose. His record also includes robbery, rape, theft, among other offences. He's a brutal, ruthless and dangerous criminal who's now at large in our city..."

"I guess you're famous too." Mate spoke to Hector.

"You also look fat in this picture, bro." Vince observed.

"And pissed."

"Well, at least I don't need any Photoshop for that." Hector responded.

Shane's face was back on TV:

"We have the situation under control, but we need your help. Those terrible people might be walking among you, decent people, right now. So, be on the lookout all the time. If you see any of them, please report to the authorities immediately..."

Tess muted the TV with the remote control.

"Sorry, folks" He said. "This is all I can take. And I believe I speak for all of you."

"I'm disappointed." Vince sighed. "How come they didn't show my face on TV? I can also look like a murderer, burglar and rapist with the help of some software."

"She surely fed the people with a truckload of nonsense." Maria spoke. "Now, everybody in town thinks we're Jack the Ripper."

"Yes, she's really good at manipulating the fear of others." Tess agreed. "And the only way to counteract such damage is by also going live on TV. To us this is virtually impossible. Now the population is afraid of us."

"What about folks in Downtown?" Hector asked.

"Oh, don't worry about them. My waiters and I did a thorough job telling people here Shane is not to be trusted." He cleared his throat "Now, enough about her for the moment. I'd like to welcome the newcomers to my humble establishment, best cuisine in town, also safe harbor for street fighters and road warriors. My name is Tess, at your disposal."

Lily and Clark nodded.

"Thank you for taking us in." The Australian girl said.

"Don't mention, dear. It's always a pleasure to defy this system somehow. Speaking which, you all meet Shane." Tess stretched an arm to the TV, for the blonde woman was still talking. "She's our local queen bee, so to speak."

"So, you met her before, I mean personally." Lily said.

"Oh yes, my darling," Tess replied. "I was once very welcome in her little wonderland. And she was so sweet to me, you should've seen it, even after I told her about my sexual orientation. That was before I committed the sin of disagreement. Shane only likes those who obey, homosexuals or otherwise. Then, she kicked me out of Heavensville, that's how she calls Uptown. But it's not so bad. I'm living out my dreams of owning a restaurant, also headquarters for all sorts of nefarious activities, which I hope annoy Shane very much, if she knew it of course. Actually, she scares the hell out of me."

On TV, Shane's image was finally gone, to be replaced by some commercials with Becky on them.

"What about you?" Hector turned to Lily. "What's your story? You've been captured, right?"

"Oh yes. Shane put me in shackles. I escaped, but not before having a little chat with her."

"And what did she say, something we can use?"

"She said a lot of things. I give you the headlines. Basically, she was tossed into a lab right after she was born, and some scientists modified, enhanced, pasteurized her, turning her brain into some kind of radio station which, among other things, allows her to control minds."

Everybody gazed at her.

"Any questions?" Lily asked.

"That's a lot of headlines." Maria commented.

"Man, if we shave her bald, we may find out she's Lex Luthor." Vince observed.

"She's not kidding." Tess intervened. "I got to know Shane a little, and there was indeed something about her I couldn't put my finger on. I felt different every time she looked at me, when she touched me, some weird feelings. And in regards to control minds, yes, I'm sure she does it somehow. I heard her saying words to people, strange words."

"Words?" Lily opened her eyes widely "As in rhymes, a poem, something of the kind?"

"More or less, it was something like *the sunshine springs, happiness it brings. Those eyes you should follow, to keep away sorrow. Seek the giant bird you must, on her you shall blindly trust. For the good science you will urge, from all impurities to purge.*"

"It looks like you memorized the whole thing." Clark said getting worried.

"Well, I heard it enough times." Tess justified himself, feeling tension rising in the air. "Shane never knew I was listening, of course. But every time she looked a person in the eyes and said those words, the person went all gaga over her."

Hector approached Tess with an unfriendly look on his face.

"So you heard the words several times." He said. "How do we know Shane's not controlling you?"

"If I was to betray you, honey, I would have done it already. Besides, if my mind was under Shane's control, you'd know it. For starters, I'd be acting heterosexual."

"He got a point there." Vince admitted. "Maybe, it takes more than just hearing the words to go gaga. Maybe, the person needs to be at the same place as Shane, look her in the eyes and hear the rhymes all at once for the thing to work."

"What about you?" Hector turned to Lily. "It seems to me Shane had all the opportunities to dominate your mind. Why didn't she?"

"She got other things in mind. She had a living dead set aside just to bite me and make me like him. Then, Shane would bring three children to be killed by the zombie-me in front of cameras."

"Why'd she do such thing?" Maria asked shocked.

"So the myth of Apocalily would be destroyed together with the kids."

"Shane doesn't like competition very much." Clark said. "And she has a very particular way to eliminate it."

"How did you escape?" Natasha asked.

"It wasn't easy." Lily answered. "Anyway, once back on the streets, I told a school principal what happened and asked her to spread the truth. But it seems Shane took care of that."

"Yes," Vince grunted "by going on TV with some story about an educational event to sell the idea you are the one trying to discredit her."

"Anything else?" Hector queried.

"Shane also said she got a high ESP. It's a short for extrasensory perception."

"And this is Australian for...?"

"She might be able to read minds."

"Oh Lord!" Maria spoke even more anguished.

"It would ruin her self-esteem if she could read my mind right now." Tess commented.

"So, these are the powers I heard about at the power plant." Maria divagated. "Michelle would've never committed suicide unless her mind was being controlled somehow."

"Who's Michelle?" Lily queried.

"Long story," Hector whispered.

"And this is all." Vince hesitated, "Right, Lily?"

"Not quite. Shane also mentioned she and some other guys were responsible for the zombie pandemic that destroyed the world."

"Do you believe her?"

"It's far-fetched, but it can explain how this virus spread so suddenly and so fast."

"I had a feeling this whole thing was much bigger than just one area." Prashant said. "It's too sophisticated."

"Great!" Vince muttered annoyed, "Just great! And I thought we had a problem! Next time I bump into a town offering sanctuary to protect me against deranged folks trying to eat me, I'll stick to the deranged folks trying to eat me!"

"But how can Shane dominate minds just with words?" Maria asked.

Everybody turned to the Australian girl again.

"My guess is, there got to be some kind of radio waves that come out of her head which, activated by the specific sound of those words she says, somehow affect the control system of people's brains, allowing her to manipulate their will."

They all kept on looking at Lily, only this time also with their mouths open.

"You got some technical degree after all!" Clark said.
"Nope, but I watched a movie with all this. It seems to fit this situation."

"Hey look!" Maria pointed a finger at the TV. "Are they rerunning her speech?"

Shane was back on the screen.

"No dear," Tess said. "This is brand new stuff. And I got a bad feeling about it." With a shaky hand, he grabbed the remote and got the sound back on.

Shane on TV:
"Good afternoon, my dear puppies in the Industrial Zone. This message is for your eyes and ears only."

Her voice also resounded from the huge loudspeaker in the city center.

Shane continued on TV:
"I know some of you are harboring the criminals who rebelled and escaped from the power plant. Then, I'll be brief."

The TV started to show a big hangar shaped liked the half of a rugby ball. Several people were being forced inside of it by soldiers. Then, images from within the construction were displayed. Many anguished and frightened faces spread around the hangar like cattle.

Shane continued on TV (voice-over):

"This is a live broadcast. It's all happening right now. I guess most of you recognize those souls getting into the shed. They are your friends, husbands, wives, sons and daughters. I know the power plant fugitives are listening to this. You shall go to Heavensville, surrender your weapons and peacefully turn yourselves in to my police force, or my soldiers will flood the hangar with cyanide. I believe you all know what that does. You have until nineteen hundred hours to comply."

"In case the rebels are too spineless to present themselves voluntarily, I'm very sure the rest of you, Industrial Zone residents, will put your best efforts to find them and bring them to me. Dead or alive, it doesn't matter. This is the only way you'll ever see your loved ones again."

"I'm really sorry I have to resort to this, but I won't let some scumbags ruin everything I worked so hard for. I'm doing this not only for me, but also for all good people entitled to enjoy a comfortable, normal life. We need to have some order."

Tess turned off the television. A big cloud of gloominess descended on everybody's hearts and spirits.

"So much for the locals sympathizing with our cause," Prashant lamented. "Now, we're definitely screwed."

"What's nineteen hundred hours?" Maria asked anxiously.

"Seven o'clock in the evening," Harper, the former military man, informed. "That gives us less than two hours."

"Residents will tear this whole city apart looking for us," Vince said, "Including this restaurant. Sorry to drag you into this, man." He turned to Tess.

"I dragged myself into this..." He whispered discouraged, looking at his waiters, who returned a pessimistic look. "Gosh, what do I do?"

Suddenly, but not surprisingly, everybody turned to Lily again.

"Okay, I'll turn myself in." The Australian woman announced. "See if I can buy you some time."

"No way!" Hector retorted. "What good would that do?"

"People's lives are at stake! I have to go there and talk to Shane. She wants me. Maybe I can convince her to trade me for the hostages."

"Shane might kill those people anyway, Lil, even if we all turn ourselves in." Clark spoke. "She can't be trusted."

"That's a good point." Vince said.

"That's a very good point." Hector spoke.

"Then what?" Maria asked.

All eyes in the room slowly turned to Lily.
Lily scratched her chin and said:

"There might be something we can do."

"I knew it!" Natasha screamed.

"But I'll need to find somebody who knows a hell lot about networking, routers, this sort of thing."

Hector and Vincent jumped with big smiles.

"You found us already!" Hector said proudly "*Hector and Vince, Routers and Since*, best products and services in the universe!"

"I heard about you." Lily spoke.

"Really?" Clark asked surprised. "No offense, but you've never struck me as someone who reads business magazines."

"My father was a Telecom technician." She reminded him. "He worked for *Lonestar Technologies*."

"Oh yes, from Texas," Hector recalled, "One of our best customers, tough but fair, not that we ever gave anyone any reason to complain of our products for that matter, unlike the competitors."

"So, what's the catch?" Vince asked Lily.

"We don't have much time. I'd rather tell you my plan as we go. You got to trust me on this one and follow my play."

"Yes, but you still need to tell us what to do in the immediate future." Clark pointed out.

"If I remember correctly," Lily said "we did have a truck when we came here. I need to find my motorized kangaroo."

"Maybe I can help you with that." A man they didn't know offered. "My name is Zachariah, but everybody calls me Zach. I run a car repair workshop two blocks from here, and sometimes I make delivers to Uptown."

"I'm listening."

"Normally, we ship spare parts always to the same addresses over there, but recently we received purchase orders for very weird items to be delivered to the TV station."

"TV station?" Clark frowned. "Why would they take a seized truck to a TV station?"

"Well, my drivers don't ask many questions because it's dangerous, but they told me they did see a very peculiar, ugly, shielded, armored truck-looking thing with the steering wheel on the wrong side."

"It's my rig alright!" Lily jumped "Can't miss it."

"Now that you mentioned a TV station..." Vince said. "Yo Hec, remember that place we've been before they took us to the power plant, with that minister guy and all?"

"Crystal clear, bro."

"There was a huge dish antenna in there."

"Yes!" Clark agreed. "I saw it too."

"We've all seen it." Prashant said "I even lost an eye on the occasion."

"Anyway, I have the address." Zach informed.

"Is it possible that Shane and the minister guy are using the TV station as headquarters?"

"Let's find out." Lily spoke. "But before we do that, we need to know how Shane communicates remotely with her armed forces."

"Good point." Clark replied. "When we fled from the hospital with Susan, a whole parade of suits and limos just popped in front of us, as if coming from the sewers."

"Cell phones?" Maria suggested.

"For some reason, cell phones are allowed neither in Downtown nor Uptown." Tess informed.

"What about walkie-talkies?"

"Yes!" Hector responded. "Harper and I brought a lot of those from the power plant when we escaped."

"And that stupid sheriff also had one." Clark recalled as well.

"But I never saw any walkie-talkie on Shane." Tess said.

"Me neither." Lily agreed. "But I don't think she needs it."

"What do you mean?"

"I tell you later. Anyway, if we are to pull this thing off, I'll need help from each and every one of you."

"You got it!"

"But first, let's pay a visit to Susan and her new doctor, to see how they're doing. We'd better keep a low profile though."

All eyes turned to Tess.

"Okay, you can use one of my delivery vans."

"How is she, doc?" Lily asked Aaron.

"She's young and strong. I pumped all *Luviximil* out of her stomach and gave her some drugs to counteract its effects. Now, it's up to her."

"Remember when I said you were going to be practicing medicine in no time?" Hector asked the doctor. "I always keep my promises."

"So, your name is Susan?" Vince talked to the patient.

"Yes." She whispered with a very fainting voice. "Susan Burkowski."

"Whoa! I'm glad people in Uptown never found out about this Polish leaning of yours."

"It's Ukrainian." Susan corrected him. "And I have a feeling they did find out." She rolled her still worn-out eyes around. "I got friends... in there. They don't know what they're doing... I need to come back..."

"You need to take a rest." Lily spoke. "Don't worry, we got everything under control."

"Hold my hand."

"O-okay" Lily stuttered before such unexpected request. She sat down by Susan and held her hand.

"I know you..." The patient whispered. "The girl on the YouTube video... My friends... showed me... You and the other guy... came back for me... I just want to thank you."

"No biggie. It's just that we are curious to see how you look like healthy."

Susan smiled.

"I can help..." She said. "Got an idea..."

"Don't worry, lass. We got that part covered. You just rest."

"Hey Hector..." Clark called him.
"Yes?"
"Why did you come back?"

"You mean, why I came here with the rest of the group after escaping the power plant?"

"That's right. Why didn't you stay out? You were free."

"Well, aside from the dead people we had to deal with, I got blood in my hands."

"Why?"

"Twenty good people perished because of what I did. I just felt I needed to come back and fight for their memories. And the group supported me. Don't forget I left you behind too. I got your blood in my hands."

"It's cool, man. I know you had to do it. Besides, I'm here now, no harm done."

"But what about the ones who died? They were my responsibility and I let them down. I should have come back for them."

"No, you should not." Harper stepped in. "You made a command decision and it was the right call."

"How can you be so sure?"

"I've been to wars. I led men and women in battle. I lost my share of them. Anybody can make easy decisions, but the tough ones are reserved to real leaders. There was nothing you could do for those people. You didn't kill them, the enemy did. Now, let's get some payback." He turned to Lily. "Ball's in your court now."

"Yes!" Clark jumped.

"I don't know what you have in mind, missy, but I just hope you know what you're doing." Harper continued. "Right now, we are deeply immersed into a catastrophic world of hurt."

ACT 27

The *Fleur du Soir*'s delivery truck was heading to Uptown when the men in the cabin heard the unmistakable sound of a police car siren.

"Sloppy version of Starsky & Hutch right on time" Mario said behind the wheel, watching the red lights flashing in the rear-view mirror.

"I'm surprised those two are still in the force." Philippe commented in the passenger's seat.

"I'm surprised they're still not cleaning latrines in Slim's butcher shop, Downtown."

The truck stopped, as well as the police car.

"Good evening." Joe said looking up at the window on the driver's side. "May I ask you where you think you're going?"

"Yes, you may ask." Mario answered with a smile. "Can we go now?"

"Cut the bullshit! We don't have time for this! Where do you think you're going?"

"Well, I think I'm going to paradise! But actually, we're going to the TV station."

"What for?"

"What does it look like? To deliver food, silly."

"I know that! How come I wasn't informed?"

In the meantime, Tony walked around the truck tapping the hull with his club as if he was checking something, a totally pointless gesture he saw on the movies.

"It's a special delivery of caviar!" Mario said. "As the cargo is too precious, one doesn't exactly announce it at the four corners, right?"

"I'll have to contact logistic at the station to check on that." Joe informed.

"Great! You do that while we go."

"You stay put, my friend!"

"But the product is highly perishable. You don't want your beloved TV stars to spend a month in the bathroom, now do you?"

"May we see the cargo?" Tony asked on the other side of the truck.

"Yes, why don't you do just that?" Philippe said.

"Door is opened." Mario spoke. "You know the drill."

Joe and Tony went behind the truck and pushed the doors up. And they were pulled inside by four strong hands. And they didn't come back outside, at least not with their clothes on.

"Alright" Hector said. "They are back in the police car, in underwear and duct tapes only. Now, you get their clothes and put them on."

"You didn't hurt them, did you?" Mario asked preoccupied.

"Nope, but they might catch a cold."

"Sometimes, I pity those guys." Clark whispered.

At the TV station, two tall men wearing police uniforms approached the security cabin by the main entrance, with Lily walking in the middle of them. They were immediately stopped by the guards who left the cabin.

"We're taking this prisoner to the authorities." Mario informed firmly. "This is Lily Master, one of the terrorists that invaded the power plant. She surrenders and wants to talk."

"Roger." One of the guards said. "Take her inside while I radio Colonel Talbot."

Lily was escorted into the cabin, following the guards. But Mario and Philippe ran outside. Some punches and kicks later, Lily walked out.

"Done" She said.

Mario grabbed a walkie-talkie "Okay, coast is clear... for the moment!"

The delivery truck materialized from behind a small building and stopped in front of the gate.

"Did you kill them?" Philippe asked Lily.
"No! I just sent them in a round trip to *slumber land*. Make sure you tie them up good."
"Don't worry, sugar, we know our way around duct tapes and handcuffs."
"I also took the liberty of taking their clothes off for you."
"Man, this place is slowly turning into a nude beach." Philippe said.
"Well, as long as there are only men..." Mario replied.

"Alright..." Hector spoke. "Grab your radios and let's do this."

Now impersonating security guards by the main gate, Mario and Philippe found the button to lift the boom barrier and the truck went through. After taking some turns around the parking lot, they finally found the south building, the one indicated by Zach. The truck stopped by its metal door.

"Okay, we're home." Hector said on the radio. "What do you got for us, over?"
"I can open the door to the building from here, but once in there, it's up to you." Mario responded. "All doors inside can only be opened by entering six number codes on keypads, copy that?"

"Got it, hang on."

"This is it, lad." Lily spoke to Clark. "You know what to do."
"Find your rig, kick ass if we have to."
"It's our only ticket into the damn hangar."
"Do you know where this hangar is located?"
"More or less, it's the same place Shane kept me captive with the zombie. I guess they fixed the garage door I broke and probably reinforced it. Then, we'll need my rig to get in."
"What time is it?" Vince asked.
"Ten past six."
"Damn, we're late! We got to go, bro!"
"Roger."
"Aren't you taking your gear?" Clark asked Lily. "It's in the truck."
"Nah, that's my zombie killing gear. When I deal with the living, I'd rather do my kung-fu dancing. Perhaps, you can take it!"
"Really?"
"Everything except for the boomerang, I'll take this one. It's not a toy and you don't have the gloves for it."
"One day, you got to teach me how to use that thing."
"Alright" Hector spoke on the radio. "We're ready, over."
"So are we." Mario replied. "We'll keep our frequencies open all the time. I did some hacking in my days, and I can tap into the surveillance system to cause some glitches. But you can't linger in front of the cameras. The glitches can only last two, three seconds top, or the real guards will get suspicious, copy that everybody?"
"Yes!"

Philippe pushed a button and the lock mechanism of the south building metal door was released. The group entered.

"Lord, I've been to this place before!" Hector realized.
"Me too, bro, it's still in my mind."
"That makes three of us." Aaron said.

"Four." Maria completed.

Hector and Lily, Vince and Clark, Aaron and Maria split to different directions, always in contact with Mario and Philippe to tell them where they were.

Lily and Hector found stairs and went down one floor.

"I've been to my share of switching buildings." Hector said. "Normally, the equipment room is located on lower floors with more refrigeration. Boards and circuits need to be cooled down all the time."
"But they need to be moist, too?"
"Yep, you're right, I'm feeling as well. This is not the right place. Let's double back."

But they stumbled on some showers distributed in a row.

"This is definitely not the equipment room." Hector observed.
"Hostile coming..."

They hid behind a pillar. A man walked past them, calmly whistling a tune. Lily advanced to knock him down, but to her surprise, Hector was way ahead of her.

"This one's mine!" He said in anger.

Hector pulled the man's arm and punched him right in the face. He fell stunned on the hard ground.

"I did some bare-knuckle fight back in the old neighborhood." Hector said proudly.
"Yes, but I just hope you keep your focus here." Lily retorted. "This is not a good time to settle scores."

"I'm focused. I just want to have a chat with the gentleman. Please, take his club, gun and radio."

Lily did it.

"Help! HELP!" The man screamed and his voice reverberated loud through the tiled walls.

The Australian girl looked at all sides nervously.

"We need to get out of here." She said with urgency. "His friends will be here in no time!"

But Hector didn't seem worried at all.

"Relax." He said. "I can tell you, a lot of people must scream for help in this place every day, including me and my brother once, but nobody cares."

Hector dragged the man by his collar to a shower booth. He crawled back in despair until his back touched a wall. Hector grabbed a hose and signaled to Lily. Even not approving her partner's behavior, she walked to the spigot.

"What's your name?" Hector asked him.
"Miller."
"Remember me, boy?"
"Y-yes!" Miller cried, trying to take his body further back with his legs, as if it was possible to go through the wall like a ghost.
"That's right, the wet nigger. But I'm not the one who's getting wet today. Lily, if you please..."

The Australian woman opened the spigot. A furious jet of water whipped Miller, compressing him even more against the wall.

"Stop! Please, stop!!!" He screamed in anguish and pain.

Hector nodded at Lily and she killed the jet.

"Alright, now that you're clean, you can tell us where the equipment room is, and the code to open the door."
"I can't, please, I can't tell you! You don't know these people!"

Hector nodded at Lily and the water jet came back to life at full power, punishing Miller's body.

"Stop, please!"

Lily closed the spigot.

"I'm not asking you again!" Hector shouted at him.
"Look, mister, I'm sorry for what I did to you, okay? I just follow orders! If you mess up with these people here, you don't know what they do to you!"
"Oh, I think I do. And I know you follow orders. That's all you do. Only now, you're following my orders. And you don't want to know what I can do to you."

With a powerful grip, Hector strangled Miller's neck to force his mouth open. Then, he stuck the hose down his throat.

"There's only one way to clean racist pricks like you." Hector spoke "By washing your dirty soul on the inside. Lily, when you're ready."

She was about to open the spigot again.

"UHHH! UHHH!" Miller grunted in dreadful horror, his eyes goggling.

"Hold it!" Hector said and took the hose out of Miller's coughing mouth. "I'm listening, boy."

Once by the equipment room, Lily typed the numeric code and it worked. They opened the door and Hector pushed Miller inside, to later tie him up and gag him with duct tape.

"No cameras in here" Lily spoke "as far as I can see."

They studied the room and all the gizmos around.

"It's not your brand." Lily noticed.
"That's why it's so inefficient." Hector replied, sitting down by a table with a desktop connected to monitor, mouse and keyboard. "Alright, time to play some piano." He snapped his fingers.

"It's that him?" Maria asked Aaron.
"Oh yes. I'll never forget that face."

The guard they saw was casually making his rounds, so distracted he didn't see Maria coming with a pipe. She hit him in the head and he fell unconscious.

"You did this kind of thing in your hair-parlor too?" Aaron asked her.
"Only to customers that didn't appreciate my work."
"Right. What we do now?"
"Have you watched the movie *I Spit on Your Grave*?"
"No."
"Follow my lead."

The guard woke up in a room, his arms and legs tied up to a chair. He was dizzy and with a strong headache.

"What... what's going on?" He screamed and struggled on the chair. "Get me out of here!"

"Good evening." Maria went into the room and closed the door.

"What are you doing? Who are you? Untie me right now, you hear?"

"Yes, I hear you. I'll untie you, but first I need you to tell me where you guys keep the heavy vehicles you steal from travelers. Is there a garage around here somewhere?"

"What?! Fuck you, bitch!"

"Oh, that's not the answer I'm looking for, mister."

"You are one of those freaking rebels, right? Oh yeah, it's you! What? Is this supposed to scare me? Oh, I'm sorry to disappoint you, babe, cause this is just the way I like it." He spread his legs as much as he could. "Come on, cunt, put your little mouth in here and do what you do best, hahahaha." He wiggled his tongue and laughed again.

"You're quite rude. Let's see how you deal with a real man." Maria left the room.

"Don't be shy, baby!" He spoke between laughter. "Come back, I'm ready for you!"

But Aaron was actually the next one into the room.

"Remember me?" He asked the prisoner.

The man narrowed his eyes a little and said:

"Oh yeah, you're that kike I shaved! So, how's the new face doing? I guess I made you pretty, huh? What's wrong, can't you remember anymore what you ate last night? Hahahahahaha!"

"Oh yes, the face's doing well." Aaron answered serenely. "You shaved me indeed, and you did it all for free. I guess it's just polite to return the courtesy."

The smile vanished from the prisoner's face.

"What are you talking about, man?" He asked.

"You shaved me, now I shave you. Only I'll start for your balls. By the way, I couldn't find any electric shaver, like the one you used on me, so I'll have to use the only item I could get my hands on." He drew a big and rusty gutting knife.

"W-wait, man! Be cool, man! We were just kidding! That whole shaving thing was just to pull your legs, man!" He began to pant heavily.

"I'm kidding too! And I'll also pull your legs." Aaron unzipped the man's pants and raised the knife.

"Hey, hey, stop! Please, don't do this, please, please! I'm sorry, you hear! I'm sorry! They made me do that!"

"Forgive me if my clumsy hands are not very familiar with this line of work. I'm not a barber, you know. I might cut the wrong thing by mistake." Aaron put the knife right into his pants.

"Stop, come on, stop!" The prisoner burst into tears. "Please don't do it!"

"The lady who was here before asked you a question."

"Yes, yes, I tell you everything you want to know!"

"And you also owe her apologies for the way you treated her."

"Yes, yes!"

"Mate, do you copy?" Aaron spoke on the walkie-talkie.

"Loud and clear, brother, copy."

"I hope your driver's license is not expired, my friend. You got some driving to do."

"How is it going?" Lily asked.

"Purring like a cat" Hector replied. "I'm almost in. Security in this thing is a joke. Even a four years old kid can break these passwords. Now, if they had used the ultra sophisticated encryption methods of *Hector and Vince, Routers and Since* my brother and I created..."

A strident blare interrupted his bragging. A loud alarm screamed to all walls. A light bulb on the ceiling spun red beams around the room.

The guard tied up and gagged on the floor beat his shoes against the ground in satisfaction.

"Oops!" Hector mumbled.
"What's going on?" Lily asked.
"Somehow, they must've connected the man-machine interfaces to the local alarm system. They did that probably because their cryptography is weak."

"Everybody, copy" She spoke on the radio. "Abort mission, we've been compromised. Try to get out of here or find a place to hide, copy."
"Is there a third option, over?" Vince queried.
"Yes, you ask them nicely not to kill you, over and copy." She turned to Hector. "Can you still do your magic?"
"Oh yes, I got access to the routers and switches, but soldiers will be all over us very soon."
"Can you open that door never mind what happens to the keypad?"
"Sure, it can only be locked on the outside."
"Good. Keep on working. I'll be right back."
"Where are you going?"
"I'll take a tour around the complex. I've never been to a TV station before."

Lily left the equipment room and closed the door. She grabbed her boomerang and destroyed the keypad with it. Some soldiers ran to her, firing automatic machine guns. She jumped around a corner to a corridor, bullets crossing the air very close to her head and shoulders. She looked up and saw fluorescent light fixtures attached to the ceiling by cables.

The soldiers stopped by the door and tried to open it, but noticed the keypad was obliterated. One of them shot a whole round of ammunition at the locks, but to no avail.

"Forget it. It won't budge. Let's get the girl." The man reloaded his weapon and ran with the others.

They turned the corner and faced an empty aisle ahead of them.

"Where did she go?"
"She couldn't have run that fast!"

In fact she did not. From one of the light fixtures, Lily jumped and landed on two of the men. The others succumbed to her nimble dance of martial arts, hitting the deck unconscious.

She searched the sleeping soldiers until finding a lighter. Running again, she tried to reach the stairs to the upper floors. But another division closed on her from the opposite direction, blocking her way and forcing her to double back with more shots.

"Guess I'm not welcome." She whispered.

While running, she also jumped and hit all water spray nozzles she found with the flame of the lighter. Water poured hard on the corridor like rain. More soldiers came from the other side and Lily had to stop. She was surrounded. Everybody was soaked.

"I don't know why you did that," one of the uniformed men spoke "but say goodbye to this world, toots."

"Goodbye to this world, toots." Lily said.

"FIRE!"

And they all fired at Lily. But none of the weapons worked.

"What the f..." The soldiers started to examine and shake their machine guns like mad.

"Wet powder" Lily explained.

"Only this water can't do all that!"

"Crappy equipment, you've been forcing people to work real hard for almost no gain. You get what you pay for."

That being said, she once again opened way through the men with precise karate blows. She found an open door and went in.

"Great!" A sergeant said. "She's just got herself cornered." He grabbed his radio. "All units converge to the showers. I repeat – all units converge to the showers. And bring some dry weapons, damn it!"

Lily closed the door, and very quick realized that was the only way in and out the room. There were some glass windows, but out of reach.

"Wonderful." She grunted.

Lily walked into a shower booth. "Please, tell me you guys dig a hot bath."

Soldiers approached the door on both sides. One of them nodded at the others and broke into the place.

"Goddamn it!" He had to leave almost immediately because of the thick steam coming out of the room.

"Alright, let's go in!"

They entered two at a time, but the overall atmosphere was unbearable.

"Man, this place is a sauna!" One private complained.

Unpleasant sounds of water hitting the floor reverberated through the walls.

"She turned on all showers." A soldier informed his sergeant "Only hot water though."

"Yes, I noticed!"

"She must have some water fetish."

"No, it's not that. She's using the steam to cover her. All right, spread out and comb the area, widest possible angle! And turn off those damn things as you go!"

"Ugh, ah, ouch!" Screams were heard.

"James, Brody! Are you there? Please, respond!"

"Man, I can't see a thing!"

"Ow, uuuuh, Jesus!"

Loud thuds echoed.

"What's happening? Somebody talk to me!"

The soldiers finished turning off the showers. A few minutes later, all steam dissipated through the ventilation system. Several men were lying on the floor, knocked out cold. And the door was opened.

"Sir, we searched every inch of this dump. She's not here."

"Are you sure?"

"Positive, sir. She escaped."

"Damn it!" He took his radio. "All units, this is Sergeant O'Herlith. We got a hostile on the loose! I repeat – a hostile on the loose..."

Lily found the break room. She decided to stay there for a while and even take a coffee.

"Too sweet!" She mentally complained.

Some men in suits ran outside.

"Lily, do you copy?" a voice came on the radio.

"Yes Mario, I hear you, um... over or copy."

"We got some problems in here, over."

"That's a switch. Tell me, over."

"A whole army of riot police is crossing the gates right now, copy."

"Are you and Philippe in any danger, over?"

"Oh no, they look too worried about whatever you guys are doing in there, over."

"Hang tight. I'll get back to you. Just a question, over..."

"Yes, over..."

"Why we have to say *over* or *copy* every time we're done blabbing on the radio, copy?"

"I'm not sure. It's a convention I guess, over."

"Okay, hang tight; over, copy and out."

"You'd better hurry, sugarplum, they have tear gas. Over and out."

The rumble caused by the heavy boots of men crossing the main gate was enough to shake the structures of the security cabin.

"Oh dear" Mario cried. "It's an earthquake outside."

"All we can do now is pray for a miracle." Philippe sighed.

Lily peeked outside. Coast was clear. She went downstairs, hoping to find a garage. She was anxious. It was a big place and she didn't have the slightest idea where to go next. She was afraid to get lost.

Sounds of steps roared on the upper floors. They were so loud they could be heard even from two or three stories down. A shadow appeared on a corner. Lily froze and got ready to attack. When the person materialized, she jumped on whoever that was, fists ready to hit the punch.

"No, no, please!" The skinny young woman gasped and Lily held her hand. "I just noticed all the fuss around and I wanted to see what was happening. Please, don't kill me! I won't tell anybody I saw you!"

"Don't fret, lass. Everybody knows I'm here already. Besides, it's not a problem, I suffer from attention deficit."

"W-what?"

"Never mind, it's just a bad joke. What's your name?"

"Becky."

The Australian woman let go of her collar and stared at Becky for some seconds.

"I remember you!" Lily said." Your pictures are all over town. Your face is showing in more billboards than mine on YouTube."

"Yes, I know who you are." Becky revealed.

"Is there a reception desk somewhere in this place?"

"Yes."

"Do you mind telling me how to get there through the least busy route you know of?"

"Go straight ahead, make a right and you'll find a service elevator. Nobody uses it very much, not even on emergencies. Reception desk is on the ground floor."

"Great, thanks. Are you alright? You don't look so good."

"I'm fine."

"You go home now."

And Lily ran to the directions informed by the youngster.

"Too nice for a scoundrel and a looter" Becky wondered in her mind, but that was all she could think of.

A headache had been plaguing her for some time. The pain grew stronger to slowly become a migraine.

"What's happening to me?" She cried while massaging her temples.

"Yes, yes, I know, we're doing the best we can!" A neatly dressed front-desk receptionist spoke nervously on the phone.

By his side, another clerk drummed her keyboard like a crazy piano player.

"Yes, we got most of the invaders on cameras, but we still couldn't pinpoint their exact location." The receptionist continued. "Somebody keeps switching channels with me. That's right. They must've tapped into the system. We're locating the source right now."

The other clerk raised her eyes and shouted "The security cabin by the main entrance."

"Did you get that, sergeant? Great, talk to you later." And he put the phone back on the cradle.

"Sorry folks, you'll have to leave the office a little earlier today." Lily said, walking behind the fancy desk.
"Hey, you can't be here...!"

Before he could finish his reprimand, Lily hit both receptionists' heads against each other, rendering them unconscious.

She grabbed the radio "Mario, you there, over?"
"Yes, sugar, over."
"Get out of there now! The soldiers know you're there, copy!"
"What about you, over?"
"Never mind. Just go!"

"Time to split, dear" Mario turned to Philippe and they jumped out of the cabin, back to the street.

Lily broke the glass protecting the fire alarm and pushed the red button. Another deafening siren blared all over the place. She also found a paper containing the building blueprints pinned to a bulletin board.

"This may come in handy."

"Everybody please leave the building and go to the extraction zone in an orderly manner, everybody please..." A recorded female voice kept repeating on the PA system.

Workers in the building slowly complied. In a few minutes, a multitude of employees, janitors, TV anchors, reporters and maintenance personnel flooded the corridors, making real difficult for the soldiers to transit. A good number of them also congested all possible entrances and exits, rendering impossible for the riot police to get in.

"What's going on?" A frowning policeman asked from behind his helmet.
"Fire alarm" an employee replied.
"It's probably a hoax! The building has been invaded!"
"Yes, I heard it too, but perhaps it's not a hoax. Invaders sometimes set places on fire, you know. In either case, we have to follow protocol."
"Ah hell! Just make it quick, okay?"

Lily was heading back to the equipment room, but found more resistance on the way. Three men in black suits ran to her unloading machine guns like crazy, forcing her to retreat back to a corner. Over there, she bumped into four soldiers.

"It's over, miss!" One of them said. "Just come with us peacefully, please. Don't make us shoot at you."
"Listen to me," Lily responded "three other guys are coming here, shooting everything. You have to get down!"
"What are you talking ab..."

The three men in suits showed up shooting and screaming. They looked more scared than determined. Lily was fast enough to duck, but the four soldiers weren't so lucky.

"Damn it!" Lily cried. "What's wrong with you people?"

The men in suits, surely too young for the job, paralyzed in horror, mouths wide open, eyes gazing at the bloody corpses stretching on the ground, with a red pool coming out of their dead bodies.

Lily left the scene aghast, once again trying to find the equipment room, following the blueprints in her hand.

"Oh man!" One youngster in suit spoke with a shaky voice and eyes full of tears.

"Hell with this!" Another man said. "I'm sick of this! I'm out of here!" He threw his machine gun on the floor and walked away.

The other two did the same.

ACT 28

In a showroom, Shane was contemplating a painting by a very famous artist, considered the ultimate masterpiece by many. Back in the days when the world was still standing, some art collectors were willing to pay top dollar for it.

"What a piece of crap." Shane commented. "Looks like somebody vomited on the canvas."

"Yes." Colonel Talbot agreed. "My artistic sensibility seems to match yours."

"Report, colonel."

"Things at the TV Station are not good."

"I'm not surprised, considering the incompetents guarding the place. I need to check on this."

"I lost contact with many of my men, some others simply deserted. Four soldiers were killed by friendly fire."

"And how do you propose we handle this situation, Mister Talbot?"

"We can beat them. A handful of rebels invading a station are hardly a threat. Anyway, it's a good training exercise for the soldiers."

"Except those rebels are not stupid, there's a reason why they're doing this; any ideas, colonel?"

"They're probably after Lily's vehicle, or whatever that thing is. They figure they can break into the hangar and free the hostages."

"Well, can they?"

"No, it's impossible. We reinforced all the entrances. The hangar is a fortress now."

"Very good, colonel. I'm glad to know I don't have to do all the thinking after all."

"Yes, ma'am."

"But this is not only about the vehicle. They are up to something else..."

"Madam?"

"I can feel it in my head.

"Now that you mentioned, I also received some disturbing reports from Doctor Blake at the hospital. It seems half this town came down with a case of migraines."

"Yes, I have to figure it out. Anyway, I trust Lily's vehicle is heavily guarded, right colonel? Can your men at least execute such a simple task?"

"Nobody goes anywhere near the truck. If anybody tries it, the order is to shoot to kill."

"Good. I don't wish to order a premature execution of the hostages. That would make me look bad. I gave my word they'd only die at nineteen-hundred hours."

"That won't be necessary, madam."

"I don't understand these people. I give them everything they need. And yet, they break out of the power plant, leaving a whole district without power, and now this havoc at the TV Station. Their reputation around Heavensville is in shambles."

"And I don't think they're planning to turn themselves in."

"That's right. They'll make me kill men, women and children. People in the Industrial Zone will hate them too."

"They act before they think."

"Indeed. They could all be living good lives, far from the horrors outside. Go figure."

"There's something else intriguing me, though."

"What is it?" Shane yawned.

"I spoke with Sergeant O'Herlith a couple of times, and he told me that he and his men only saw Lily in the complex."

Shane turned to him with a serious face and said:

"And why are you so intrigued? She's attracting attention, so her friends can walk freely around the complex and make a mess. This is called strategy, something you should learn. If she wasn't such a nasty sociopath, I would recruit her."

"Well, apparently, the nasty sociopath took most of the soldiers down all by herself."

"This is not possible. She can't be that good. Did you get all possible information about her from the records, as I requested?"

"Yes. Actually, I didn't get much on her, except that she played cricket sometimes."

"Well, she's too young to have a long record. Please, continue."

"However, I found a lot of stuff about her father. Peter Master was a golden medal Olympic athlete."

"That's interesting. What sport?"

"More than one modality actually; from Olympic gymnastic to martial arts, he won champions trophies from tournaments all around the world, including Japan. When he got too old to be a gymnast, he took some interest in mechanics, microelectronics, but he actually worked with telecom, also proving to be very competent. I tell you, if Lily inherited only half of his gifts, we're in trouble."

Shane laughed "Oh, I guess she inherited them all, not to mention the things he must've taught her."

"Do I detect admiration in your voice?"

"I do admire her. That's why she must die, or be controlled, not necessarily in this order, of course. I underestimated her and I won't make the same mistake again."

"Yes madam."

"Colonel..."

"Yes?"

"Get rid of this painting. It makes me nauseous."

ACT 29

"Hey Hector!" Lily shouted, banging on the door. "It's me, open the door!"

The man inside let her in.

"What the heck happened out there?" Hector queried. "It sounded like world war three!"
"Sort of. How is it going?"
"I shut down all local interfaces, now I have to finish installing the *little nosy* to kill the remote ones. What about you and the rest of the team?"
"There's a bunch of guys outside dying to stick tear gas down our throats. I managed to buy us some time, but they'll be coming soon."
"Yes, I heard the fire alarm and the voice on the speakers. I figured you did that. What about the security forces in here?"
"I neutralized them all."

A volley of bullets ricocheted from the half open door, almost hitting Hector and Lily, who had to jump behind a rack.

"I'll be right back." The Australian girl said.
"What...?"

Lily took a small table made of hard wood and left the room. She ran to the aggressors holding the tabletop in a way to protect her head and body from the bullets.

Some shots, punches, roundhouse kicks and screams later, she came back inside, without the table and with minor wounds.

"Now I neutralized them all."

"Hey Lily, do you copy?" Clark came through on the radio.

"Hey partner! Are you still in the building?"

"Yes, we couldn't get out, but we're safe for the moment, so are Aaron and Maria. They'll be joining us soon."

"Listen, I didn't have a chance to tell you this before, but stay away from the cameras. Mario and Philippe were compromised and they had to go."

"It's okay, it doesn't matter now. I have good news for you. We found your rig."

"Really? This is great!"

"But we can't get to it. That's why I'm calling. There must be at least twenty guys armed to the teeth guarding it."

"Wow, I'm flattered! Hang on, partner, I'm a-coming."

"Roger."

Lily turned to Hector "It seems I didn't neutralize them all again."

"We need to have a serious talk about your raid techniques."

"What time is it?"

"Twelve to seven o'clock."

"Oh boy! Time to go, Hec."

"I can't. I still got stuff to do in here."

"Can't you do it remotely?"

"No, it's impossible."

"Then, I stay with you. Our friends can save the hostages."

"They can't pull this off without you."

Lily hesitated "I'll get you a machine gun. There're plenty idling by outside."

"No. I don't want more blood in my hands. But you don't have to worry about me. Just close the door and I'll be fine."

"Are you sure?"

"Oh yeah. Now go. Save those people."

"I'll come back for you. I promise."

She left the room and closed the door.

Mate and Vincent were looking over the guardrail down at the parade of soldiers walking around Lily's truck.

"Aaron and Maria should be here by now. Why are they taking so long?" Clark asked anxiously, the parts of the dismounted hockey stick making metallic noises in the sheath strapped to his back.

"Perhaps they stopped for a milkshake or something. Relax man, they're coming."

"I hope they understood when I said first parking lot, not second. Otherwise, they'll bump into those men."

"They know how to take care of themselves."

"Maybe I should radio them again."

"This is no longer possible, dude. My brother is shutting down communication as he goes."

"Is it me or our rebellion techniques need some work?"

"Yeah, I think it gets easier in the second or third rebellion."

"This waiting is killing me. I got to do something, man."

"Yes, you got to sit here and talk to me. Now tell me, how do we know the key will be in the ignition when we get to that contraption of yours?"

"We don't, especially because it doesn't need a key. You push a button to start the engine."

"Man, I like it already."

"But it only works with Lily or her dad. Well, only Lily now. The button reads her fingerprints."

"That's some high-tech shit!"

"If those jerks didn't break it trying to start the truck."

"Don't worry. I can always hot-wire it."

"Let me guess, sister also taught you how to do this."

"No, that was Hector. But sister was the one who taught him."

Clark shifted position impatiently and glanced at Vince's wristwatch.

"Man, we're definitely running out of time!" He said. "I can't just sit here!"
"Calm down!"
"You stay here. I'll go downstairs. See if I can find them in the ramp."
"It's dangerous, man! You may find somebody else."
"I'll be fine. I got to do something!"

Mate stood up and went to the stairs.

"Come back here!" Vince spoke. "Damn it!"

He turned to the guardrail to watch the guards on the lower level. That was when he heard the unmistakable sound of a hammer cocking and felt the cold barrel of a gun touching his ear.

"It seems I got myself a black swan." The man with the pistol said.
"Cool, man." Vincent said raising both hands. "Cool, man."
"You tell me, friend. Should I kill you now?"

"Only if you want to die first!" Clark appeared behind the man, pressing one of Lily's knives against his neck.

The man's eyes goggled.

"A bullet goes way faster than a knife." He said.
"He got a point there, dude." Vince said shaking and sweating.
"I'm dangerously close to your jugular." Clark replied. "You'll bleed to death before you can even wink. Besides, you know I wouldn't hesitate to kill you, right Drake?"

The man chilled in horror by finally realizing who the guy with the knife was. Very slowly, he uncocked the hammer and put the gun away from Vince.

Clark snatched the pistol from Drake's hand and dragged him far from the guardrail. Then, he hit Drake with his own gun. The man fell on the floor bleeding.

"I gather you remember me and my freckles, right?" Clark said and kicked his face. "Are you a tutti-frutti?" He kicked the man in the belly. "What? Say that again? I can't hear you!" And another kick followed. "I guess you need to man up a little!" Mate hit his head again with the gun. "Toughening up already, huh?"

"Hey, whoa, man!" Vince held Clark. "I understand this man gave you a real hard time, right?"
"You bet he did!"
"Yes, but you're not like him."

Mate stopped hitting Drake and gave the gun to Vince.

"I just don't like the way he thinks." Clark said.
"No problem. He just needs to go out at night a little more to develop his social skills. And we both know just the place. But first, we got to go."
"What?"
"You're right, man. We can't afford waiting for our friends. We need to get to the truck, hot-wire it and try to find that goddamn hangar. And dickhead here is our ticket."

"HEY!" Vincent screamed.

All guards around the vehicle turned and pointed weapons at the three newcomers. Drake was walking between Vincent and Mate. Vince had a gun on his neck.

"You all lower the pieces and move away from the truck!" Vincent shouted. "Or the dude here will be the next headless horseman!"

"Do what he said! Do what he said!" Drake cried in despair.

But the soldiers didn't seem willing to comply.

In a desperate act of fury, Drake elbowed Vince's stomach and pushed Clark, dropping him on the floor. He ran behind a car screaming "Shoot them! Shoot them!"

Vince and Mate shrank in their clothes, just waiting for the bullets to cross their bodies.

However, before somebody could pull a trigger, a boomerang spiraled down, striking soldiers in the head, enough to make them bleed and fall stunned, but not actually killing them.

Lily descended from somewhere, taking back the boomerang in midair. Once on the ground, she neutralized the remaining guards with precise blows.

"Sorry I'm late." She said. "I found some hostiles on the way."

One soldier was still awake. He grabbed his machine gun and aimed at Lily. But Maria rendered him unconscious with her pipe.

"You also took your sweet time!" Clark complained. "Where the heck have you been?"

"We had some trouble going through crowded corridors." Aaron answered for Maria. "It seems somebody activated the fire alarm for no reason."

"Can't trust anybody these days. We got to go now!" Lily said urgently.

"This guy is riding with us." Clark pushed a sobbing Drake inside the vehicle.

"Just make sure he's tied up and doesn't occupy too much space."

"He's small enough."

And the truck accelerated out of the garage, hitting boom barriers and security cars on the way.

"Do you know how to get to the hangar?" Vince asked Lily. "We're really out of time."

"I'm not sure. I've just been there once."

"The walls of that hangar must be made of stainless steel, virtually unbreakable." Maria said. "It looked that way on TV."

"This is bad, because I have no time to pick locks." Vince spoke.

"There may not be enough room in this truck for all of them." Aaron pointed out.

Lily remained quiet. Her face denounced how pointless she considered all that pessimistic whining.

They made it out the building and were greeted by machine gun fire and rocket-propelled grenades. The bullets died on the shielded hull, but a volley of grenades almost caused the vehicle to overturn.

The truck destroyed the complex main fences. Lots of armed men had to jump out of the way. The vehicle also crashed against armored cars, but they didn't stop it.

"They're getting away." Colonel Talbot informed, looking at the whole scene through binoculars, from a window.

"This wasn't in the plans." Shane responded upset. "Call your men at the hangar and tell them to commence execution."

"But it's not time yet."

"I'm changing the deal. As they were going to die anyway, technically I'm still keeping my word."

"Hello, copy?" Talbot talked on the radio "Anybody, copy? Please respond, over?" He turned to Shane. "This is odd. I can't get through for some reason."

Shane closed her eyes. After a few seconds, she opened them again and said:

"I can't reach them either. I knew those rebels were doing something more than just stealing back their truck. Never mind. Your men got orders to spill the cyanide at seven o'clock sharp anyway, right Mister Talbot?"

"Yes madam." The colonel said nervously. "The truck will never get there on time. They don't even know where the hangar is."

"Yes, but just to be on the safe side, call your troops and get them ready for a full-scale attack on the Industrial Zone."

"You mean... a full-scale attack to kill people?"

"No, to give them all foot massages. Yes, Mister Talbot, to kill them."

"But..."

"What happened today was child's play, but it can't go unpunished. Order must prevail. The status quo shall remain in force. Examples have to be provided. And this is the only language they understand. I gave them everything, but they threw it all away. They don't deserve my benevolence. If only one single hostage gets out of the hangar alive, I want the entire Industrial

Zone reduced to ashes. Then, I'll just send my Center of Refugees outside again to get replacements."

"Madam, perhaps… if we just try to…"

"Follow orders, colonel. I visited Hartford recently. He's not doing so well. Doctors said he's eating through straws."

"Yes madam."

"Let me know when the hostages are dead. I need to start a campaign to blame it all on the rebels. Now, if you excuse me, I got an errand to run."

Seven o'clock in the evening.

Soldiers wearing masks began pumping cyanide into a protective chamber on the roof. From there, the gas proceeded to the hangar ventilation system. The poisonous substance quickly spread around the interior.

Frightened men, women and children stumbled on each other with anguished looks on their faces, minds lost in bewilderment and dreadful fear.

Some people started to cough. Others fell on the ground, fighting asphyxiation. The ones who were still standing definitely surrendered to panic and cried in despair. The toxic gas was taking its toll, flooding each and every corner.

A thunderous metallic roaring startled the few souls who could still breathe. From a small tool shed attached to the hangar, a truck burst through the walls like a giant shark.

"We crossed those things like they were made of paper." Clark gasped in the passenger's seat "How come?"

"I also don't know how we did that." Lily replied. "I guess we should thank my dad for this too."

The new door torn by the vehicle made the air inside a little more breathable.

Vince opened the side door and screamed:

"Alright, everybody inside, suck your bellybuttons and get ready for some squeeze."

Aaron and Maria jumped out of the truck and helped those who could no longer walk. But even they were getting dizzy. Maria brought a hand to her mouth.

"Try not to breathe." Lily advised.
"That's a little hard to comply." Clark responded.

Soldiers came and shot at the intruders. The truck blocked the bullets and worked as a natural barrier, but the military men flanked the vehicle, walking around it.

"I have to close the shop!" Vince announced, also getting nauseous. "Please hurry, folks!"

ACT 30

"Alright, almost there" Hector whispered to himself.

He watched his program loading on the screen, the percentage increasing in a very slow pace.

"Like in any telecom site, they really cut corners around here." Hector thought.

"I don't really see any need for processor speed. All these computers do is communicate with machines." Shane said, surprising Hector.

He stood up and took one step back in an instinctive gesture of self-defense.

"How did you get in here?" Hector asked.
"I just opened the door."
"I can see that! But the keypad outside is broken."
"A very expensive piece of equipment by the way, but it doesn't matter. The point is I own this town. I have the key to everything here."
"Wait a min... how come you answered my cutting edge comment? I've just thought that, I've never said it."
"Ah!" Shane smiled. "A natural gift of mine, enhanced for the common good."
"I see."
"Well, I don't think introductions are necessary. If you watch TV like any average American, you know who I am. And you are Hector, right? I'd recognize this face anywhere!"
"Yes, especially after you trashed my face on this same TV you mentioned."

"Oh, nothing personal, just a little response to you and your group after you destroyed property, left several blocks without electricity, got twenty workers killed…"

"What do you want?"

Shane walked to him. Hector stood his ground, but a chill came down his spine. To show determination, he looked her in the eyes, which was actually a mistake, for he could no longer dodge her look.

"You got a lot of stamina, Hector. You're a lousy strategist, but brave anyway."

She turned to the side and noticed the guard on the floor, tied up and gagged, staring at her with puppy dog eyes.

"Oh, that's a nice touch." She removed the gag and untied him. "I need to have a private conversation with this gentleman. Get out."

Miller staggered out the door.

She fixed eyes on Hector again to his despair, although he disguised it well.

"You proved your value." Shane said. "You surely got a strong heart. All you need now is some reasoning. You're such a worthy foe. Imagine the things we could do as allies."

"Are you trying to recruit me?"

"No. I'm proposing a partnership."

"And it doesn't bother you anymore the fact that I'm black?"

"I guess we can put our differences aside and see the big picture. Let's end this madness and work together."

"Do you really expect me to join you when I know you run a vacation resort powered by the blood of slaves?"

"*Powered by the blood of slaves*, I love it! You're really a man of many talents, somebody who once benefited so much from the gears of capitalism, yet partial to Karl Marx, whom I most admire by the way."

"Who's Karl Marx?"

Shane smirked.

"I think you know what I'm talking about." She said.

"No, but I'm pretty sure you know what I'm talking about." Hector replied.

"Indeed I do. But some people call it organization."

"Well, I call it segregation!"

"Segregation... So that's what I am, a bigot, a racist pig."

"That's right!"

"Uh-huh. You ran a business if I'm not mistaken."

"Yes."

"Then, let me ask you something. Let's suppose there's an opening in your company and two candidates are disputing the position. Both can do the job real well, only one is married with children while the other is a confessed homosexual who lives with another man. Now, which of them would you choose?"

Hector didn't answer right away. Shane grinned.

"That's what I thought." She said. "You don't even have to say it. I've already read your mind."

Hector growled.

"And I send gays to the Industrial Zone..." Shane spoke, "How awful of me!"

"Hey, I could always change my mind, this *don't* mean *nothing*! You and I are not alike in any way! I know what you do to people in the Industrial Zone and especially in the power plant, remember?"

"Yes, guess I have to mend my ways and come back to how things were done in this fair, marvelous world we used to enjoy, full of men just like you, real entrepreneurs working during the day, studying at night, to finally achieve the dream of a successful business with fame and fortune."

"What's wrong with that?"

"Nothing whatsoever, come on, I admire you. And of course, as opportunities were the same for everybody, all people without exception could get a big slice of the pie. All they had to do was work. That's why there was no poverty anywhere..."

"Now, wait a minute!"

"...except for those who chose not to be successful, right? Anyway, it's fun to roam the streets living on other's charities, eating from garbage bins. Not to mention those poor bastards who spent their whole lives on a paycheck, busting their backs for no money, but it's their fault, they wanted that way!"

"You're twisting my words!"

"On the contrary, I'm totally agreeing with you. Before me, you all lived in this magic utopia, without difference of classes, a world where wealth was not concentrated in the hands of a few while millions starved to death..."

"You stop right there, miss!"

"...a perfect world without segregation or bigotry or racism, no discrimination of any kind... Oh, how terrible of me, it seems I created all those."

"There was social consciousness for crying out loud!"

"Sure there was, politicians making laws to favor minority groups just to win the next election, millionaires donating to charity funds to get tax deduction."

"I know things were not perfect. But my brother and I are the proof that no matter whom you are or where you came from, you can always improve yourself and your situation if you're not afraid to work a little harder."

"Of course, not to mention the ones you stepped on in your climbing to the top."

"I never did that. Once again, you're twisting everything."

"No, I'm not, you are. Face it, Hector. I'm the demon that inhabits the darkest paths of human soul people are afraid to walk. I'm the reflection in the mirror you cover with a hypocrite mask of benevolence."

For a moment, Hector couldn't say anything. Shane's look was all over him.

"No!" He finally spoke. "There's still a difference. You got a reign of terror going on here."

"I beg to differ. Reign of terror means war, genocide, bloodshed. Oh, but I forgot you also didn't have those in the world of before. You probably don't have the slightest idea what I'm talking about."

"We need to have freedom!"

"Oh yes, freedom to judge and torment those who are different, freedom to mock and destroy your own species."

"Well, that's exactly what you've been doing. You're the hypocrite here, not me. Every time things don't go your way, you get cruel, you kill people!"

"We need to have at least a little order. Is it such a high price to pay for all security and stability I offer? Have you taken a good look at the horrors outside the city gates?"

"Yes, I've been there, alright. And it's a horror you helped causing, or so I heard."

Shane studied his face. After some seconds, she said:

"We did nothing this greedy humanity wouldn't have done to themselves sooner or later. You were consuming everything, without giving anything back."

"True, but it wasn't your place to interfere."

"Well, this is academic now." Shane lowered her voice. "What's done is done. Now, we have to think of the future, don't we?"

"How? What're you talking about?"

"You're just making things greatly worse, can't you see? People are confused, they're all scared and I'm not the one frightening them. Truth is everything was nice and peaceful until you came. You can't possibly win this, so let's negotiate. Join me and I'll release the hostages in the hangar and this is just for starters. Then, we can study better ways to get the necessary tasks done around here, with your suggestions. It's a win-win deal. What do you say, Hector?"

He hesitated and put some efforts to avoid her look. Naturally, her eyes stayed on his, trying to read his mind. Some moments of very awkward and uncomfortable silence followed.

"No!" He finally decided. "I think you're just bullshitting me. This is all a trick. You don't really intend to hold your end in this little bargain, do you? Anyway, I can hardly trust a person who's willing to poison innocent people only to get things her way."

Shane took a deep breath and shook her head. She also grabbed Hector by the neck to force him to look her in the eyes.

Hector could fight neither her grip, nor her look.

"What the hell are you?" He mumbled, stunned.
"In a few seconds, your new master," she replied.

Hector tried to resist as much as he could, but his mind and senses collapsed and surrendered to the huge energy emanating from Shane's eyes.

"I tried to talk some sense into you, how naïve of me." She said. "You made me waste precious time. Now I have to do this the hard way. Listen to this, please."

And Shane spoke:

"The sunshine springs, happiness it brings.
Those eyes you should follow, to keep away sorrow.
Seek the giant bird you must, on her you shall blindly trust.
For the good science you will urge, from all impurities to..."

BANG!

A bullet hit Shane right in the side of her head.

"Ouch!" She screamed and tumbled to the floor.

"That's for Frank, you bitch!" Susan shouted from the doorway, smoke still coming out of her gun.

She ran to Hector and said "Are you alright? Are you still you?"

He blinked like mad, but then he stopped.

"Yes." He answered rubbing a hand on his head. "Thanks. I almost didn't recognize you standing up. By the way, what the heck are you doing here? You should be in bed!"
"I got all the rest I could take. You probably thought I was raving on that hospital bed when I said I had an idea. Well, it turns out I do have an idea, time to make it work."
"How did you get here?"
"I drove. Nurses in the hospital didn't like it very much, but I convinced them and the rest of the group to tell me where you guys were hanging."
"And what is this idea of yours?"
"Can you get me some machine guns?"
"There're plenty of them idling by outside, thanks to Lily."
"I only need three."

Shane stood up.

"This is so blasé..." She said with hands on her waist "You coming in here shooting like Wyatt Earp..."

Susan screamed in anger and decided to simply unload the pistol on all parts of Shane's body. She fell down again.

"She bleeds, but I don't think bullets can hold her down." Hector observed.
"I agree. Let's get out of here."
"Just a sec..."

He checked the monitor connected to the desktop and his program was still loading, fifty-five percent and progressing slowly. He blocked that station with a password and smashed some racks and printed boards in the vicinities with powerful kicks. Susan twitched in surprise.

"You surely have a gentle way to deal with delicate electronics." She commented.
"I don't need those anymore. I don't want to risk that somebody may undone what I just did."
"And what did you do?"
"You'll see. Now, let's get out of here before blonde over there resurrects again."

They ran through corridors. To their horror, they stumbled on four dead bodies on the floor, with seven machine guns lying around. Hector took three of them and gave one to Susan.

They took a lot of turns and came back to the same place a couple of times.

"We're walking in circles." Susan realized.
"Lily forgot to leave those blueprints she found with me." Hector spoke.

They walked past the showers to finally find a staircase leading up.

All places were strangely empty.

"How did you get into the building?" Hector asked Susan, his guts telling him something was terribly wrong. "How did you pass security?"

"There was no security." She revealed. "I found it strange too. I saw some folks getting back into the building after a fire alarm or something. It was remarkably easy to get in."

Hector froze all of a sudden, his wide opened eyes almost jumping out of the sockets.

"What?" Susan asked, stopping as well.

"Shane…" He replied "Oh my God! I know what she's up to!"

He gave Susan the two machine guns with very anxious moves.

"What's going on?" She queried.

"Can you handle things here?"

"Yes, but…"

"Listen, I have to go back to Downtown. Maybe, it's too late already. Do whatever it is you came here to do and pray."

"Alright, take this" She gave him car keys "Blue Volvo parked right in front of the main entrance. A guy named Zach let me drive it."

"Thanks."

Hector ran upstairs, leaving a puzzled Susan behind with three loaded machine guns.

In the equipment room, Shane stood up, full of holes but composed.

"What a silly bird! She ruined my blouse, my brand new blazer and even messed up my hair!"

She walked to the desktop and monitor Hector was working on. She took a look around and saw some equipment destroyed.

"This is all coming out of his salary, if he ever works for me again."

She sat down by the station, making faces of pain while extracting nine slugs from her body and head with forefinger and thumb.

Shane tried to get into the system. But she couldn't because it was blocked by a password.

"What are you doing, my little ebony chap? What are you doing?"

Suddenly, she felt like she had lost a good portion of a sense, like an individual who goes partially blind, or deaf.

"What did you do? WHAT THE HELL DID YOU DO?"

At her private dressing room, Becky could no longer stand the horrible migraines splitting her skull in half. Her legs faltered and she was forced to get down on her knees, bending the upper body, hands strongly compressing her head.

"Make it stop! MAKE IT STOP!" She considered that only a merciful dead could stop the pain, but her condition no longer allowed her to stand up.

Then, her eyes simply met the ceiling, staring at some emptiness.

"Oh my God, Frank!" She began to cry copiously.

ACT 31

"How are they?" Lily asked behind the wheel, speeding like crazy to the Industrial Zone.

"Some of them are stable, some are still unconscious." Aaron answered.

"Are they going to make it?" Vince queried.

"We need to get them to a hospital."

"That's where we're going."

"It's very tight in here." Maria observed.

"We'll get there. Then, I'll come back for Hector. I promised him."

"So, what's the deal with this boomerang of yours?" Clark asked in the passenger's seat. "It kills the dead, but only hurts the living. Is it trained or something?"

"It's all about how you toss it." Lily explained. "If it flies clockwise, the blades on the concave side slash everything in its path. But if the boomerang flies counterclockwise, only the side without the blades hits."

"Man, I'm surprised it doesn't come with a chip and a remote control," Vince commented "like a boomerang-drone or something."

"That was next on my father's list." Lily said. "Too bad he didn't live enough to make it happen."

"But tell me, what Hector was doing after all?" Maria queried.

"He shut down all interfaces he could locally in the main router." Lily replied. "But there were many others he couldn't touch from there."

"But a little virus we created can do the trick." Vince stepped in. "It's not actually a virus; I'd rather call it medicine. But it takes some time to kick in."

"But, what's the purpose of all this?" Aaron questioned.

"Cut all possible communication" Lily responded "and significantly decrease Shane's influence, hopefully."

"How?"

"As I figure, Shane is basically a mini broadcast station." The Australian woman continued. "Her brain can transmit and receive information, not to mention control minds."

"But her range is limited, right?" Clark said.

"Precisely" Lily answered. "She needs to use all those antennas spread around rooftops in town as repeaters."

"And that big dish antenna at the TV Station is her link to such repeaters" Vince spoke "so her thoughts can be everywhere, in shops, offices, pubs and people's homes, reading everybody's minds and tapping into the will of those under her control."

"And the idea is to shut down this entire network, so Shane will be reduced to her limited transmission range." Lily concluded.

"But even if it works, she still can dominate your mind if you're close enough, right?" Maria observed.

"Probably yes" Lily replied.

"And why are cell phones forbidden?" Aaron asked.

"Because they interfere too much with Shane's broadcast capabilities" Lily answered "too many people yakking at the same time, congesting lines, increasing traffic, stealing network resources..."

"But she allows walkie-talkies."

"She needs them to talk to her military forces, cops, secret police, etc." Vince responded. "But radios don't bother her cause she knows who have them, at least she did until now."

Clark looked at Lily.

"And how do you know so much about networking and stuff?" He asked her. "I mean, I'm not surprised Hector and Vince got all this knowledge, it's their business anyway. But what about you, how come you know it?"

"I watched a lot of movies." Lily replied.

"Oh no, you love to hide under a veil of cynicism so you don't have to talk about yourself, but I know you better than this."

"Then, how do you figure I know all this stuff?"

"Your dad, it got to be him. My guess is he taught you not only his hobbies, but also his daytime work."

"My guess is daddy always dreamt of me becoming, you know, a good wife and mother, in a lovely home paid by a steady job. He could never imagine I would end up on the road, driving the very contraption he put together, fighting zombies in a dying world."

"Well, you can still have a family, kids, a lovely home… Only the steady job could be a problem these days."

"Yes, but then I'd have to clean gutters, worry about bills, cable TV and neighbors, ask them to low the volume of their stereo and all. Nah, I'll think about it later."

At Downtown, Drake was thrown inside the *Fleur du Soir* restaurant like a sack of potatoes. The first thing he saw after standing up was Tess staring at him.

"Uh-oh, homophobic bee twelve o'clock…" Tess spoke.

"You!" Drake said.

"Oh yes, little me! I'm so glad you still remember me! Oh, this is flattering! I hope you also remember the way you treated me when they kicked me out of your dear Heavensville. That was pretty unpleasant, with your filthy mouth and all, you and your friends beating the hell out of me and laughing. I spent a whole month in a hospital bed."

"L-look madam, I mean mister, I was just…"

"Oh, no apologies needed, honey." Tess said waving arms and hands in an exaggerated manner. "I know you're just a jerk. Everything's forgiven and I'm so happy you made it."

"Made it…?"

"To the party, silly! And you are the guest of honor!"

Drake looked at all sides. A big entourage of men dressed like Village People, except for the Indian war bonnet, stood all around, smiling directly at him.

"Oh no!" Drake mumbled and turned to the main glass entrance.

However, five muscular waiters were blocking the way, all grinning in anticipation.

"Don't be shy, darling." Tess spoke. "How do you know you don't like it if you never tried it? Or did you?"
"No, NO! Stay away from me, I'm telling you!"
"Don't worry, dear. We'll be gentle."

All men closed on Drake.

"Stay away from me! STAY AWAY FROM ME! Oh boy!"

ACT 32

Several residents left their homes and workplaces, partially crowding the main streets of Heavensville. Most of them rubbed their heads in confusion. Susan walked fast among them, going around those standing in the way.

She was lost in her thoughts when she noticed that everybody was gazing at a big screen hanging from a pole on *Happy Trails Boulevard*, one of the many in the city. All eyes were paralyzed in genuine horror. They had to be really focused not to notice a woman walking around with three machine guns.

Susan also stopped to see what was going on in the latest TV news. And like everybody else, she also felt sick in her stomach, a dreadful fear possessed her spirit.

Her walk had turned into a run when she rushed into the glass office building. She couldn't wait for the elevator and went upstairs in a mad dash toward the construction company floor.

She found Nick and Paul in the break room. No surprises there, but she froze by the doorway, not knowing what to expect from them. However, they seemed scared and perplexed. She considered that a very good sign.

"Sue!" Nick said. "Jesus, what happened to you? You look like hell!"
"What's with the weapons?" Paul spoke.
"Are you alright?" She asked.
"I'm glad to see you!"

Both men came to her. Clumsy as she was for carrying three machine guns, she still managed to point one of the weapons at them. They stopped immediately.

"Christ, what are you doing, Sue?" Paul asked.

"Put that thing down!" Nick said.

"This is far enough. I asked you if you are alright!" Susan insisted.

"We are now." Nick answered. "We got this real bad headache cracking our skulls…"

"Like everybody else in town, it seemed." Paul interrupted him.

"…but then, everything cleared up totally out of the blue, and it was like we were out of some terrible nightmare."

Susan lowered the gun and ran to hug her friends.

"Sorry about that." She said. "I'm a little edgy. Have you seen the news on TV?"

"N-no" Paul stuttered. "What's happening?"

"People are dying and things are going to get worse. You got to listen to me. I have to talk to you about Shane. We've been fed lies from the moment we set foot in that Cinemark. I need your help and I need to find Becky!"

"She's right over there."

Susan turned to the place he nodded at, and saw that in fact Becky was quietly sitting on a sofa, legs crossed with feet touching the worn-out quilt.

"Hold this." Susan handed two of the machine guns to the men, one for Paul and the other for Nick. "And be careful, the trigger is sensitive."

Susan walked to Becky. The girl stood up and hugged her friend crying.

"I'm sorry, I'm so sorry." Becky said.

"It's okay." Susan whispered. "It's not your fault."

"We know about Shane." The young woman revealed. "I still had memories of everything when I snapped out of that wacky spell of hers."

"How come we snapped out of it in the first place?" Nick queried.

"I'm not sure." Susan answered. "Some people I associated with in the Industrial Zone must've done something to interrupt the flow of her energy, or whatever it is. But I don't know how they did it."

"Industrial Zone?" Nick frowned.

"This is one of the things I got to talk to you about."

"Forget it!" Becky complained. "It's Shane we have to worry about now. How we stop her from dominating us again?"

"That's why I need your help." Susan gave the third machine gun to Becky, who accepted it. "Do you think you can handle it?"

"I'll do my best." Becky promised. "It's the least I can do after I killed Frank. Damn it, I was so busy being a piece of meat folks devoured with their eyes I couldn't even see what was happening."

"You didn't kill Frank. It was Shane. You were under her control. There was nothing you could do to stop it."

"F-Frank is dead?" Paul asked with shaking lips.

"Shane put a gun against his head and pulled the trigger."

"My God!" Nick bent his body to cry.

Becky lowered her head and sighed.

"Whatever you want us to do, never mind how crazy it is, I'm in!" Paul announced raising the machine gun, eyes sinking in tears.

"Same here!" Nick declared.

Susan turned to Becky and said:

"After all this time you've been working at the TV Station, you got to know the premises rather well, right?"

"Every bit of it" The girl replied. "Why?"

ACT 33

But reality in Downtown was far more terrorizing than what was shown on TV. Armed forces from Uptown fell upon the place like the army of apocalypse, shooting and leaving behind corpses, whose blood painted the streets red, as an anchorman said.

Citizens sought protection as best as they could, while their houses and shops were either reduced to pieces by gun fire, or blown to shreds by RPG (rocket-propelled grenades). Desperate, panic-stricken women ran with children to the local orphanage, but even such institution was made a target.

The first line of defense when the deadly army started its destructive campaign was Lily's truck. She barely had time to position the vehicle across the road to block the advance of the enemy. Nobody was expecting such sudden attack. Anyway, the truck did its job as much as it could.

Soldiers shot the vehicle with the thunderous firepower of M249 light machine guns. The hull was resisting the punishment, but it was beginning to crack. Lily and Clark clumsily returned fire with M16s, the only weapon they got. And they clearly didn't know how to shoot.

With very anguished eyes, Colonel Talbot followed the entire action from an outdoors garage on the second story of a commercial building, a reasonably safe position. Shane came to him.

"You're late." He turned to her.
"I had some problems leaving the TV Station."
"What the heck happened to you?"

"I was shot several times, but that doesn't matter. How is it going?"

"What do you think? They are not a match for us, not in a million years."

"They had it coming. Have you seen Lily?"

"She's in the truck, together with her friend. And the vehicle is really complicating matters, but we can deal with it."

"Just bomb it out of the way like anything else. As I said, there's more than one way to kill a myth and this time I mean it literally. Lily is pretty good, but she's not bulletproof."

Realizing the action was taking too long, the soldiers themselves took the initiative to call the man with the RPG. He fired at the truck and the grenade directly hit the ground right below the vehicle, causing it to fly a few feet from the asphalt and roll down the street toward an abandoned liquor store, clearing the way for the armored cars of the attackers. Although the truck overturned several times, it landed on its tires, but Clark and Lily were unconscious inside, bleeding like waterfalls.

"Nice shot." Talbot praised after watching everything through the lenses of a binocular.

And the army of doom was free to ominously strike down upon the frightened city, leaving nothing but destruction in its path, like a hurricane.

A small militia of street fighters tried to make a stand with the few weapons and ammunition they had. Most of them had already been gunned down, including Raul, shot dead. Hector, Vince, Prashant and even Maria led a reduced squadron of courageous individuals who didn't even know why they were being attacked. Aaron had to stay at the hospital, taking care of the hostages rescued from the hangar.

Former sergeant Harper and some volunteers, all with wife and kids, fought to hold the attackers back in another battle front.

But eventually, they all had to retreat to avoid getting massacred. Many lives had already been wasted.

Every resident who was crazy enough to hold a gun was shooting at the powerful enemy behind light poles and dumpsters; however, they looked more like criminals trying to resist a huge police raid in a godforsaken neighborhood. And they were also forced to seek shelter behind constructions, some of them died trying to get there.

Harper and his men managed to get into the hospital in one piece. Hector, Vincent and their group had to seek protection in a bar. None of them could reach Tess' restaurant. But it would be pointless anyway. All places in town were on the path of total obliteration.

"Hey Phil, how are you doing?" Vince asked him.

"Trying not to be shot to pieces, and you?"

"Where are Lily and Mate?" Hector asked.

"Their truck got hit by one of those missiles, or whatever that thing is."

"And what happened?"

"I don't know, man. After the hit, I just saw a big ball of fire, a crater on the road and the truck had disappeared. I think it was blown to pieces."

"Ah, Jesus!"

"I don't think Lily and Mate had time to jump out of it." Vince took a deep breath. "They're gone, bro."

"This is the end of Apocalily." Pedro said. "This is the end of us all."

"Everything we did only brought us tragedy." Prashant lamented. "We need to stop this madness before more people die and I lose the only eye I got left."

"Alright" Hector said. "Somebody find me a piece of white cloth, it could be anything but your underpants."

And, some minutes later…

"Hold your fire!" Colonel Talbot screamed.
"Hold your fire!"
"Hold your fire!" The message was passed along the troops.

The shooting stopped.

"What's happening down there?" Shane asked rudely and snatched the binocular from Talbot's hands.

And she saw it as well. Hector was walking on the shattered main street, followed by his group. He was holding a stick with a white cloth attached to it.

"We're all yours!" He screamed. "Just leave the rest of the residents be!"

"Great!" Shane said, giving the binocular back to Talbot. "That makes it easier. Colonel, tell your men to gather fifty people in the street, including the rebels that's just surrendered. Make them kneel down and cross fingers behind their heads."
"Y-yes, madam."

Talbot screamed the order to Major Henderson, his second in command down at the sidewalk, and he passed it along to his lieutenants, sergeants and privates.

In a few minutes, the fourteen who escaped the power plant plus thirty-six other residents were brought by the soldiers and organized in several rows along the street, all kneeling down, as per Shane's orders.

"Good. I appreciate your expedition." She said. "Now, tell your soldiers to shoot them all dead. Then, gather another fifty and do the same until there's nobody left in this dump."

"But…" The colonel was sweating through every pore. "I can't do that!"

"I'm sorry if I didn't make myself clear when we first had this conversation. This is neither an invasion nor a raid. This is a cleaning and replacing operation. Now, do as I said, then we discuss with the Center of Refugees the best strategy to bring new people in."

"You are aware of course we're about to shoot unarmed civilians who want to surrender!"

"Well, they know why they are dying. We need people who follow the rules as they are. We can't afford the kind of indiscipline they showed. Otherwise, we have no order. Otherwise, we have no peace."

"Let me arrest them and give them a chance to answer for their crimes!"

"Too late for that, they were surely given more than a fair chance. Now follow orders, colonel."

Talbot hardened his look.

"Colonel!" Shane insisted. "I'm not asking you again!"

"NO!" He retorted furiously. "I'm not doing this!"

"It will happen with or without you."

"Then it'll be without me! You know something… I'm sick of you and your ways! Like you said before, I guess I can stop kissing your ass now." He ripped the military patches off his uniform sleeve and threw them on the floor, by Shane's feet. "I resign my commission!"

Shane looked at him really disappointed and grabbed him by the neck. She fixed eyes on him and forced the man to return her look.

"Resignation accepted. Now, listen to this." She began reciting "The sunshine springs, happiness it brings. Those eyes you should follow... ah, what the heck!"

Shane decided to simply snap Talbot's neck and toss him on the sidewalk. His dead body crashed against the ground, very close to his second in command.

"Major Henderson..." Shane spoke to the air and her words were carried by radio waves that emanated from her brain until they reached the major's walkie-talkie.

"Um... yes madam?" He responded stunned on the radio.

"It seems you're in charge now. You see those people on the street?"

"Yes."

"Tell your men to shoot them dead. Then, gather more fifty and do the same."

The major hesitated.

"Do you want to end up like your colonel?" Shane pressed him.

Henderson looked at Talbot's horridly twisted body on the sidewalk. He turned to his soldiers with a heavy face. They all stared back at him with anguished eyes.

"Weapons ready!" He finally gave the order.

His men obeyed him.

"Aim!" The major ordered after a brief pause.

All machine gun barrels pointed at the rows of human beings crowding the street. Hector didn't take his eyes off his killers. Maria closed hers. She and Vince held hands.

"FIRE!"

"Stop everything you're doing! Please!" Susan's voice resounded from the giant loudspeaker hanging right above the soldiers ready to shoot. "Please, stop whatever you're doing! I'm talking to the ones doing the killing in the Industrial Zone. I beg you to stop and listen to me, please!"

"HOLD IT!" Major Henderson screamed.

The soldiers stood down. Maria opened her eyes.

Susan's face was also on television sets all over Downtown, as well as on the big screens spread around Uptown.

Susan on TV:
"My name is Susan. I'm a teacher at Heavensville's Elementary. If I'm getting through somebody, just know I'm addressing you all, but especially the people of the so called Heavensville. I plead you to listen to what I have to say. Shane is nothing more than a cruel and ruthless assassin and torturer. She's been misleading and deceiving you all along…"

"I knew I should have killed that bird when I had the chance." Shane spoke grinding teeth.

"I knew she was a good girl the moment I set my eyes on her." Tess said to Mario, both watching the plasma TV on *Fleur du Soir*.

At the News TV Set, while Susan spoke, Nick, Paul and Becky walked around with weapons in hand to assure full cooperation of the audio and video crews. They only had to shoot at the ceiling once in a while.

"I've always wanted to produce my own show." Paul commented.

Susan continued on TV:
"...and when I found out the truth about the Industrial Zone, also called Downtown, I tried to take the problem to Shane, expecting that she would look into the matter in a fair and reasonable way."

"I deal with her later." Shane thought. "Major Henderson!" She called him again. "You got your orders! Follow them now!"
"Shut up, Shane!" He responded and turned off his walkie-talkie.

Susan continued on TV:
"But what she did instead was shooting my friend in the head. His name was Frank, a citizen like you and me. Then, she imprisoned, drugged and tortured me! Following her orders, some men injected something in my veins and threw me in a prison cell. Then, they took me outside the city gates to be torn apart by those deranged drifters some of you call *lamebrains*."
"Thank God Lily Master and her friend Mate Clarkson came and saved my life. But Shane betrayed them too, like she did to all of you!"

"This is a scheme, can't you see?" Shane screamed with all the strength of her lungs from the garage two stories up. "It's a dirty scheme plotted by these scumbags kneeling down before you! Shoot them, damn it!"

The soldiers turned to Shane in confusion, then back to the loudspeaker. One civilian kneeling on the street tried to stand up.

"Go back down!" A soldier shouted, pointing his rifle at him. "Go back down!"

Scared, the man knelt down again.

"Did you see that, bro?" Vince asked Hector.
"Yes. Susan is doing a good job, but it's not enough. The soldiers are not killing us, but they're divided. Some of them don't trust her. We need something stronger on that loudspeaker, a voice all people know and trust."

However, it was clear no soldier would fire a single shot in the immediate future.

"Fine, if that's the way you want!" Shane spoke, more determined than ever. "I'll just kill them myself. Like they say, if you want a thing done well, do it yourself!"

Shane turned around to go back to the street, but froze in surprise before the woman standing in her way.

"You'll have to go through me first, lab rat!" Lily said.

ACT 34

"Oh, look who's here!" Shane smiled. "You've been better, sweet heart."

"I can say the same about you." Lily replied. "Looks like you're fresh out of a Swiss cheese factory, pardon the cliché."

Lily walked to Shane, who was standing by the edge of the building. The Australian woman slightly limped on her left leg, also with a broken rib.

"Somehow, I had a feeling we'd meet again." Shane said with a smirk. "Isn't this great?"

"And this is the last time we'll ever meet, because I'm ending this right now."

"Oh, make no mistake, sweetie. You're a tough cat, but you definitely exhausted your nine lives."

"I'm here to exhaust the only life you got."

"What are you going to do, fight me?"

"And kill you."

"You don't even know if I can die."

"I got a few ideas. I'll have some fun testing them."

"Such a powerful line, you heard that in a movie, or perhaps in a cartoon?"

"Nope, it was in a movie."

"Always the daddy's little girl, aren't you?"

"Yes, guess I'll always be. But at least I had a dad who loved me very much. What about you, lab rat?"

Shane frowned "You're still powerless against my very particular skills."

"Maybe, but we killed your coverage."

"No, you merely reduced it. Just so you know I have people working to repair the damages you did."

"They can't stop the virus installed in your systems. That much I know."

"Even so, my personal sphere of influence covers a good fifty yards radius in all directions. And you're well within range. I can control your mind as I please, very silly of you coming to me like this."

"You'll have to catch me first!"

Shane lifted a hand towards Lily's head.

Lily deflected Shane's hand with a karate defense technique and struck Shane with each and every kind of blow she knew from her martial-arts training, including several types of punches and even roundhouse kicks. But the blonde woman didn't seem bothered at all by such attack.

When Lily finally got tired of punching and kicking, Shane said "Not bad for somebody who's so wounded. Now, it's my turn."

Shane hit Lily with the back of her hand, and that was enough to toss Lily backwards like a tennis ball, making her collide against a concrete wall almost at the other end of the roof. Blood was pouring from her right eyebrow.

Shane came to her and said "This is a punch. Now, let me show you what a kick really is."

And she kicked Lily right in the chest, causing the Australian girl to fly in a parabolic trajectory and crash violently against the windshield of her truck, which had just arrived. Lily groaned in pain, with yet another rib shattered.

"Goddamn it!" Clark said behind the wheel. "Are you sure you can handle this?"

"I'm exhausting her." Lily talked breathlessly, a cutting pain hammering her thorax.

Mate's left arm was broken and hanging in an improvised cast. And he needed such limb to shift gears.

"Ah, I can see your friend and your contraption also have nine lives!" Shane observed. "Thanks for dragging more people to my sphere."

She walked to the truck.

"If I wasn't so sophisticated, I'd separate your head from your shoulders right now." Shane spoke as she went. "But as it is, I'll just make you my slave and then I'll smash the head of your little freckled friend, I have no use for him."

"There are better ways to exhaust a super being." Clark spoke. "Let's do this *Fast and Furious* style."
Still on the windshield, Lily said "What is *Fast and Fu…* AHHHHH!"

Clark stepped on the gas pedal with everything he got and the vehicle accelerated, hitting Shane with fury. The impact was such that she burst through a wall, disappearing somewhere into the construction.

Lily rolled down the vehicle hood and fell right in front of it. Mate hit the break with both feet, bringing the truck to a stop, only inches from the Australian's head, after burning a good amount of rubber.

"Jesus!" Clark said. "Are you alright, Lily?"
"Yes." She grunted. "Nice driving. Only next time you decide to test metal efficiency against a super being, let me know first."
"Sorry about this. It was kind of a spur-of-the-moment thing. Besides, I'm not comfortable driving on the right side."

On the street, soldiers were still pointing weapons at civilians kneeling on the asphalt.

Down at the station, a mildly attractive middle aged woman stepped into the News TV Set and went to Susan. Immediately, Becky, Paul and Nick pointed machine guns at her.

"Hold it! Don't shoot!" Susan screamed. "This is my boss."
"Far from me to shoot a boss and save the world for democracy" Nick commented.

"Turn off the camera for a minute, will you?" Susan told the camera operator and he obeyed. "What can I do for you, Missus Hildenbrandt?"
"Call me Agnes, my darling. I'm here with some parents. They're waiting in the lobby. Now that you got everybody's attention, I just thought I might add something to your little speech, if you don't mind. You see, Shane called me a fool in front of the whole city. Now, there're a few things I want to say about her as well."
"Be my guess, Missus... I mean, Agnes."

Susan stood up, so Agnes could sit down on the anchor's chair. She adjusted her glasses, organized her hair and nodded at the camera operator. In a matter of seconds, she was on the air.

Agnes Hildenbrandt on TV:
"Hello citizens of Heavensville and Industrial Zone. Most of you know me, but for those who don't, my name is Agnes Hildenbrandt and I'm the principal at Heavensville's Elementary. Susan here is one of my teachers and a darn good one by the way. And I'm here now not only to confirm, but also to emphasize each and every word she's just said to you."

Soldiers at Downtown gazed at the loudspeaker, although they could only hear a voice. Hector and Vince exchanged meaningful looks.

Agnes Hildenbrandt on TV:
"After Shane delivered her speech in this very network, I did some research on my own. And I found out everything she said is a filthy lie. For starters, Mister Hector Dryland is by no means a criminal. On the contrary, he's a good, law abiding, hard working man who bravely tried to put an end to Shane's reign of terror. If some bloodbath was committed, it wasn't by the hands of Hector or his friends. Shane and her henchmen did all the killing and slaughter!"

"You brought it all on yourself, Shane." Minister Robert Hedgiest talked to himself in an undisclosed location.

He turned off the television and sat down by his desk, with a monitor and keyboard protruding from it. Hedgiest typed some commands and grabbed the phone.

"Hello Harland, it's me. Yes, I'm ready. You can give me the final codes now."

Agnes Hildenbrandt continued on TV:
"And I was about to start a research on Lily Master, but I didn't have to actually. Some parents came looking for me. And they told me some of my students, their sons and daughters, once studied at that very elementary school that was attacked by a huge horde of those dead creatures roaming outside the gates. Oh yes, these children were eye witnesses of everything that happened in there. And they said Lily Master indeed saved their lives, also saving teachers and law enforcement officers. If it weren't for her, they would all be dead."

"I am now addressing the soldiers who are attacking the Industrial Zone at this very moment. It came to my knowledge that some of your kids also studied at that elementary school and they were rescued by Lily as well. Yes, you heard me! You're trying to find and kill the woman who saved the lives of your sons and daughters! But the powers of Shane were somehow clouding your minds, stopping you from remembering this."

"I know that Shane's influence is strong. However, I plead you, just search your memories and you'll find the truth."

By hearing those words, one private, also father of two, threw his weapon on the floor. One by one, the other military men followed his example, including Major Henderson. They helped the people kneeling on the street standing up and introductions took place.

"Hi, I'm Sergeant Arthur O'Herlith." He said to a citizen. "If you need anything, just let me know."

"Thank you, boy" the man replied, shaking hands with him. "I'm Jake Harper, former sergeant of the United States Army. What's your division, son?"

"None actually" He answered embarrassed. "All ranks in here are complimentary. We were taught how to deal with weapons and this sort of thing, but that's pretty much it."

"Then you got a lot to learn as to what being in the military is really all about. And believe me, it's not only about fighting, shooting, going into battle or to a war. Most of all, we protect people that can't stand for themselves."

"Yes sir."

"And you don't just go ahead and shoot unarmed folks who are surrendering to you, son!"

"I know that now." He whispered.

The hospital in Downtown was already full, all beds occupied either by patients recovering from cyanide poisoning, or by those wounded in the invasion. Nevertheless, Heavensville

Hospital agreed to have some patients moved there, as per request of Major Henderson.

Tess also accommodated people with minor injuries in his restaurant.

"What did you do to Drake?" Vince asked, curiosity killing him.

"Nothing really" Tess disappointed him. "I abhor violence in any form, you know. We just scared the bejesus out of him. We didn't even touch him. He peed in his pants though."

"You're kidding me, right?"

"No. It was kind of embarrassing, actually. Two of my waiters had to wear latex gloves to lock him up in the bathroom, the only place he belongs now. But I guess the real question is what're you going to do to him?"

"Well, he has to answer for his crimes against humanity, not only him of course, like in that Nuremberg thing."

"And let's not forget about Susan's case." Aaron pointed out. "We also need to arrest a certain doctor in Uptown on multiple accounts of medical malpractice."

"But, where are you going to find an unbiased judge and jury in this neck of the woods?" Tess queried.

"Well, there're always the zombies." Vince replied.

"Do you think she's dead?" Lily asked, examining the hole on the wall, together with Mate.

"Well, even if she's not, her bones will be sore in the morning."

"Alright, let's get into the truck and see if our friends need some assistance."

"Sounds like a plan."

"Damn it!" Lily cursed, stopping in front of the vehicle.

"What?" Clark mumbled scared.

"It scratched the painting!" She rubbed a finger on the spot that hit Shane. "Daddy would be furious if he knew it."

"And what would daddy say about all crushes on the hull and bullet holes?"

"Well, I guess it's going to need a paint job anyway."

They got into the truck. Lily put it in reverse and accelerated. But the vehicle only burned rubber without going anywhere. The Australian looked in the rear-view mirror and saw Shane holding the truck in place without many efforts.

"So much for that" Lily said. "By the way, she's still alive."

Lily stopped accelerating. Shane walked around the truck toward the driver's door with demonic, angry eyes.

"What we do now?" Mate asked.
"She's awfully close to the hull. Let's try some tickling."

Lily pulled the lever below the dashboard and lots of pointy spikes came out of the vehicle. One of them impaled Shane's left shoulder. She screamed in pain.

"Those are still working!" Clark said.

"You're making a fool out of yourself!" Shane grunted. "Grow up, Lily!"

By firmly gripping the spike with both hands, Shane managed to push her body backwards, getting rid of the spike and falling on the floor, groaning. But she stood up fast and kept on coming.

"What now?" Mate asked anguished.
"Now, we go old school. Wait here."
"But..."

"No matter what happens, do not leave the truck."

Lily opened the door all of a sudden and hit Shane's head with it, dropping her again. Taking advantage of the favorable moment, the Australian woman jumped on her opponent and punched her face repeatedly; then again, not nearly enough to hold Shane down.

And Lily was exhausted and extremely hurt.

"Thanks for the massage." Shane said and stroke another hit on Lily's face.

Once again, she was tossed far behind, rolling toward the roof edge, disappearing from view.

"Oh no!" Mate shouted.

"Why you riffraff have to be so tacky all the time?" Shane complained.

Lily was holding on to the edge with her finger tips, not to fall off the building. In normal conditions, she would climb back up easily, but at that point her body was too punished by cuts and bruises.

She tried to pull herself up with the strength of her right arm, but her broken ribs could not stand the effort. A dreadful pain caused Lily to moan, also forcing her to lower her right arm. She was now relying only on her left hand not to fall.

Shane came to the edge. The Australian woman could visualize her knuckles being crushed by the other's high heels and her body plunging two stories down. She considered ways to position arms and legs to better break her fall.

But surprisingly, Shane pulled Lily up and dragged her to a wall.

"Has your dad never told you karate should only be used for defense?" Shane asked.

"Only when we fight honorable opponents, positively not your case! By the way, thanks for pulling me up."

"I just thought it would be a pity to let your many talents go to waste. Besides, it's only two stories down, you might have survived. Everything I do is for a reason. I'm not a monster, Lily."

"You're not a goddess either. And your reasons are all wrong."

"No, they aim the common good."

"A good that only serves your purposes, I have to stop you."

"How? Do you still think I can die?"

"You also seem to have nine lives, but I can finish them all."

"I have a million lives!"

"You bleed. Then you can die."

"Yet another cliché from a movie. My wounds can heal a lot faster than yours ever will."

"And what happens now?"

"Well, this should be the part when I break your neck, but I'll just break your mind instead. Once you're in my power, I'll make you bark like a dog just for fun. Then, I'll find something better for you to do as my slave. Now, if you could please look into my eyes and listen to this..."

However, a thunderous rumbling rattled in the distance, the sound of several explosions taking place all at once. Shane turned her head brusquely to the side, her eyes wide open.

"NOOOO!" She screamed. "Hedgiest, you son of a bitch, I would've handled it!"

"What just happened, Shane?" Lily asked.

"This is all your fault!"

"Yes but, what just happened, Shane?"

"All walls around the city have just collapsed down due to the detonation of explosives strategically placed. This is what we call *Termination Factor*, to resolve a *Delta Status* situation. It's just a bunch of code names to say that when a certain site is no longer viable, a cleaning process is initiated."

"Cleaning as in..."

"That's right. You got a big zombie problem in your hands."

"What happens after this cleaning?"

"The powers that be just pack their gear and move to another site. We got similar ventures going on in other parts, here and around the globe."

"Except there's no *we* anymore, right? By the looks of it, the powers that be don't hold you in high regard. Why don't we get these bastards the two of us, what do you say?"

"I'll get them alright, you can be sure of that. Then, I'll start my own personal project."

"Listen to me, Shane! They betrayed you. We got a common enemy now! It's not too late for us to join forces as friends and allies. Let's take care of the zombie situation and rebuild the walls, get this community back on its feet, only this time giving the population freedom and equal rights."

"Sorry, honey, no can do."

"Come on, Shane! You're strong, a natural leader, we can do this! What's wrong with letting people decide their own destinies, regardless of where they come from?"

"That's what was killing the world in the first place."

"We can right the wrongs of the past, this time with more wisdom and less manipulation, eh?"

"Truly sorry, but this is not what I'm programmed to do. Besides, there can't be two of us. First, I'll smash Hedgiest and the rest of the puppets. And you'll help me, once I have your mind under my control. I don't care for these people here, they may die. Now, let's get this over with."

"You're making a mistake."

Shane grabbed Lily by the neck and forced the Australian to look her in the eyes.

"Clark!" Lily shouted "Time for another metal efficiency test!"

"Oh, alright" Clark replied.

He moved to the driver's seat as fast as he could with a broken arm, which hurt a lot every time he had to shift gears.

"Ouch!" Clark moaned "My arm, my beautiful tennis arm!"

Even so, he managed to accelerate the truck right to the girls. Shane got distracted gazing at the vehicle coming at high speed, and Lily could jump out of the way.

"I hate YOU!" Shane screamed.

Again, the blonde woman took a direct hit from the heavy truck, this time bursting through four thick walls, to finally crash against the toilet seat of a common restroom downstairs.

"This is really getting annoying!" She grunted.

The impact also caused the wall on the second floor to tumble down, with huge blocks of concrete falling on Lily, also hitting and bending two spikes on the truck.

"Oh my God!" Clark cried again. "Why this action always backfires somehow?"

He jumped out of the vehicle and ran to his friend, almost tripping on his own feet.

"LILY!" Mate shouted, desperately trying to take big concrete rocks off her back with his right hand. "Are you alright? Are you alive?"

"I'm hunky-dory." She grunted with a very fainting voice and bleeding from almost every pore. "Make a note of this, partner, let's stop using my rig as a goddamn ram."

"My very thought exactly." Clark breathed in relief with tears in his eyes.

"Do you still have my hockey stick?"

"It's in the truck."

ACT 35

Prashant rushed into the bar breathlessly. His only eye goggled as if he had seen a ghost.

"So, what's the word?" Pedro asked him.

"It's true, man. The walls are down. Lamebrains are getting in."

"Jesus!"

Everybody in the bar lowered eyes and souls. Heavy hearts pounded sadly and frightened.

"That's rock bottom." Phil whispered.

"Can we deal with the zombies?" Pedro queried.

"We can in the Industrial Zone." Prashant replied. "Gingerbread Dam is a natural barrier. Lamebrains can only get in a few at a time, and the barbed wire fences around the power plant are still standing. But Uptown is something else entirely."

"Why?" Maria asked.

"Zombies will flow into there like a goddamn waterfall. There's nothing protecting the city now, no obstacles of any kind. And people there won't know what to do. They'll be easily overrun."

"Then we have to go there with weapons and help them." Maria spoke with urgency in her voice.

"Why?" Pedro retorted disdainfully.

"What do you mean why?" Maria narrowed her eyes. "People are going to die! We got to help them."

"What did they ever do for us?"

"I don't understand."

"Come on Maria, you've been there too. Like you, I was humiliated, tortured, beaten and starved half to death. Then, I was forced into a work I knew nothing about for bread and water.

I had to suffer, so people in Uptown could go on living lavish lives, with running water at will and electricity to keep them warm and cozy."

"But they didn't even know we existed, for crying out loud!"

"How do you know that? As far as we know, they might have chosen to look the other way, because life was just too comfortable to be spoilt by social issues. Now, I'm the one looking the other way."

"Listen, I know folks there might've done a lot of things wrong, but it doesn't matter now. The point is they need..."

"It matters to me!" Tears welled up in Pedro's eyes. "It matters a lot to me! Raul is dead, remember? He was like a brother to me!"

"I know and I'm sorry. Then, let's help those people in his memory."

"His memory means nothing to them. They just used us as stepping stones."

"I can't believe I'm hearing this! Human beings are going to die and you'll just sit here and do nothing?"

"That's right. You go save them if you want. As for me, I had my share of bloodshed for a lifetime. I'll help barricading the roads to Downtown, but that's it. If folks in Uptown want my help, they'll have to come here and beg me."

"You chicken shit!" Maria hardened her look. "You can't simply let people die! We need you!"

"Hell with you! I'm not going to fight for people who treated me like garbage!"

"Then, you're no better than them! How could I ever put my life in the hands of such a small person like you?"

"I don't need this shit, okay? I don't need moral lessons, not from you, nor from anybody!"

"Hey, this won't get us anywhere!" Phil intervened.

"Stop this nonsense right now!" Prashant yelled at them.

"Stay out of this!"

But their loud voices were silenced by a powerful rifle shot.

"Are you yakking like old ladies on me now?" Hector said. Smoke was still coming out of the barrel in his hand.

He came into the bar accompanied by Vince and Harper.

"After all we've been through together, haven't you learnt a damn thing?" Hector continued, "We don't help people because of what they are. We help them because it's the right thing to do."

Maria looked at him tenderly. Pedro lowered his eyes. Hector walked to him and said:

"Everybody dies one day, right partner?"
"Yeah, and it seems you're always trying to get me killed somehow." Pedro replied. "You don't like me very much, do you?"
"Well, I don't exactly love you, but I'm starting to grow a little fond of you."
"If that's supposed to change my mind, you are a lousy diplomat. But a thought just hit me, after I save the asses of those snobs, they'll owe me big."
"That's the spirit!"

Pedro turned to Maria "I'm really sorry, chica."
"No apologies needed, muchacho. You're a loudmouth. It's part of your charm. And, unlike Hector, I love you exactly because of this. I also loved Raul. He was my friend."
"Thank you."

"I talked to Major Henderson." Harper stepped in. "And he told me the troops are more than willing to accept me as their new commanding officer. Just say the word, my friend."

"Take the soldiers to the power plant and free the workers." Hector spoke. "You may encounter resistance, not all guards there know what's going on. Then, perhaps we can talk about work on wages with a better package of benefits."

"It sounds reasonable enough. But I'd keep some men around this perimeter, in case zombies decide to show up."

"Good idea, you do that. The rest of you follow me. We got a whole town to rid of zombies. Are you coming, Pedro?"

"Oh yes, and remember this when we discuss those wages and package of benefits."

ACT 36

"Hello, anybody there?" Lily carefully asked. "Hey Shane, is your nose still in the air somewhere?"

She searched around the restroom, investigating the debris resulting from the destruction caused by Shane's little charter flight around the building.

"I'm surprised she's not in front of the mirrors." Lily thought.

She went through the hole of one wall, then upstairs, to finally come back to the upper floor garage, crossing the remaining cracks. Lily walked to her truck, which had the door on the driver's side open.

"Looks like she's gone, mate." Lily said while climbing into the vehicle. "I guess she's probably..." That was when she realized the truck was empty. She was talking to nobody. "Clark, are you there? Where are you, boykie?"

"Right here, sweetie" came the very well known voice from the outside. "Boykie's with me. And by the way, I got better things to do than hanging in front of mirrors."

Lily looked in the rear-view mirror. After a few seconds, Shane appeared, walking past the spikes protruding from the hull, one of them covered with her blood. She was dragging Clark and squeezing his throat real hard. He was gasping for air in despair, his face even redder than normal.

"Lil..." He tried to speak, but his voice got lost due to lack of oxygen.

"Damn it." The Australian girl cursed to her t-shirt. "Boy, boy, boy... Hang on, mate." She whispered more to herself. "I'm a-coming."

"You see, things would be much easier if you just admitted that you lost." Shane continued, walking around the truck with Clark panting on her hands and dragging his feet. "There's no way you can stop me. And yet, you're not being very cooperative. Then, I decided to apply persuasion. It's really simple, actually. You come out here and let me take control of your mind, or I kill your boy. What do you say, sweet heart?"

Shane stopped by the side of the truck and squeezed the man's throat even harder. His face turned purple and his eyes were almost popping out. He was being slowly smothered and about to pass out for the last time in his life. Supply of oxygen to his brain was rather low at that point.

Inside the truck, Lily looked around. She found the sheath with the hockey stick, good for nothing in a hostage situation. She caressed the boomerang in her belt, but there was nothing she could do with it as well, Shane had Clark too close to her. Mate had the two knives, but he wasn't in any condition to use them whatsoever.

Lily saw the pistol they took from Sheriff McBeattie.

"He's dying, Lily!" Shane pressed. "What's the problem? Are you forsaking your friend because you're too spineless to face me?"

Two shots were heard, muffled in the vehicle interior, but still very audible.

Shane was mildly surprised by that, but no bullet actually flew out of the truck.

"Were those meant for me?" The blonde woman scoffed. "Jeez, your friend is definitely a lousy shot." She spoke to Clark, but he was no longer in any shape to do anything.

Lily jumped out of the vehicle and landed in front of Shane.

"Let him go." The Australian said. "This is between you and me."

"You never get tired of using movie jargons. Yes, I let him go because this is between you and me, only if you give me your word you're going to listen to my rhymes nice and easy, like a good girl."

"Yes... Whatever."

Shane dropped Clark on the floor disdainfully. He brought both hands to his massacred throat, still purple. He didn't seem to be breathing. Lily looked at him afflicted.

"He's no longer your concern." Shane spoke and forced the Australian woman to fix eyes on her. "Now, listen very carefully."

And Shane recited:
"The sunshine springs, happiness it brings.
Those eyes you should follow, to keep away sorrow.
Seek the giant bird you must, on her you shall blindly trust.
For the good science you will urge, from all impurities to purge."

Lily's eyes were wide open, her look seemed lost.

"Very well, now you get this boomerang of yours and slit your friend's throat." Shane ordered. "Right now, his windpipe's good for nothing anyway. And don't you think for a minute that

I'm not keeping my end of the deal. I said I'd let him go and I did it. Now, do as you're told, dear."

Lily turned her back on Shane and walked to Clark. He couldn't stand up, so he tried to roll away from her. However, he was too weak. Lily knelt down by him, drew the boomerang and brought it to the man's gullet.

From Mate's point of view, it looked like the whole planet had frozen. Flashes of his youth danced before his eyes. In a very distant foggy mountain rising in the horizon, he seemed to hear Lily say "She definitely pisses me off."

And Lily slit the throat.

...But not Clark's.

She jumped back to Shane and slit her throat instead. Totally caught by surprise, the blonde woman gasped with torrents of blood pouring from her windpipe.

But that didn't stop Lily.

"How about a tracheotomy, eh?" She said while slashing each and every part of Shane's body with the sharp side of her boomerang. "You got no dignity, you got no honor. You're not even as good as your word. I tried to make you see the truth. I even tried to be your friend. But you're just a balloon filled with ego, you only think of yourself and how to satiate your blood thirst. Now, you bleed while I decide what I'm going to do to you!"

Grinding teeth, Shane held Lily's hand to stop the next attack and pierced the other's broken ribs with very pointy fingernails. The Australian girl screamed in terrible pain.

Shane compressed Lily's wrist with her thumb to make her drop the boomerang. Then, she gripped the Australian by the neck and tossed her to the nearest wall.

Mate Clarkson crawled back to the truck. He tried to climb into the vehicle, but fell heavily on the ground.

Bleeding like mad, Shane walked to Lily and grabbed her throat, forcing her to stand up.

"Very clever" She said "Deafening yourself to avoid my rhymes. It seems mind control is too sophisticated for you. No more miss nice girl from now on."

Clark managed to get into the truck. But the engine was off. He pushed the button to start it again with all fingers and thumbs; however, none of his fingerprints were recognized by the system.

"I won't even break your neck this time!" Shane continued speaking to Lily. "That would be too fast."

The tennis player reached for the hockey stick and started to assemble it. However, some parts got jammed at some point, delaying his actions.

"Why do they make these things modular?" He complained to himself with the little voice he had left.

"You might be deaf, but you still can see." Shane said "Time to look into my eyes and get a real taste of my powers. I'll give you way more than just a stroke. I'm going to break all synapses in your brain. You'll be a vegetable for the rest of your life!"

"LILY!" Clark tried to scream, but almost no sound came out of his mouth. It would've been pointless anyway because Lily couldn't hear a thing.

Just the same, Clark tossed the already mounted hockey stick to his friend.

Lily had her eyes stuck on Shane's. Using her last drop of strength, the Australian thrust a finger into one of Shane's many bruises. The pain caused her eyes to roll around the sockets. Such momentarily distraction allowed Lily to move her head a bit to the side and she saw the hockey stick coming. She grabbed it with both hands and impaled Shane with it, from her chest all the way to her back and out of the body.

"Gghhh, ughhhh…" Shane coughed, vomiting blood.

"Thanks for helping me decide." Lily said in triumph.

"This… is… not… even… classy…"

"You've never been classy, lass, only selfish."

"It… doesn't… matter… any… you… can't… stop… the… Undertaking…"

"Right now, I settle for stopping you!"

Lily snatched the hockey stick out of the other's body with violence. Shane fell on her face lifeless.

"Boy, she was shallow!" Lily commented.

Mate Clarkson staggered to her. Lily held him.

"Are you okay, partner?" She asked.

"Yes." He answered, with his oxygen levels and voice slowly coming back to normal, as well as his natural rosy color. "I won't be playing much tennis for a while, but I'm fine. What about you?"

"I need to take a bath."

Clark laughed boyishly at that comment. Lily couldn't resist and laughed as well.

"Why are you talking so loud?" Clark queried.

"Because of the bloody white noises in my ears, they're really annoying!"

"So, that's how you dodged Shane's mental powers."

"Yes. Vince was right. In order for her mind control to work, she needed three things happening at the same time. You had to be at the same place as she was, look her in the eyes and listen to that stupid poem of hers."

"But if only two of such prerequisites were met, it wouldn't work, right?"

"Precisely. Back at the truck, when Shane took you hostage, I fired the sheriff's gun twice very close to my ears, and the noise deafened me."

"But then, how did you hear Shane's order to slit my throat?"

"I didn't. I read her lips."

"Like daddy taught you."

"Yep."

"That's a good use for it."

"I couldn't agree more. Anyhoo, my hearing is coming back. The ringing in my ears is dying down."

"Glad to know that, partner."

"Let's go."

"Um, Lily... You'd better take a look at your hockey stick. Something got caught on it."

Lily checked the sport gear and she was also disgusted by what she saw. Shane's heart was hanging from the tip. It beat a couple of times and then stopped.

"Well, that's a way to kill a super being" The Australian woman said "By snatching her heart out of the chest."

Lily rubbed the stick on Shane's body until the organ was out.

"I hope it doesn't find its way back in." Clark observed.

"I don't think so. It's an illustrative symbol, though. Shane's never had a heart. Scientists try to create the perfect leader. They add a lot of stuff in the brain, but it seems they keep forgetting the most important part, what really counts."

At that moment, a very young man ran to them.

"Jeez, I've been looking all over for you." He said breathlessly "My God!" He saw the dead body on the floor, with a heart on the nape and a pool of blood surrounding it. "Is that Shane?"

"Yes." Lily replied. "But don't worry about her now. She's taking a little rest."

"With her heart outside the body and everything, this is so Mortal Kombat!"

"What can we do for you, lad?"

"My name is Tobias. I was selected to be the official scout of the troops. Listen to this. Situation is under control in the power plant. Soldiers led by Harper encountered little resistance and the guards surrendered fast."

"What about the zombies?"

"We got some in the Industrial Zone, but not many. Locals are taking care of them. But Uptown is practically overrun and that's why they sent me to find you."

"How's the situation over there?"

"Pretty bad, Hector went there with his friends and some soldiers, but the zombies outnumber them about thirty to one. They are out of ammo and squeezing as best as they can in a supermarket. The population is scared and about to be overwhelmed."

"Thank you, Tobias. Do you have a knife?"

"Oh yes."

"Good. Try to reach Tess' restaurant. Do you know where it is?"

"Oh yeah, everybody does."

"Go there and kill some living dead on the way, if it's safe enough."

"Yes madam!"

"Name's Lily, not madam."

"I know! Lily, the Apocalily!"

Tobias exchanged high fives with them and ran to the street.

"So, what do you say, partner?" Lily asked Mate "One last crusade to save the world for democracy and the highest values?"

"I'm with you, partner. Let's save the day for the American and Australian ways!"

Lily grabbed her boomerang. She and Clark got into the truck and sped toward Heavensville. Lily pushed the lever beneath the dashboard back to its original position. All spikes retreated inside the hull except for the two that got bent.

"It seems we got something to fix." She said.

"I'm surprised something in this rig could break."

"Hopefully not us."

"Thirty to one..." He pondered. "We need to even those odds."

"No worries, we got a few weapons and some diesel in the tank."

"I guess you want your two knives back."

"No, you'd better keep them. You're not really planning to kill zombies with your teeth, right?"

"Are you sure? I'm afraid I'll just slow you down."

"No way, boykie! On the contrary, you set me on fire!"

ACT 37

At Heavensville supermarket, Hector and Vince tried their best to reinforce the barricades blocking the main glass entrance. But they had to pull back fast. Living dead creatures were everywhere. The city was under siege.

Number made all the difference in the end and lots of cadavers broke into the store, spreading in all directions. Hector used each and every sharp object he found. He killed some, but more beasts came to replace those who died. He was cornered and defenseless.

Reanimated corpses surrounded Maria and were about to bite the guts out of her. The same happened to Pedro, Prashant and Vince, the last ones in the front line, trying a last stand to protect all other living souls inside the place, a battle they had already lost. Men, women and children screamed in desperate, hopeless anguish.

But then, everybody heard it, especially the dead creatures. A powerfully loud honk roared outside, attracting the flesh-eating monsters, which left the supermarket, and other places, one by one.

The *Apocamobile* rode slowly along the streets, so the zombies could catch up with it. In a matter of seconds, the vehicle was completely surrounded by hungry beasts, pounding and shaking it real harshly. Lily pulled the lever and the still functional spikes did part of the work. When the corpses were far enough from populated areas, the Australian girl brought the vehicle to a halt.

"Alright" She said. "This is all we can do in the truck. Now, it's time for some field work. Are you ready?"

"I was born ready!" Clark responded. "It's also time for me to finally reach that flag on top of the Empire State."

"Yes, I know I said that, but I myself don't know what it means."

"Oh, I got a pretty good idea."

"Do you have my..."

Before she finished the question, Mate gave her the hockey stick, already mounted.

"This is cheating!" She complained.

"Nah, don't worry about it. You're concentrated enough."

They jumped out of the truck. And that was it, Swashbuckler and Ninja Knight fighting evil dragons - hockey stick chopping, knives piercing, with an occasional boomerang flight to slash monsters skulls.

And so, Lily was no longer the daddy's little girl, but a woman with dad's strength in her heart. And Mate walked a long, arduous path to become a man, however keeping the amount of innocence necessary to exercise the sometimes lost art of understanding.

"Look at her going!" Nick said, watching the spectacle through the supermarket glass door.

"I told you she was for real." Paul replied.

"She's everything they say and more." Susan commented.

"But her hair is awful." Maria spoke. "I'll fix it when I get the chance."

"Who's the guy with her, the one with the little knives?" Becky asked.

"Mate Clarkson," Hector answered, "a tennis player who would've surely been number one if the planet hadn't come to an end."

"He's cute." Becky said.

Paul and Nick looked at her.

"I dig freckles!" The young woman explained.

As Lily and Mate walked toward the city centre, the army of reanimated dead beasts seemed to increase in number.

"Man, there're a heck lot of these things." Clark observed.

"Just think of them as oversized, angry, growling, dead Chihuahuas." Lily replied.

"Right," Mate grunted.

"Well, we got no choice," Lily decided, "Let's get them, Mate!"

"Yes, let's get them, Mate!" A young man carrying a big wrench screamed.

Behind him, a mob of residents from Downtown armed with a wide range of tools joined forces with Lily and Mate. Very soon, people in Uptown also armed themselves as best as they could, and together they stampeded against the horde of monsters.

In twenty-seven minutes and fifteen seconds approximately, all creatures from that batch were finished, harmlessly littering the streets.

ACT 38

"We just killed this bunch." Lily announced to the crowd in the supermarket. "More will come."

"Yep, it seems we never run out of them." Vince observed.

"Well, a lot of people were infected." Clark spoke. "This disease, this fever, whatever they call it went global. Damn it, we don't even have a name for it."

"Let's call it *zombities*." Vince suggested.

"You have to rebuild the walls around the city" Lily said "and quick."

"No worries" Hector replied. "We got more than enough qualified people for the job, they're already on it. Nick and Paul are taking care of the details."

"What about that minister guy?" Clark queried.

"I searched the whole TV Station with some soldiers and no sign of him." Vince replied. "It's like the bastard vanished in thin air."

"Have you guys decided what you're going to do from now on?" Lily asked.

"We're going to need a new mayor." Maria responded. "Susan here got a lot of possibilities. She's been on TV and all. But Nick and Pedro also have their eyes on the chair, with good chances too. What do you think, Hector?"

"I don't care who is next in command, as long as there is a vote."

"Oh, there will be."

Hector turned to Lily "What about you?"

"I'll continue." She answered.

Maria frowned and said:

"You mean... you're not staying?"

"You guys can take care of things." Lily replied. "You don't need me."

"I think we do!" Vince intervened. "I talked to Tobias on the radio. He told me how you released Shane from the burden of carrying an evil heart in her chest."

"And your performance at the TV Station, taking the soldiers down all by yourself, wasn't bad either." Maria pointed out.

"It was a team effort." Lily responded.

"True, but indeed you brought us together." Hector said.

"I don't understand." It was Lily's turn to frown.

"When I was in the equipment room, Shane paid me a little visit." Hector spoke. "And she said that she's the demon that inhabits the darkest paths of human soul people are afraid to walk. In a way, she's right. That's why we also need an angel in our hearts to counterweight the devil, so we won't feel so bad next time we look in the mirror."

"Maybe" Lily responded "but this angel has to have your name, not something as crude as Apocalily."

"I agree, but sometimes it feels good to know there's someone out there you can take inspiration from in difficult moments. Perhaps, you shouldn't be so resistant to this title. It brings good in people."

"Are you running for mayor, Hec?" Maria asked.

"I've never been a politician." Hector replied. "Sure as hell I'm not starting now. I was thinking of taking care of the power plant for a while. Run a business is not new to me."

"Yes, but high voltage is not exactly our thing." Vince pointed out.

"We need to keep water and power coming. Besides, it's always a good chance to expand our horizons."

"And I'll surely make a great manager. What do you say, bro?"

"Manager? We are partners!"

"Well, pay is better anyway. But the work is tougher."

"See Vince, I told you we'd be right on top again."

Missus Hildenbrandt came to Hector and said:

"And I'd really appreciate if you could please take some time to address the students of my school, and tell them all about the benefits of honest, hard work. My teachers and I would be very honored."

"The honor is all mine." Hector agreed.

"Me too," Vince said. "I'll also speak to the students. I'll teach them everything they need to know about picking locks, pockets, hot-wiring cars and all. Then, I'll give a lecture only for the boys, to tell them how to get girls."

Not very friendly eyes turned to him at the same time.

"What?" Vince spoke. "This is also hard work."

"Do you really have to go?" Maria asked Lily with sad eyes.

"At least for the time being, my future is there." Lily nodded at the truck. "I'm not sure where I'm going, or what's waiting for me on the way, but I'd rather find the answers on the road."

"I can understand that." Vince said. "Anyway, there'll always be zombies to fight, cities to release from ruthless dictators, prefab villains to face..."

"I hope not!"

ACT 39

"Mister Chancellor," Robert Hedgiest politely approached the man in impeccable blue suit, looking out of the window at a wondrous landscape.

"Mister Minister," he returned the courtesy.

"You sent for me, sir?"

"Oh yes. No need to say the stockholders are very unhappy and they are not the only ones. Project Sunshine, North America Site UNO A, failed miserably." He turned to face his minister. "And I'm holding you responsible."

"I know that, sir, and I apologize for my mistakes. However, it was just an experiment anyway. Shane was unstable. The important thing is we learnt all we needed from this first experience. Now, we know exactly the vulnerabilities we should address in the other sites."

"And I fully trust you'll do a better job this time. Your position is rather debilitated right now."

"I made Project Cleaning work like a charm, didn't I? The virus delivered as expected with a perfect timing. Population of Earth was drastically reduced. Very soon, it will be only a matter of picking up the pieces."

"I hope so, for the sake of your future in the Undertaking."

"You won't be disappointed."

The Chancellor cleared his throat and spoke:

"And I suppose you are very aware of a vulnerability we most certainly shall address."

"Yes, the girl..."

"She might be a bit of a problem, yes. Try to find out more about her than we already know."

"Right away, sir."

A beautiful young assistant knocked on the open door.

"Yes, Miss Tulips" The Chancellor turned to her.

"They are here." She said with a very congenial smile.

"Oh, send them in!"

"Excuse me, sir." Hedgiest understood that was his cue and left.

Almost at the same time, a boy and a girl went into the room, four and five years old respectively.

"Grandpa!" They happily shouted and ran to the Chancellor.

"Hey, come here you!" He answered joyfully.

And they all rejoiced in a delicious collective hug.

"When are we going to meet the Big Mambo King, grandpa?" The little boy asked.

"Oh, very soon, Tommy, very, very soon."

"Where's mommy?" The little girl asked.

"Listen, um... I'm afraid we're not going to be seeing mommy for a while."

FINAL ACT

After a round of goodbyes, Lily walked to her truck. She opened the door and threw the sheath with the hockey stick inside. She looked around and found strange the fact she was alone in there.

Mate Clarkson was sweeping glass shards off the supermarket floor, but he clearly had his mind somewhere else. Lily went to him.

"Aren't you coming?" She asked.

"Um, me?"

"Yes, you. Who else? We're leaving, mate."

"Do you still want me to go with you?"

"If you want to come. Why, are you giving this second thoughts or something? They're not building many tennis courts in town, not a priority. Besides, we can always find some nets and flat areas on the way, if you want to improvise something."

"No, it's not that, it's just..."

"It's just what?"

"I wasn't so sure you would want me to keep on riding with you. I mean, I really appreciate you giving me a ride and all the first time you saved me from zombies, but..." He choked on his own words.

"I really don't know where you're getting at with all this." Lily walked to him. "What's your point?"

"My point is you don't need to cope with me anymore, if you don't want to. I... I'm safe in here now."

"Cope with you? What kind of talk is this?"

Lily sweetened her eyes all of a sudden.

"Well, do you want to go with me?" She asked.

"Of course I want. I'm just not sure if you want me around."

"Why wouldn't I?"

"Well..." He spoke rubbing the back of his head. "It's just that sometimes I think you saved my life only out of obligation, like you would've saved any lamb from the wolves, and the only reason why you took me in your truck was because you felt sorry for me."

"Hoy! So, that's the problem."

"Yes."

"This is nonsense, mate. This is nonsense!"

She came even closer to him and spoke:

"You said once you were my comic relief, you couldn't be more wrong! When we were captured and forced to split, you were the only one I could think of."

"Really?"

"Oh yes! In all that time we've been apart, I remembered the moments we spent together, and I missed our conversations, I missed how well we do things, I missed... Well, I missed everything about you. I need somebody smart to discuss Pink Floyd's lyrics! If you are so concerned about my standards, just know that to me, we make a hell of a team! I need you, man."

"Do you really mean those words?" He asked with tearful eyes.

"Yes, I do mean those words. My life would suck without you."

"Like Kelly Clarkson."

"Yes, but especially like me."

"So, what are we waiting for?"

"Right now, we're waiting for you."

"Not anymore!"

Once on the road again, Mate said:

"You need to teach me how to use the boomerang."

"I'll do that."

"And some of your kung-fu moves."

"Sure, you can be my pupil."

"And you'll be my master, I mean, from now on you're not only Lily Master, but also Master Lily."

Clark glanced at her preoccupied.

"Yeah, yeah, I know." He grunted. "You must've heard this pun several times before. You probably think it's another stupid playing with words."

But oddly enough, Lily smiled.

"Actually, it's the first time I hear that pun." She revealed. "And I love it!"

"Thanks!" He cleared his throat. "Then, when are you going to start teaching me all your stuff?"

"No hurries. Next ghost city we stop by for supplies, we also try to find a gym."

"Come on! I can't wait that long! I want to carry my weight as soon as possible."

"My truck is carrying both our weights right now."

"You know what I mean. You can't do everything alone. Even Apocalily needs to have a functional co-hero."

"Would you stop talking like this? I'm not Apocalily, nor any road warrior for that matter! I'm also not a street fighter, nor Sonya Blade, Mario Bros, Super Sonic, nor the Oceania version of Resident Evil! I'm just me and you are you! Damn it, I don't even know who I am!"

"I know who you are. Do you want me to tell you?"

"Yes, why don't you?"

"Remember when you first found me on that prairie, with the zombies trying to eat my guts?"

"Yes."

"Well, before you came, some cars passed by. None of them stopped. I screamed for help with all I got, I'm sure they saw me, but they just kept on going. And there were those who slowed down, not to help, only to get a kick out of my misfortune, some even took pictures to show their friends, perhaps post them on the internet."

He took a deep breath and continued:

"We live in a shitty world, with some shitty people in it, but there are those who try to be good and they're all we got. And I'm really glad and even relieved they take you as a role model to change this world. You were the only one who stopped to help me and you didn't do it because your truck broke down, the same way you didn't stop by that elementary school because your truck broke down. You stopped because you are just this kind of person. Like father, like daughter."

"You know something," She said with tearful eyes "I'm glad I took you in!"

"Thanks!"

"But maybe it's too late to change this world."

"Are you willing to find out?"

"Yes, I'm not doing anything important right now. Just for fun, we may try to find out more about this Undertaking thing the creepy blonde mentioned."

"And perhaps stop for an ice cream on the way."

"I like chocolate syrup on mine."

And together they rode to the end of the world.

THE END....?

"Now, wait a minute!" Clark screamed. "Not so fast!"

"What's wrong, mate?" Lily asked.

"I almost forgot. You never told me how you escaped from Shane's captivity, when she put you chains, with the zombie trying to bite your ear."

"Oh, that. Nothing to it, really. Actually, the zombie did most of the job."

"Care to explain that?"

"I was there, with my ear glued to the wall, with that creature trying to eat my other ear. I bet you think I just got scared and nearly peed in my pants, right?"

"Well, did you?"

"Yes, of course. But then, the bloody zombie gave up my ear and went for other parts of my body. Eventually, he crouched and tried to bite my ankles, but he ended up chewing off the shackle holding my ankle."

"Are you meaning to tell me the rotting teeth of a dead cadaver were strong enough to chew through metal?"

"It was a bad quality material manufactured by means of forced labor! You get what you pay for. Anyway, once my ankle was free, I could use my foot to push the creature's skull to my other ankle. And the silly thing chewed off the other shackle, too!"

"Let me guess, you killed the zombie with your feet."

"Nope, I still needed him to release my hands. Then, I grabbed the critter with both legs..."

"Like Sonya Blade."

"...sort of, yes. With both legs, I brought his head to the shackle holding my right hand. Spine flexibility was never a problem in my family. After he chewed through the metal tying up my hand, I brought his teeth to my other hand."

"And you were totally free."

"There was still a strap holding my neck to the wall, but I took care of it myself. I didn't want that zombie anywhere near my neck. Lucky the bolts holding the strap to the wall were also poor quality. Then I was totally free. All I had to do next was hit the zombie's head against the wall repeatedly until it cracked wide open. After that, I found a bolt cutter and broke out of the shed. That was when I found the school principal with the three children. And you know the rest."

"Uh-huh." He glanced at her. "Is that really how it happened?"

"I've just admitted I almost peed in my pants out of fear, why would I say such thing if it wasn't true?"

"Yes, got a point there, very ingenious of you."

"Thanks."

Clark looked out of the window and saw a dead woman roaming around at random.

"Things are just going to get worse, right?" He observed.

"I guess so."

"What we do then?"

"We ride to the end of the world."

APOCALILY

vs.

THE SUNSHINE DAME OF DOOM

In loving memory of
Virgilio Fizzotti, Piero Dimitri Fizzotti & Susana Sguizzardi
Bevilacqua
Great Fathers and Uncles, Great Mother and Aunt